Her fingers clutche
connection zinged
ending, sending sci
over his skin.

It was as if together they created a sort of sensual electricity. And Lars couldn't get enough of her mouth, her tongue, her sighs.

Pressing a hand against her back, he coaxed her forward and bowed to continue the kiss. Her moan said everything he was feeling: yes, yes, all the yeses in the world. This tiny witch felt so right in his arms. He had to thank the gods for putting him in her backyard, even if it had been a strange night that had scared the hell out of him.

Michele Hauf is a *USA TODAY* bestselling author who has been writing romance, action-adventure and fantasy stories for more than twenty years. France, musketeers, vampires and faeries usually populate her stories. And if Michele followed the adage "write what you know," all her stories would have snow in them. Fortunately, she steps beyond her comfort zone and writes about countries and creatures she has never seen. Find her on Facebook, Twitter and at michelehauf.com.

Books by Michele Hauf

Harlequin Nocturne

Her Werewolf Hero
A Venetian Vampire
Taming the Hunter

The Witch's Quest

The Witch and the Werewolf

The Saint-Pierre Series

The Dark's Mistress
Ghost Wolf
Moonlight and Diamonds
The Vampire's Fall
Enchanted by the Wolf

In the Company of Vampires

Beautiful Danger
The Vampire Hunter
Beyond the Moon

Visit the Author Profile page at Harlequin.com for more titles.

THE WITCH AND THE WEREWOLF

—

MICHELE HAUF

Recycling programs
for this product may
not exist in your area.

ISBN-13: 978-0-373-13998-9

The Witch and the Werewolf

Printed in U.S.A.

™ www.Harlequin.com

Dear Reader,

This is my sixtieth book for Harlequin. I've created and written a lot of heroes! Each one of those remarkable men means something to me. Learning about my fictional heroes can remind me that love can be won by simple kindness, or something so complex that it takes me on a journey to explore past lives and how we are all connected.

Lars Gunderson, the hero of this story, has touched me in a way no other hero has. He might not be the strongest, the most handsome, even the wisest, but he is genuine and true. And he faces some incredible challenges in a way that only he can. He is a simple man (werewolf) who takes life as it is given to him. I shed many tears when writing Lars's story because I knew, going into writing this tale, that he represented someone very close to me.

We fiction writers tend to put truths to the page, then we alter them, and we pretty them up or dirty them down. But either way, there's always a piece of me imprinted in my stories. And I love Lars for allowing me to place a piece of my heart in print.

Michele

For Jeff. Our souls agreed to this.

Chapter 1

Feet floating up so her toes peeked out of the frothy bubble bath, Mireio Malory wiggled the little pink beads as she sang to the music filling her bathroom. She sang along with the Meghan Trainor tune about loving herself and not having time for a man because she was all about having fun. A fitting theme song for Mireio at the moment.

Guys were great, but she didn't have the time to focus on a relationship if her plans to achieve immortality came to fruition. A simple spell could prolong her life a hundred years, guaranteed. But to actually perform that spell—which involved drinking the blood from a live vampire's beating heart? She'd been avoiding the spell for years, but she couldn't do that anymore. It was time to honor her departed mother, and to take back her power.

Baths were a common ritual for her in the evenings, after a long day of work at the brewery, or after she'd flexed into a few yoga moves and watched an episode of *Bones* on Netflix. Born a witch, yet pretty darn disappointed she'd not been born a mermaid, Mireio honored her water magic by feeding her body's innate craving for water. Surely she owned the biggest bathroom in the city. It was hexagonal, tiled like a Moroccan temple and the big round marble bathtub sat at the center of it all. It was the size of a hot tub, but there were no bubble jets in this tub beyond the sensory explosions from her homemade bath bombs.

Singing loudly, she blew a handful of bubbles skyward and laughed when some landed in her pinned-up red hair. The water was starting to cool, and she'd been in for forty-five minutes. Her fingers and toes were pruned, providing her traction—if she were an amphibian. Or a mermaid.

With a reluctant sigh, she rose from her watery haven and reached for a toasty towel hung over the towel warmer. It wasn't the wet porcelain tile floor that almost caused her to slip upon exiting the bath—it was the scream.

And a very familiar scream at that.

"Really?" Mireio wrapped the towel around her ample curves and padded wet tracks to the back window to peer out, though she knew she couldn't see into her neighbor Mrs. Henderson's yard from here. The windows were also fogged.

She often mentally compared her neighbor to Mrs. Kravitz, the nosy neighbor on the 1960s TV show *Bewitched*. They didn't look at all similar, but they possessed the same snoopy, and unwelcome, curiosity and annoying voices.

Yet another scream, this one curling the hairs on the back of Mireio's neck, prompted her to use the side door in the bathroom that walked out onto the patio.

Pushing open the screen door, she leaned out into the cool spring air and scanned her backyard. It was close to midnight, yet her yard was always illuminated from the house light above the door where she stood, and the dozen solar lights pushed into the lawn at five-foot intervals that framed the backyard.

Suddenly something ran into view. A deer? Wildlife always dashed through the neighborhood yards. Raccoons, beavers, deer, once even a black bear.

Mireio stepped out onto the bamboo patio rug, holding the screen door open with two fingers. She peered into the night, thinking her species, witches, had gotten ripped off because they didn't have cool night vision like vampires and werewolves. Suddenly an animal stopped, twenty feet away, in the middle of her yard.

She recognized the creature with an ease that made her heart sink.

"A werewolf," she gasped.

Removing her hand from the screen door to put her fingers to her mouth, she suddenly felt a cool breeze skim her bare skin. More skin than should have been exposed. The towel had gotten caught in the door and fallen away, leaving her standing naked beneath the house light, unable to form words as she met the werewolf's golden gaze.

The creature, who in fully shifted form was half wolf, half man, thrust back his shoulders and lifted his chest, looking ready to howl. But when his gold eyes dragged away from hers and down her body...

Mireio tried to cover herself as she actually said, "Eek!"

The wolf snorted and a low growling noise rumbled in the night. It didn't sound threatening. In fact, to her it sounded...amorous.

Mrs. Henderson's scream sounded again. It was the catalyst to setting the werewolf off in a dash out of the yard.

Released from the spell of the creature's piercing gaze, Mireio grabbed the door pull and opened it, reaching for the towel and quickly wrapping it around her body.

Just in the nick of time because from around the corner of her backyard appeared a policeman, and in his wake, Mrs. Henderson.

"Did you see it?" Mrs. Henderson, wrapped in a thick

white terry robe, scampered over to the patio, the ears on her bunny slippers bobbing.

Tugging the towel up higher and this time clasping it firmly, she stood before the elderly policeman, whom she knew lived on the other side of Mrs. Henderson. Mireio nodded. "Uh, yes?"

"I told you!" Mrs. Henderson slapped the policeman's back, who shrugged and winced. He was accustomed to answering Mrs. Henderson's cries of wolf at all hours of the day.

But had this been a true cry of wolf? Best not to let humans know that.

"It was a deer," Mireio hastily tossed out. "Or maybe a moose. Yes, I'm sure that's what it was."

"A moose?" Mrs. Henderson jammed her bony fists to her hips. "It was Bigfoot!"

"All right, all right," the policeman said, placating his neighbor with a pat to her back. "Miss Malory here says it was a moose. She's got very good eyesight, and her backyard is well lit. So if she says it was a moose, I believe her. Let's go home now, Mrs. Henderson. Leave Miss Malory to...her bath."

To his credit he didn't eye her blatantly, only tipped a nod to her and turned Mrs. Henderson around, walking her back to her yard. All the way they argued over why a moose would be wandering through the tulips when it had very obviously been Bigfoot.

Mireio stepped inside the bathroom and closed the door and locked it. She peered out the now-defogged window, attempting to sight the werewolf. Perhaps spy a wolfish shadow backlit by the moonlight.

Whispering a protection spell to encompass her yard, she sent it out with a blown kiss.

Why had a werewolf been wandering through the neighborhood? That wasn't common. Too risky. And it wasn't even the full moon. Werewolves were much smarter than that. They knew to stay away from humans when shifted.

"It was a good thing for him I scared him off."

Mireio winced. She had scared the wolf away with her naked body? Not one of her finest moments.

On the other hand, that look it had given her. Definitely animal, but also…maybe kind of…sexual.

She shook her head. "You're a silly witch. Just be thankful you didn't flash the whole neighborhood. Ha!"

The music now blared Taylor Swift. Dropping her towel, Mireio performed a hip shimmy as she reached to drain the tub and then blew out the candles one by one, blessing the water goddess Danu as she did so.

Three nights later, Mireio stayed late after her shift at The Decadent Dames. She and her three witch friends owned the microbrewery in Anoka. Mireio was the master brewer. They all brewed and worked shifts and took turns scheduling, but Mireio was the early riser, so she generally arrived around six in the morning to start the day's brew and finished about an hour before they opened in the afternoon. Today, she'd gotten a late start so had finished the brew hours after opening.

A local band that covered current pop hits was set up before the front windows and the house was packed. At the moment, the lead singer belted out a cover of Meghan Trainor's "NO," which was an anthem to a woman not needing a man.

Singing the chorus, "Untouchable, untouchable," Mireio danced by herself amid the crowd on the dance floor, arms thrust high and hips swaying her short red-and-blue-tartan skirt. Nothing felt better than a beer buzz and dancing. And she had new, red, five-inch heels to break in, so much dancing was required. Tossing her bright red corkscrew curls over a shoulder, she let out an exhilarated hoot.

Eryss, the brewery's principal owner, danced up to Mireio. She and her boyfriend, a former witch hunter who lived in Santa Cruz, California, split their time between cities during the year and soon she'd be headed for the sunny West Coast. Her friend's long skirts dusted the hardwood floor and she grasped Mireio's hands and the twosome danced for a few seconds.

"You look happy," Eryss said over the noise.

"I am! I'm always happy!"

"It's contagious!" Then Eryss leaned in to speak close at Mireio's ear. "Did you notice the hunk at the bar who has been eyeing you up fiercely for the last ten minutes?"

"What?" Mireio abruptly stopped dancing and glanced to the bar, which was fronted by rusted corrugated tin in keeping with their rustic theme. She scanned from the left end of the bar to the right, and there at the end a big, beefy man with a mustache and beard, and long brown hair tied behind his head, lifted his pint glass to tip toward her. Handsome. "Huh." But. "Didn't notice. I'm in my zone, don't you know?"

"Yeah, I got that. I wish I could find the zone so easily nowadays. Whew!" Eryss blew a strand of long hair from her face. She had a six-month-old at home who lately had been keeping her up nights because of teething. "But don't be too untouchable tonight, okay? That man is sexy times two."

"Don't tell me that, Eryss. I'm not in the market for a— Oh, my goddess, he's coming over here."

"Then I'm going to leave you to him."

"No! Eryss!"

The man pushed by two people and deftly avoided a bull terrier sitting beside his owner's table. (Yes, the brewery was dog friendly.) He was halfway across the room.

"Please don't be a creeper. Please don't be a creeper." Mireio performed a hip swinging turn and he stood right before her. "Oh!"

Big brown eyes looked into her soul almost as deeply as if he could do a soul gaze. Of which, only witches were capable. And no one in town knew the owners of The Decadent Dames were witches. Well, mostly no one.

"Oh, hey," she offered.

Eryss had been right in her assessment of the man. But more like sexy times infinity. His dark brown hair was tied behind his head and his beard was trimmed neatly to reveal a snow-white smile. Chocolate brown eyes? Dreamy. Dimples? Oh, mercy. And he smelled like a forest after the rain.

"My name's Lars." He leaned in to be heard over the music. "I don't normally walk up to pretty girls and introduce myself." He looked aside briefly, then cast his eyes toward hers for only a few seconds. Nervous? "But there's something about you. Do I know you?"

"I've never seen you before. Unless you come to the brewery often. I work here," she said, unable to keep her hips from swaying to the beat. "You like to dance?"

The man shook his head. "I'm not a dancer. Was hoping you wouldn't mind a little conversation."

He seemed nice enough. And he hadn't tried any pickup lines on her yet, so that earned him points. But, as she'd told Eryss, she'd been in her zone. And some nights a girl just wanted to be with herself. Maybe she should reinforce her white light. She always warded with a white light against psychic invasion—or energy vampires—before going out. It tended to wear down as the night went on.

"Sorry." He shrugged and smirked, interrupting her thoughts. "I think I'm out of line here. You don't seem interested—"

"No, wait!"

Ah hell, she wasn't a mean girl, and the guy was cute. What could a little conversation hurt?

"That table is empty. I need a break anyway. New shoes, don't you know." She didn't need the break, but again, the man was a tall order of nummy, so she'd be a fool to send him off like a stuck-up witch.

He wandered over to the table and Mireio assessed him as he did. His jeans were snug and showed off incredibly muscled thighs and legs that stretched much longer than hers. Good thing she was wearing the heels. But she still came up a head or two shorter than him. He wore a soft blue-and-green flannel shirt opened to reveal a plain white T-shirt beneath. And that shirt stretched over abs and chest muscles that screamed *this man works out*. A lot. Add in the beard, mustache and well-groomed hair and he sported the whole lumbersexual vibe.

She could dig it.

She stepped onto the lower rung on the stool to boost herself up to the high table. Hey, she was five-two on a good day. Here at the back of the taproom they were set off from the dancers but it was still loud.

"Lilacs," he said.

"What?"

"You smell like lilacs." His dimpled smile was accompanied by a shy dip of his head.

She didn't wear perfume, save for essential oils once in a while, so if he smelled lilacs, then... "Oh. I was in the garden this afternoon. That must be what you smell on me. The lilacs are blooming. I love spring. Everything is so lush."

He nodded. "A familiar scent. I like it."

"You're a big one," she said absently. Then she realized what an idiot she'd sounded like. "Uh, I mean... Oh, witch's warts. I need another beer."

"I'll get you one."

"No, I got it." With a wave, she caught Eryss's attention behind the bar and made the pouring signal for another beer. "I work here. Not right now. But I own the place along with my friends. They know the fill-me-up signal."

"You ladies make excellent beer."

"Thank you. I brewed that oatmeal stout you're drinking."

"It's nice and creamy."

"I'm the head brewer," she said over the rising noise as the band kicked into a rousing '80s tune that everyone started to pound their fists to and bounce up and down.

"You say it's newer? Yes, I like it." He tilted back the drink and offered her a cheers with his half-empty glass.

She was never going to have a conversation with him surrounded by this noise. And she did want to get to know him better. Because why not? He was sexy and nonthreatening. And she wasn't against having a conversation with a handsome man.

"So, Lars, eh?"

"Yes. Officially Larson Gunderson."

"That's a fine Scandinavian name, if I've ever heard one. I'm Mireio Malory."

"Muriel."

"No, Mir-ee-O."

"Oh. It's loud in here with the band singing. My hearing is usually…much better." He winced then, as if thinking of something he'd forgotten. He shook the sudden lost moment away and offered her a smile that flashed his pearly whites from beneath his trimmed mustache.

"Muriel will do." She thrust up her hand for him to shake.

His hand clasped hers gently, wrapping with ease about it and up to her wrist. And then he held her more firmly, and the heat of their connection gave her a shiver. One of those really good, how-could-a-girl-get-so-lucky kind of shivers that she felt from head to nipples to toes—and everywhere in between.

And yet… She sensed something in his handshake. Something not quite human. It was the same feeling she got whenever the Saint-Pierre brothers stopped into the brewery. Those four ranged from werewolves, to a vampire and also a faery.

With a gasp, Mireio pulled her hand from his. He didn't notice her surprise, thank goodness. She was a water witch and spent a lot of time in nature working with streams, ponds, lakes and otherwise. She also communicated with the animals, and could always sense when one was near.

And Larson Gunderson gave off a distinctive animal vibe. Could he be? Oh, mercy, he wasn't. Please, do not let him be the one who…

Mireio swallowed. If the lilac scent was familiar to him—witch's warts. He was the one.

Eryss suddenly popped up beside the table and handed her another pint of blueberry cream ale. She winked and sailed off before Mireio could grab her as an anchor. Something to hold her down so she didn't float too near the curious man who— This couldn't be an accidental meeting. But did that mean he'd followed her here?

She tilted back a swallow, then set the pint down on a coaster that featured their logo, a sexy witch casting a spell over a foamy brew. "So, Lars, uh…what can you tell me about yourself? I mean, I don't want this to sound like fifty questions."

"Fifty? You have that many questions for me in such a short time? I'm impressed." He pushed his glass aside and leaned his elbows on the table. She wanted to touch him once more. Just to be sure that what she'd felt was real. "I live out past Oak Grove. I come to town once a week for groceries and a pint. Just remembered this place was here so thought I'd stop in. I'm definitely coming back."

"And what is it you do, exactly?" Because if he didn't have a real job, she'd get suspicious. And fast.

"I…well, you could sort of call it security. On a private compound."

"Ah-huh."

That was vague. And she was getting more nervous about the guy by the second. But really, if he was the one, would he know things about her? Things she didn't want him to know.

"I'm also remodeling the cabin I live in. I like making things with my hands." He splayed them both on the table to reveal long, calloused fingers.

Oh, those were some fine hands that could certainly cover a lot of area on her if she was in the market for such handling. Which she was not. Was she? Mercy. Maybe giving up on men to focus on a spell she was too freaked about to give more than a few moments consideration to daily was too extreme?

Could be. But even more so? Talking to a man who may have very likely seen her naked a few nights ago was even more extreme. She couldn't deal with this. Not right now.

"Do you want more stout?" she asked and nodded toward his nearly empty pint.

"Probably." He tilted back the rest of the drink.

"Head to the bar." She reached over and touched the back of his hand. There was that sensation again. Hiding a cringe, she nodded toward the bar. "Eryss will give you a refill. On the house."

"Thanks. I'll be right back."

"I'll be here!"

No, she would not be here.

Mireio grabbed her little black purse, shaped like a fish, swung it over a shoulder, and beelined it for the door behind the band, well out of view of the bar, and the mysteriously delicious Lars Gunderson's eyesight.

She'd had three drinks, so she wouldn't drive home. If she were lucky, she might catch a bus this late.

Chapter 2

When he returned to the now empty table, Lars saw the sassy little skirt slip out the door. The woman with the bright red curls and sexy, deep cleavage had dashed out of the brewery.

He gaped. Really? Had he made that terrible of a first impression? She'd kind of seemed into him. Had touched his hand. Had even fluttered her thick lashes at him as she'd smiled a sweet pixie smile. And he hadn't gotten to ask her the burning question. The one he'd been wondering about since the scent of lilacs had led him here.

Devastated that the woman had taken off, Lars sulked. He should chalk it up as another rejection. And yet a deep, visceral part of him would not allow him to mark this off as defeat. He had to know if she was the one.

So, leaving his beer on the table, he pushed through the dancing people and slunk around the electric guitarist and pushed open the door. He could hear her high heels clicking on the concrete, though he couldn't see her. But he smelled lilacs…that way.

Turning left, he passed three storefronts, then swung another left and there she stood, near the bus stop, stepping nervously from foot to foot. He heard her mutter softly, "Oh, shit."

That utterance stabbed Lars right in the heart. Never had a woman rejected him so soundly as to run off. So he stopped about twenty feet away from her and put up his hands placatingly.

Should he really do this? Was he that desperate for more cruel treatment? She seemed almost *afraid* of him. Threatened? He didn't want her to feel that way. That wasn't his style.

But the heady scent of lilacs wouldn't allow him to turn away.

So what to do?

The woman wore a short skirt that looked like one of those tartans the Highlanders wore, along with a blousy red top that emphasized her ample cleavage. Sky-high heels matched the blouse color. And white ankle socks with a delicate ruffle kept drawing his eye down there. She was short, a good head shorter than him, even in the heels, but the shoes did make her legs look long and slender.

"You keep staring at my legs like that, I'm going to have to slap you," she said.

"Sorry."

She offered him a smile and a shift of her hips. "I don't do things like slap men."

He took that as a sign it was okay to approach. But only a few steps. "Couldn't help but stare. You've amazing gams. I, uh…did you have a previous engagement you forgot to tell me about?"

She rubbed a palm up one of her arms. A black fish swung near her waist. What was that? A purse?

"Sorry. I suddenly got a weird vibe about you. No offense."

"Really? Because if you think I'm weird I do take offense from that."

"No, I don't think you're *weird* weird. Just—hey, weird is good, right?"

"Still offended here."

Her wince was accompanied by a shrug. "I'm usually much better at explaining myself. I think you're a…" She bit her lower lip. Her lips were so red and plump. Kissable. Yet juxtaposed with her appeal was also her strange fear of him. What had he said to her to make her flee?

"I'm a what?" Lars prompted.

"I'm not sure how to say it. You said the lilac scent was familiar to you."

It had been in his nose since three nights ago when he'd been out of his head and had woken in the morning knowing he'd shifted again without volition. It had been happening with a disturbing frequency lately. And each time he risked being seen by more than a few humans.

Yet, he also sensed this woman wasn't necessarily human.

"I did, and do, smell lilacs," he said. "There's only wildflowers growing out where I live. I keep bees. They make me happy." *Ramble much? Just out with it, you idiot!* "So anyway, the lilac scent stood out to me the moment I entered the brewery. Let me see if I can approach what I think we're both trying to avoid. Okay?" He took a step toward her.

She clung to the bus stop pole fiercely.

"Tell me," he asked, "if the rumors I've heard about the owners of the brewery are true?"

Thankfully, no one else was out on the sidewalk, and the streetlights illuminated their conversation. Around the corner, the band could be heard singing a Billy Idol tune. Lars would love to give a rebel yell right about now.

Anything to release his anxiety over talking to this goddess of a woman.

"What?" She teased a bright curl about her forefinger and her stance relaxed. That wasn't a motion that Lars could look at for long without wanting to do it himself. Tangle his fingers in her hair, that is. "That we spike the beer with a little something extra?"

"Is that a rumor? Huh. No, I'm talking about the one where you bewitch the beers. Because you're witches."

"Oh, that one." Her shoulders dropped. The fish purse slid down her arm to dangle near an ankle. A heavy sigh preceded her nod. "Well, we try to keep things as normal as possible for the human patrons. But…" Her pretty blue eyes dallied with his. "You have a problem with me being a witch?"

"Nope. I was raised by a wolf who was married to a witch."

"Which means…" She teased her tongue along her upper lip as she eyed him carefully. "I'm guessing you're not human either, are you?"

Lars dared a few steps closer to her. He cast a glance around toward the parking lot across the street—no one in the vicinity—then said quietly. "I'm a wolf."

"Shit." An accusing finger pointed at him and Lars couldn't be sure if it might possess a magical zap. "It's you."

He actually flinched. "I…don't even know what to say to that."

"You were the wolf the other night, weren't you? The werewolf in my backyard."

"Uh…yes?"

Talk about being caught out. Guilty as charged.

"Oh, I can't do this." She started across the street but avoided the parking lot.

If she'd been waiting for the bus, did she not have a car?

Was she veering off course to get away from him? He'd
gone about this all wrong. He'd scared her when he had
only wanted to meet her and get to know the compelling
woman who had not left his thoughts for days.

"Muriel, wait!"

"It's Mireio! And don't follow me, please. I'm embarrassed enough as it is."

"You shouldn't be. I can't remember much."

"What?" She suddenly stopped in the middle of the
street that stretched down a quiet area between the parking lot and a closed restaurant. "So you admit it was you
the other night?"

"I think so?" He approached with his hands splayed up
and out. "When I'm in werewolf shape I know things and
see them as the wolf, but my wolf mind shares space with
my man mind. Things get a little confusing."

"Not confusing enough for you to be unable to find
me tonight."

"It was the lilacs. I smelled them that night. Haven't
been able to stop thinking about them since. Or of the soft
woman I saw standing in the doorway."

"Oh, my goddess. You do remember that! I was naked!"

He offered a weak shrug. "Yes?"

"You said things were confusing. Do you remember
me naked or not?"

He wobbled his hand before him. "Kind of? I don't
have a good image of you, just sort of a memory imprint
of seeing something really nice."

"I don't even know what to say." Gripping the purse
strap with both fists, the fish wobbled before her as she
took an exaggerated step backward. "You are freaking
me out."

"I don't want to. I'm not like that. I'm not a guy who
can— Do you know how hard it is for me to walk up to
a woman and talk to her?"

"Couldn't have been that hard. You followed me out here!"

"I wanted to start over and hoped that maybe you'd talk to me." He stopped moving closer, knowing he'd blown it. He should not torment this beautiful woman anymore. Where the hell were his manners? "Forgive me. I've no talent approaching women. I mean, I do it all the time. Not like a stalker or anything—ah hell. I just... I'm embarrassingly awkward when it comes to this kind of stuff. I wanted to see the pretty woman who smelled like flowers once more. Sorry to have bothered you."

He forced himself to turn and walk off. *Idiot, Lars!* Way to spoil the chick's night. And to spoil his chances of getting to know her better. Yes, he'd seen her naked. And he remembered that image much better than he would ever admit to her. Soft, generous curves, and so much golden light glinting on her skin, which still had beads of water on it. Hell. His werewolf had been attracted to her. *He* was attracted to her.

"Wait!"

Now across the street, he stopped and turned back to her. The tiny witch toed the opposite curb with one of those sexy shoes, and offered a shrugging smile. "It was a remarkable beginning, that was for sure. You didn't do anything wrong, Lars. I couldn't be sure if you were leering at me that night—"

"Oh, never, no. I mean, I don't know. Honestly? I might have leered a bit. You're worthy of a long, lingering look."

She clutched the weird purse tightly, and he realized what he'd said.

"I'm not saying anything right tonight." He checked his watch. Almost midnight. Shit. He had to stop by the compound, and soon. "It was nice meeting you, Muriel."

"Mireio."

"Right. You make great beer. And you have the prettiest blue eyes I've ever had the chance to look into. But I promise I won't come back to the brewery. I wouldn't want to make you uncomfortable."

He turned away again, and this time when she spoke, his shoulders straightened.

"Can we start over?" she called.

He nodded, and turned a look over his shoulder. All his anxiety swept downward and flooded out across the sidewalk. Offering her a confident smile, he said, "I'd like that."

She approached him and, as she did, tugged something out of her purse. It was her cell phone, which she handed to him. "Put your number in there for me, and we'll try again."

He almost shouted *score!* but controlled his nervous energy. If she knew how much courage it had taken him to cross the taproom to talk to her, and then to follow her after she'd run out on him...

And now he was entering his number into her phone. Some kind of awesome, that.

"I'd like to get to know you better." He handed her back the slim pink phone. "What would you think about going out for something to eat tomorrow night?"

"I have to work tomorrow night."

"Oh."

"But lunch tomorrow could work. Why don't you stop by my place around noon? I think you know where I live, right?"

"I should be able to figure that out." He tapped the side of his nose. "Lilacs. Thanks for the second chance, Mireio."

"It's—oh. Right. Mireio."

He winked at her, because he'd known her name since she'd first told him, then turned and wandered off. Halfway across the parking lot he turned and waved at her.

She remained in the middle of the street. Probably waiting for him to leave before she returned to the bus stop. He wouldn't be rude and force her to wait long. Picking up his pace he aimed for his truck around the corner.

He'd talked to the girl! And it had turned out almost okay. Which was about how he rated his life right now. Almost okay, with a side of what the devil. The almost okay waited for him right now, so he shoved the key in the ignition and fired up the truck.

As for the what the devil? He'd been having weird symptoms for over a year, more than just shifting without volition, so had finally gone to see a doctor a few days ago. The doctor told him he'd give him a call in a week when the test results were complete.

But he wasn't going to worry about that. He'd been invited to a pretty witch's house tomorrow for lunch.

So he did indulge in a shout out loud. "Score!"

Chapter 3

Lars strode up the sidewalk to the little red cottage placed at the end of a cul-de-sac. He didn't recognize the area by sight, but by scent? He'd been here before. Yet, besides the naked woman, it hadn't been a pleasant experience. He remembered someone screaming, and then the sight of a beautiful woman—naked. He wasn't going to tell Mireio that as werewolf he saw things as he did when in man shape. His instincts and thoughts were more animalistic, but he did recall sights and sounds and smells.

And she had the sweetest curves on that tiny package topped with red curls and a Kewpie doll smile.

Now as he took the steps up to the door, he inspected the flowers he'd picked up at a gas station on the way here. Blue daisies. He liked blue. Her eyes were blue. But the flowers didn't have a scent and now he studied them closer, they actually looked...dyed.

"I can't even do flowers right." Thinking to toss them aside in the little flower garden that hugged the front of the redbrick house, he paused. "She'll see them there."

For once he would like to get it right with a woman. It would be a bright spot in his life. And he really needed one. But his nervousness around the female sex could never be allayed by his usual confident alpha surety. Women made him go all stiff and fumble for his words. And hiding the stiff part could sometimes prove a problem, as well.

Smirking at that thought, he grabbed the door knocker and muttered, "Please let her like me. Give me this one, okay?"

Who he was asking, he wasn't sure. He believed in the possibility of God, so if there existed a higher power, he hoped his words would, at the very least, be noted by some force.

Rapping the knocker a few times, he then waited. After ten seconds the door swung open to reveal the flour-dusted face of a witch who sported a surprised look on her face. Hell, he should have called first. But she had told him to stop by for lunch. He must have misunderstood. Par for the course with him.

"Uh...?" Thick black lashes blinking over her blue eyes, she glanced to the flowers in his hand. "Oh! Right! Lunch! I forgot."

"I should have called."

"No, that's fine."

"You weren't expecting me. I can leave and—"

"Don't be silly." She grabbed him by the wrist and coaxed him over the threshold. "Come in! I was baking some bread."

"It smells great." He followed the scent toward the kitchen more than he followed her. Yeast and warmth and crisp browned crust. Mmm… He scanned the many loaves on the kitchen counter. He counted eight but also noted the oven light was on and there was another loaf inside. "That's…a lot of bread."

"I know, it's crazy!" She flung up her hands in surrender, then noted the flour on her fingers and wiped them across her pink frilled apron, which was covered with a white dusting of flour. "Whenever I get the urge to bake homemade bread I always go overboard. I really like the kneading process." She punched the air with a tiny fist. "Gets out some of my frustrations."

Lars wasn't sure if he should sit on one of the stools before the kitchen counter—that might seem too presumptuous—so he stood there holding the bouquet with both hands. Feeling out of his element and, as usual, awkward. "You're frustrated?"

"It's because of a decision I've been mulling over recently. A witch thing. A spell, actually. So, you brought some pretty flowers for me? I love blue."

"I do too. I can't smell them, though. It's kind of strange."

He handed her the bouquet and she pressed the oddly colored blooms to her nose, then sneezed. "Whew! Nope, no smell, but I think I got a petal up my nose. Ha! Sit down. Oh, we were supposed to go out for lunch, right?" She glanced to the oven.

"We can do it some other time. I can see you're busy. It was nice to see you again today. I thought I freaked you out last night. I know I handled things wrong."

"Don't worry about it. Today's a new day. And I have an idea. Because I certainly need to do something with all this bread. How about sandwiches and lemonade out on my patio?"

Spend time with the sexiest woman he'd met in a long time? "I'm in."

The opportunity to have lunch with the sexy werewolf was just the thing to knock Mireio out of her incessant worrying over how to locate a vampire for the immortality spell. It would also complement the fruitful results of her bread-making endeavors. Sure, she would hand out loaves to her girlfriends, and freeze a couple, but seriously, what witch needed that much bread?

So she sliced up a loaf of oatmeal rye, making the slices extra thick. The steam rose with a seductive invitation as she spread on some cucumber yogurt sauce, covered that with spinach, pickled onions, peppers and some slivered carrots and radishes. Top that all with broccoli sprouts and finely shredded red cabbage, and voilà!

With a glance and a wink to the candle she kept above the stove, she felt as if her mother was watching over her. She lit the beeswax candle once a year on her mother's birthday. It was her way of keeping her memory close.

Ten minutes later, the werewolf didn't seem to mind that there was no meat in the sandwiches. He was on his third half when Mireio returned to the patio with a refill on the blueberry lemonade for both of them.

"This is really good," he said. He sat on the wide-backed white wicker chair before the tiny wrought iron table. His big form seemed to suck up the chair and his knees kept hitting his elbows. It was doll furniture for the man. "What's that sour tangy stuff in the middle?"

"Pickled red onions."

"Love them. Thanks," he said as she poured him more lemonade.

"I'll send you home with a loaf of bread too, if you don't mind. I obviously have some to spare."

"I'd like that." He met her gaze only briefly over the sandwich.

He was a shy one, which surprised Mireio after his bold approach last night. But she'd sensed his nervousness then, as well. And knowing what he'd known about her, it had to have been tough to get up the courage to approach her. Especially when she could have reacted badly—and did.

She noticed his distraction as he looked over the small backyard, framed in on one side by ten-foot-high lilac hedges and low boxwood on the other. As he narrowed his eyes she suspected he was remembering. Merciful moons, she might as well rip off the Band-Aid and get all the painful stuff over with.

"Yes," she offered, "I was standing right there—" she pointed over her shoulder "—by the door that enters into the bathroom."

"Sorry. I didn't want to ask. It's the lilacs. They are what brought me to your doorstep today, and to the brewery last night. The scent is heady."

"You wolves have good sniffers. Did you happen to remember an old lady screaming from that night?"

"I, uh…" He set the remaining quarter of sandwich on the plate. "Yes?"

Mireio chuckled at his obvious confusion. "It's okay. Mrs. Henderson is a drama queen. She stopped over the next morning. Wanted to talk about the monster."

"Monster?"

"Yes. And get this—she'd changed her mind from her original assessment that it was Bigfoot. Now she's sure it was a Sasquatch."

"A—really?" His mouth dropped at the corners and his big brown eyes saddened.

"You're not a monster." She felt the need to reach over and pat his knee in reassurance. "But it's a good thing she thinks that, isn't it? If she was telling everyone she'd seen a werewolf, that could cause trouble for you. How many people actually believe in Sasquatches?"

"About as many as believe in werewolves?" He rubbed his palms on his thighs.

"Right. But don't worry about it." She sipped the lemonade. "So you said something like it wasn't normal for you to tromp through yards in werewolf form. Why *were* you in my yard the other night? Were you lost? Had you come through the cornfield that backs up to the yard?"

He picked up the lemonade and drank half of it. The man seemed nervous again. Yet much as she shouldn't push, curiosity was a witch's best tool when it came to making good choices and weeding out the wrong.

"Well, I mean, aren't werewolves much more cautious about shifting near humans? And it wasn't even a full moon."

"I don't know why it happened," he blurted out. "It's something I'm looking into."

"Really? Like, something is wrong with you?"

He shrugged. "I went to a doctor a few days ago and he checked me out. Said it was probably nothing to worry about. Might have been sleep shifting."

"Sleep shifting? I can't imagine."

"Neither can I. The doc took a bunch of blood and did some other tests."

"And?"

"And? Uh, he hasn't called with the results yet. It's nothing. I don't think you have to worry about finding me in your backyard in werewolf shape anytime in the future."

"Well, I'd rather you in *my* backyard than Mrs. Henderson's. You have to be careful."

"I am," he said forcefully.

And Mireio took that as a warning to curb the conversation topic. She did love an alpha, but she wasn't stupid. When you poke a wolf with a stick, it'll bite.

She prodded the bread crust on her plate. "So you said you're some kind of security guy?"

"That was just my roundabout way of saying I'm scion of the Northern Pack without actually telling anyone I'm a werewolf."

"Right. Gotta be careful. But since I know… What does being a scion entail?"

"At the moment? Not much." He chuckled and his

shoulders relaxed. The wicker chair creaked as he settled into it. And those sexy dimples returned. "The pack I grew up in has been shrinking every year. A few years ago, Ridge Addison handed over the principal reins to Dean Maverick, which bumped me up to scion, his second-in-command. But there are only two other pack members at present, and the only one who lives on the compound is Maverick and his woman, Sunday."

"I know Sunday. She's good friends with one of The Decadent Dames owners, Valor Hearst."

"I know Valor. I've sold her queen bees for her hives. I'm also a beekeeper. I think I mentioned that last night?"

"That's so cool. I love bees. They're so fluffy."

"And industrious. They fascinate me. And Sunday is awesome. Lately she's been helping me with…a project."

Mireio leaned across the table and caught her chin in hand. "What sort of project?"

"Just something—" he held his hands in the air to suggest something bread-basket sized "—small."

A small project that he obviously didn't want to talk about. The man was either shy or shifty. Mireio would stick with shy. And he was a cute shy, so that made his reluctance to expound easier to accept. On with the next topic. "You said you've been remodeling a house?"

"Yes, my cabin. I'm fixing it up. I intend to add on two rooms to the back before winter. I live about a run away from the pack compound."

"A run?"

"I can jog back and forth from the cabin to the compound in about five minutes, or take a leisurely stroll in fifteen minutes. I moved into the old, single-room cabin years ago. I've got the outhouse all finished, but now—"

"Wait." Mireio set down her lemonade and sat up straight. "You have an outhouse? Like…no indoor bathroom?"

He laughed, and the sound of it felt like rough water rushing over river stones to Mireio. And for a water witch that was a very sexy sound. "It's how the place was when I moved in," he said. "But thanks to my remodeling it's all modern and has running water with good quality plumbing in the outhouse. Not a hole in a board."

"Whew! For a second there you had me worried. I'll have you know the bathroom is the most important room in my house. There are not too many nights I miss my bath."

"You were taking a bath the night I saw you standing outside the door. Uh, sorry." He rubbed a palm over his face and swiped across his beard nervously. "I have to stop bringing that up. It's rude of me."

"Not rude, just..." Mireio sighed. "So you've seen me naked. Just gives you something to desire, doesn't it?" And she sat back, satisfied that she'd stepped beyond the weirdness of the event and made it something she could control. If not a little weirder. *Ha! Go, Mireio!* "Anyway, my bathtub is huge. It's because I'm a mermaid."

Lars's jaw dropped open. "You are? So you're like a mermaid witch?"

"I mean, figuratively I'm a mermaid. I love water. I work water magic. I think I was probably a real mermaid in a past life. You know?"

"I can imagine you swishing around in the sea. But would your hair have been green?"

"Maybe." She twirled the ends of her hair around a fingertip and fluttered her lashes at him.

And Lars fell into that puppy-dog, lovestruck expression again. Oh, dear, but he had it bad for her. And she wasn't beyond encouraging him, because now that she was getting to know him, she really liked the strong silent alpha.

Had she intentions to avoid a relationship? Silly witch.

"Mireio!"

At the shrieking female yell, Lars sat up abruptly, kicking the table and upsetting the plates. Mireio made a grab to keep them from falling onto the stone patio. "It's just Mrs. Henderson," she said quickly, as if to calm a spooked dog.

The old woman popped around the back corner of the house with a notebook in hand. She wore an olive green pencil skirt that Mireio imagined she'd probably worn in her heyday back in, well…whenever the skirt had been in style. Her black-and-gray hair was piled into a messy bundle atop her narrow skull and on her feet were the ever-present and quite beaten pink bunny slippers.

"Oh." Mrs. Henderson eyed up Lars. "I didn't realize you had a guest, Mireio."

"Mrs. Henderson, this is Lars Gunderson. Lars, Mrs. Henderson, my next-door neighbor. We were just finishing lunch. And I have a loaf of oatmeal rye for you that I'll bring over once it's cooled, Mrs. Henderson."

"Oh, that's lovely. You're always so generous with the baked goods. And quite a talent too." She still couldn't drag her assessing gaze from Lars as she held out the notebook before her. "I don't mean to interrupt but I wanted to show you the sketch I made of the—" she dropped her voice to a whisper "—you-know-what we saw the other night."

Mireio glanced to Lars, who, no doubt, had figured what the woman was talking about, but he didn't show that he had.

"Lars, was it?" Mrs. Henderson asked him. She tilted her head, taking him in with a discerning gaze. "Have we met before? You seem very familiar."

"Never," Mireio blurt out. "I mean, we've only just met, so of course you've never seen him here or in my yard before. Let me see what you've drawn, Mrs. Henderson. It's okay. I mentioned the, uh, incident to Lars. So he's in on it."

"Oh?" The woman's eyes brightened, pleased to have another conspirator present. "She told you about the Sasquatch?"

"That she did." He leaned his elbows onto his knees, giving her his full attention. "You must have been frightened something fierce."

"Who me? Oh, gosh, no. I may have been initially surprised to see such a big, ugly, hulking beast tromping through my prized tulips, but that didn't stop me from getting a very good look at the monster."

Lars's jaw tensed. It was a good thing he wasn't holding the glass of lemonade because Mireio guessed his clenched fingers might have sent shards flying.

Mrs. Henderson laid the notebook down on the table and Mireio turned it so both she and Lars could look at the—quite talented—sketch of what looked similar to an ape-like man with long hairy fingers and a hunched back and shoulders. The head was all wrong, not matching the werewolf's actual wolf head and long toothy maw, but instead more resembling a man with large ears and a flat monkeylike snout.

"Remarkable," Mireio said with a secret glance and smile to Lars.

"Is it how you remembered the beast too?" Mrs. Henderson asked eagerly. "I intend to bring this sketch in to the police, but I'm still not so sure I got the nose right."

"Oh. Well…" Mireio shrugged. "I didn't get a very good look at it. I had initially thought it was a moose… but I'm sure what you've drawn here is very close."

"But you said it stopped and stared at you for a moment. Surely you must have seen details? Did you look into its big glowing yellow eyes?"

Mireio met Lars's lift of his brows. He was smirking

now, thank the goddess. He obviously understood there was no fear of him being found out with such a drastically wrong drawing, no matter who the woman showed it to.

"Maybe a little longer," she said, tapping the nose. "And did you get the tail?"

"The tail?" Mrs. Henderson picked up the sketch and studied it. "I'm not sure I remember…oh. Sure. A tail. Of course, Sasquatches have tails."

"Do they?" Lars asked.

"Oh, yes," Mrs. Henderson replied with knowing authority. "I'll have to add that. Thank you, Mireio. Oh." She placed a hand on Lars's shoulder. "Will you be around more often? To, you know, keep an eye on our sweet Mireio?"

"Uh…"

"I think I hear the oven timer for the last loaf of bread," Mireio interrupted. "We'll talk later, Mrs. Henderson. Lars, would you help me bring in the dishes?"

"It was nice meeting you, Mrs. Henderson," he offered as he dutifully and quickly followed Mireio's escape route into the kitchen.

The two of them watched out the window until Mrs. Henderson had turned the corner at the back of the house, then they both started laughing.

"That was the most awful rendition of—" she made air quotes "—'the monster,' I've seen. You don't look anything like that."

"Yes, I'm relieved. Must be interesting having that woman living next door, eh?"

"Never a dull moment." She opened the oven door, which emitted a whoosh of delicious bread scent.

"Mmm, now that scent will lead me back to your door over and over."

"Good," she said decisively. "Because I like you, Lars. I'm glad you had the courage to approach me last night. Maybe we can do this again tomorrow night? More like an official date? Because right now I have to go change and head in to work."

"I'd like that. Ah, but tomorrow night won't work. I won't be able to find a..." He winced, pausing to think his words through. "I have a previous engagement. It's not with another woman. Just something I can't get out of. How about this Saturday?"

Two days away. "Saturday works for me. But you'll have to pick me up at the brewery because I have the early shift."

"It's a date."

"Great! Let me wrap up a loaf of bread for you to take along." She pulled out some brown paper she kept for wrapping baked goods, and with a few folds and tucks fitted it perfectly about a warm loaf and handed it to him.

He took the gift and then glanced to the front door. Back to her. He rubbed a hand along his thigh. "Yes, I suppose I should leave. Thank you for lunch. It was really good."

"It wasn't that great. But you're a guy. Usually guys like any food that's been made for them that isn't a TV dinner."

"So you've seen the inside of my freezer?"

He smiled, and she fell into that pretty white gleam of his. He had no idea the impact those pearly whites had on her. And was she blushing? Parts of her suddenly felt very hot.

"Uh. Right. Then I suppose I should go." He turned, but didn't walk to the front door.

So Mireio stepped up before him, sensing what he couldn't say or do. And finding it sweetly endearing. "Did you want to kiss me before you leave?"

He nodded. Eagerly, but with a sheepish shrug. "I wasn't sure it would be okay."

The guy had scored one simply by being a sweet, uncomfortable lunk of shy. Mireio crooked her finger, gesturing that he should bow down, and when he got close enough to kiss, she met his lips with hers.

His mouth was not tentative, finding its place against hers with a surety and the promise of more confidence than his speech gave. He didn't open her mouth, but he lingered, and the pressure of him against her worked a delicious tingle in her core. Mmm, now that was a very not-shy kiss.

When they parted, his eyes darted back and forth between hers. Then his dimples dented his cheeks and his smile caught up. "Saturday can't come fast enough." He kissed her quickly, and then turned to leave.

Standing on the threshold and watching his long strides out to his pickup truck, Mireio touched her lips and whispered a blessing for the fact she'd not been a stuck-up witch last night and had decided to talk to the man.

"Good call," she said to herself. "May the witch and the werewolf get along. At the very least, have some fun."

Well past the midnight hour, Mireio startled from her sleep and cried out. She sat up, seeking in the darkness for a creature—with fangs. Heartbeat thundering, she pressed a palm to her chest and, realizing she'd had another nightmare, breathed deeply in and out to calm her fears.

It was always the same. The vampire stood before her holding a bloody heart that dripped onto the toes of her white shoes, forever staining her memories of a younger, more innocent time.

She hadn't had a nightmare in over a year, but the fact it had returned now disturbed her. She had to perform the immortality spell. But if so focused on preparing for the spell, could she then also concentrate on dating the shy but sexy werewolf?

"Am I doing the right thing?" she whispered into the night.

No one answered. Which was a good thing. That meant she was alone. No creepy vampire anywhere near her. Yet the only way to ensure she was safe from vampires was to rip the heart out of one of them and consume its blood.

She dropped back into the pillows and closed her eyes tightly.

Chapter 4

Saturday evening Lars stopped into the brewery. Mireio was ready to go, waiting for him by the door. She bounced on her high heels and her short multiruffled purple skirt caught his eye. And dangling near that skirt was the black fish purse. The woman was a character. And she was going out with him tonight.

He was the luckiest guy in the world.

Mireio waved goodbye to a woman behind the bar with dark hair and a calm, knowing smile, whom Lars waved to, as well. He hadn't been introduced, but did know Valor Hearst, who also worked here. She and Sunday, his pack leader's wife, were friends, so Valor popped up at the compound once in a while. They always chatted bees for a while when she did so.

"Where are we going tonight?" Mireio asked as she joined him and slipped her hand into his.

Momentarily captivated by the warm slender hand in his, Lars took a few seconds to answer. It actually took a squeeze from her hand to lure him back to what she'd asked.

"Uh, where? There's a new place in Tangle Lake. Supposed to be fancy and the scenery is pretty cool. You like a steak house?"

"Sure. I like all food. Your hand is so big and—" she turned it over to inspect as they strolled toward the parking lot "—rough. You must do a lot of physical labor."

"I've cleared out some fallen oaks from the forest near my place, so I've been chopping and stacking wood for winter fires. As well as doing some repair work on the plank path that leads to the outhouse."

"I need to see that outhouse one of these days. I can't imagine having to walk outside to get to the bathroom."

"I'm sure your bathroom with the big tub puts my little outhouse to shame."

"Oh, I'm sure it does." She skipped a few steps up to the charcoal gray truck. "This is yours? You men and your big trucks. You're going to have to boost me up for this one."

He opened the passenger door for her and held her hand as she stepped onto the lower step. Even then she had to stretch up a leg, and…he put a hand to her hip to guide her. He wanted to give a shove to that sweet little derriere, but that might be too forward. He was the kind of guy who would never manhandle a woman. Unless she'd given him permission to do so. And then he would enjoy touching her with abandon.

"I'm in!" she announced with a clap. "Let's do this!"

Chuckling at her enthusiasm, Lars rounded the front of the truck and hopped inside and started the engine. "How's business tonight?"

"It's a Saturday," she said as he drove out of the lot. "Comedy night."

"Really? Like stand-up?"

"Yes, and tonight is locals only. It's a big hit. There are some ridiculously hilarious people living in Anoka."

"You like music?" he asked, turning on the radio low.

"I love the oldies stuff like the '80s tunes."

"I think I know the station for you." He turned the dial to an '80s hit station, one of his favorites too, despite having missed the era because he'd been born in the late '80s. Culture Club was playing and Mireio gave him a thumbs-up.

"Did you eat all the bread I sent home with you?" she asked.

"Most of it. Had sandwiches for lunch, with enough left for a French toast breakfast tomorrow. You make great bread."

"You'll have to stop by when I'm in a cupcake-baking mood."

"Don't tempt me."

"Temptation is my thing, don't you know?"

He waggled his brows at her.

She giggled. "You're starting to loosen up around me. You were pretty shy initially."

He shrugged as he turned onto the freeway that would take them to their destination. "You're just so pretty. I admit I'm intimidated by most women. You're all so... tiny."

"That is understandable, coming from a big beast of a man. How tall are you?"

"Six and a half feet? Something like that."

"Good thing I like wearing heels. Oh! I love this song!"

Adam Ant's "Desperate But Not Serious" started playing and Lars turned it up. He would never consider himself desperate for a woman. But would he like to get serious with one? Hell yes. And Mireio Malory seemed a very good option.

The view was gorgeous, as promised. They sat on a patio situated about thirty feet from the lakeshore. The sun settled above the jagged line of pines across the lake, casting pink and silver shimmers on the water and the night air was surprisingly warm for spring. A fountain nestled in the center of the small lake burbled and a pair of white swans floated close by. Fortunately it was too early in the season for mosquitoes.

The brown butter shrimp with Gouda grits was excellent. The red wine sweet and not too dry. And the man sharing shy glances with her was slowly moving up to broadcasting more confidence in his brown eyes.

Mireio had never dated a man who wasn't in her face and always dropping innuendos about them *doing it*. Sure, she had dated a few who were polite, but none so sweetly masculine and devastatingly charming as this guy. A werewolf? She'd dated witches, faeries and once even a demon. But a wolf was new to her, and she was excited about the possibilities of learning more about this sweetie.

"I lost the muskie after that struggle," Lars said, ending his tale about ice fishing without an ice house or a line in the middle of what had turned into an ice storm.

"Do wolves have a greater affinity for cold weather?" she wondered.

"Yes, we can handle the Minnesota winters well. But I do like to bundle up when I know a storm is headed our way. That one took me by surprise. Froze my beard something fierce."

"Ha! I hope you had someone to help you defrost it with snuggly kisses."

He shrugged, that bashful move that endeared her to his big, awkward appeal. "I was out with the guys. We never mix fishing and women. You ladies just don't get it."

"Oh, I think Valor is into ice fishing. But there are times I wonder if she's more a guy than a girl. I don't think I'd like to lie on the ice and dip my hand in the cold waters in hopes a fish will find me of interest," she said. Which was exactly how Lars had explained they'd done it. "I admit the winter bothers me. I need a big thick sweater to keep from constantly shivering. I prefer spring and summer. And warmth."

"Your tail would freeze in the winter," he said with a wink.

"Which tail are you talking about?" she asked teasingly.

"Both?"

"Ha!" She tilted her wine goblet to his and he met it with a *tink*. "To breezy summers and warm winter nights. And while we're at it, let's toss in a long life of immortal dreams."

"Immortal dreams?"

She shrugged. "It's a witch thing. Just a spell I've had on my mind lately. Anyway, back to the fishing. I certainly hope to never get hooked by a fisherman anytime soon."

"Is that so?"

"He'd rip my tail. And besides, we mermaids would never be caught swimming in any of Minnesota's ten thousand icy lakes."

"What sort of bait do you think would attract a mermaid?"

She leaned across the table and the small heat from the candle warmed her cheek. "Kindness and a sexy shy smile."

And there it was again! Those dimples were mermaid bait for sure. But to think about it, she'd hooked him. And this was one catch he wasn't eager to toss back.

The waitress stopped by with the bill and Lars dug out his wallet from a back pocket and handed her his credit card.

"So what do you like to do for fun?" he asked. "I've already marked ice fishing off the potential date list."

"I don't have to be entertained in any wild or elaborate fashion. A movie. A book club. Dancing, or even just sitting in a park. I'm a chick who can find fun in most anything."

"I get that. You're what they call one of those eclectic women," he said with a wink. "Your bright hair and frilly clothes tell me that."

"How else is a girl supposed to dress?"

"You won't hear me complaining. But what's with the purse?"

She lifted her purse. A cool find on Etsy, crafted from black suede in layers that emulated a fish with scales. "Mermaid, remember?"

"Right. Let me guess… You're the chick at the summer festivals with the flowers in your hair, dancing in the mud with bare feet and not a care?"

"You got it."

"I think I'm the guy always standing off to the side, wondering if that beautiful blossom of a chick will ever notice him."

She placed her hand over his. "I have noticed you, Lars. And I think you're pretty cool. I'll get you in daisies and bare feet before the summer is out. Promise."

"I'd actually wear daisies for you. So why don't we…" He paused, staring off over the lake with the swans floating by.

The pause was…quite long. "Lars?"

"Huh? Oh. Sorry, lost my train of thought. What were we talking about?"

Daisies and flirtation. "Nothing much." But it was time to move it up to the next level. "Now do you know what I want to do?"

"What?"

"You said you live close?"

"About ten miles north."

"Then I want to see this mysterious outhouse with the modern plumbing."

He smirked and collected his credit card as the waitress swung by with it. But instead of dimples, he rubbed his jaw, with a wince. "I'm not sure. I have to make a stop on the way home, actually..."

"Am I being too forward? I'm not suggesting anything. I mean, am I? Maybe? If you're not ready to take me home with you, just for chatting, I get that. You're a guy who works more slowly than most."

"Not at all. I can do fast. I'm very fast. I mean..." He swiped his fingers over his beard in what Mireio was learning was a nervous gesture. "I want to spend more time with you tonight, Mireio. I just, uh...well..." A heavy sigh surprised her. "You'll need to know sooner rather than later. Guess now's as good a time as any."

"That sounds absolutely mysterious. But I'm in. Let's go!"

Ten minutes later, they drove up the long driveway to the Northern Pack compound, which was where Lars had to make a stop. It wasn't like a big military compound, which Mireio had expected, but rather a white plantation-style home with a massive tin-sided building out back that housed all kinds of building materials and lots of junk.

"So none of the pack members live here except Dean and Sunday?"

"Nope. We all live in the area, though. Packs used to share close living conditions, but you know, it's the twenty-first century. We like our privacy as much as we like the family we get from being in the pack." He parked before the house and swung around to open the door.

Just when she thought to step down, he lifted her and swung her out, setting her down carefully until she could get a sure footing with her heels on the gravel drive. How many times had a man helped her in and out of a vehicle?

Exactly twice. Both of those times had been tonight. She could get used to this kind of chivalry.

"Shall we?" He offered his hand and that pushed her over the edge and into a giddy swoon.

She clasped his hand and beamed as he led her toward the front door, which opened to reveal a waving Sunday. The chick sported long, white-blond hair and was built like Valor—straight—and she seemed accustomed to hanging out in jeans and greasy T-shirts as opposed to frills and lace. She was a cat-shifting familiar, married to Dean Maverick, a werewolf and the pack principal.

"Hey, Lars!" A shout from near the storage building drew their attention to Dean standing near a huge steel beam he held at a diagonal, one end of it digging into the ground. "Come give me a hand!"

"Be right back," Lars said. "Uh, you know Sunday?"

"We've met once," Sunday confirmed.

Lars winked at Mireio. "This won't take a minute!"

"Hey, Mireio." Sunday gestured she come inside and held the screen door open for her. "I didn't know you and Lars were a thing."

She entered the house, which was dimly lit. The sun had set, and the soft kitchen lights gleamed on the white marble kitchen counter and copper toaster.

"Lars and I just started seeing one another. First official date tonight. Oh!" She spied a munchkin sitting in a baby seat on the kitchen table and her maternal instincts rushed her to check it out. "Who is this little sweetie? Can I hold him?"

"Sure, I just fed him. We call him Peanut."

Mireio picked up the warm bundle of blue fleece and baby softness and he nuzzled against her chest. The scent of warm baby was better than baked bread or chocolate any day. She rubbed her palm lightly over the thick crop of black hair swished to a wave on top of his head. "So much hair! And it sticks straight up. Adorable. How old is he?"

"Uh, about four months?" Sunday leaned against the counter, her T-shirt falling from one bare shoulder and her hair a little tangled as if she'd been through a tough day. Or she simply wasn't a fashion queen and didn't often bother to comb her hair.

"Did you and Dean adopt?" Mireio knew, from Valor, that Sunday couldn't have kids. Well, she could, but a cat shifter simply could not make a baby with a werewolf. Just didn't work that way.

"No. He's uh…" Sunday straightened and scratched her head. "You don't know who Peanut is?"

"Should I?"

The front door opened and Lars and Dean wandered in, chuckling about almost dropping the steel beam, but finally getting it loaded into the back of Dean's truck. Lars took one look at Mireio holding the baby and activated the nervous beard swipe.

"Hey," she offered. "Isn't he the cutest little button ever? He's called Peanut."

"I know that." Lars exchanged glances with Sunday.

"I'll leave you two." The cat shifter left the kitchen swiftly, grabbing her husband's hand and heading toward the front door. Dean protested with a "What's up?" as his wife tugged him outside.

"What was that about?" Mireio bounced as she held the baby. It was a natural motion, instilled from years of babysitting. His plump little body felt so good snuggled against her breast and neck. Someday she would have a million kids. Or at the very least three or four. "She must be babysitting for someone, huh?"

"She is." Lars smoothed his hand over the baby's hair. "Peanut is mine, Mireio."

"What?"

"He's my son."

Chapter 5

Mireio blinked a few times, then realized Lars was talking about the baby she cuddled against her shoulder. He held out his arms for the boy, and she handed him over. The big hulking werewolf gently cradled the sleeping infant in his arms as if he were a wise old granny who had been doing so for generations. He stroked the baby's hair and kissed his forehead.

"He's a sweetie," she offered because she was taken aback. But then she realized she was only surprised because she'd never expected such from Lars. "You're not married, are you?" came out too quickly.

He snickered and began to rock the baby with a gentle bounce. "No."

"Good. I mean—well, I don't date married men."

"I would never be so cruel to another woman. He's my boy, Mireio. I wasn't going to tell you like this. And I thought I'd wait a bit longer. But when you suggested I show you my place I figured now was as good a time as any. If you're not into kids, that's cool. At least you found out early on and can walk away."

"No." She touched his arm, and tapped the baby's tiny fingers. "I adore babies. And I'm fine with this. I mean, we're not lovers or anything. We've only seen each other a few times."

"Sure." But his wince told her he had high hopes for what might happen between them.

And she did too. Did she still have such high hopes with the introduction of this little number? It shouldn't change things. This was all a bit sudden and new. But if the guy had a baby, then she could deal.

"Let's take things as they come, okay?" She waited for Lars to meet her eyes. And when he did, she winked at him. "You should probably get this little guy home and tucked in."

"Yes, and he needs to be changed too. I uh…" He grimaced again. "I took the car seat out for our date tonight because, well, like I've said, I wasn't sure when or how to spring this on you. Usually I walk through the forest to drop him off and pick him up. Would you mind driving the truck to my cabin? It's just a winding road from here."

"That big monster truck?" Mireio gulped.

"I'll help you move the seat forward so you can reach the pedals."

"Do you trust me?"

He pressed his head against the baby's head and kissed his nose. And Mireio suddenly realized that the man probably trusted her more with the vehicle than he did with his child.

"Hand me the keys. I can do this."

The path through the woods had been there for decades. Lars knew that the very first pack members had built the compound and the cabin where he lived. He liked having his own place and had lived there alone since he was fourteen. But also, when the pack had been larger, he'd liked being close to friends, whom he also considered family. Now, it was nice for the two-mile distance between the places because babysitting was just a wander through the woods.

Sunday had been the one to suggest he get away from the cabin and go out and have a little fun. Lars had been cooped up with Peanut for months and generally walked around with baby spit on his shoulders, and who knew when he'd last washed his hair?

Yet in the process of "getting out" he'd hooked up with a pretty woman.

"I sure hope she likes us both," he said as he strode the beaten path over fallen leaves, cracking branches and crops of mushrooms that edged the lane. "What do you think, Peanut?"

The boy was awake and alert, taking in the surroundings, even though it was dark. Lars pressed a kiss to his bushy crop of thick hair. He loved that stuff. It was soft and black and smelled like nothing he'd ever known but everything he wanted to have forever.

Had he done things wrong tonight? Should he have kept Peanut a secret until he felt sure that he and Mireio might have a real thing between them?

No, better to give her opportunity to run now before they did get to know one another. And better for him. He'd hate to fall in love with her and then lose her because he had a baby. Much as she had claimed to enjoy babies, being a parent was different. It required dedication and sacrifice. And love.

Lars had never been in love. Until now. He hugged Peanut and strode swiftly toward the truck lights that approached his cabin.

He arrived at the truck in time to help Mireio down and tell her how to turn the lights off. The truck really was a monster in her hands, but she'd gotten here safely.

"Whew!" she said when she stood on the ground beside him. "That thing is huge and the road is narrow and winding. I think I just passed some kind of endurance test! Hey! Don't laugh at me, you little giggle butt," she said to Peanut.

Lars high-fived her and nodded that she should follow him in. "The road is crazy twisty. I've considered getting a smaller truck, but I haul a lot of wood and well..." He opened the front door, which he never kept locked and gestured she enter before him. "I do like a big truck."

"Men and their toys." Her heels clicked across the clean wood floor. "Wow, this place is cute. It's all just the one room?"

She turned, taking in the living area with the blue-and-green-plaid couch and low table made from half an oak trunk. The kitchen offered a small fridge, a porcelain sink and an old gas stove. A round kitchen table sat at the end of the foyer, which was right before them. Immediately to their right stood the queen-size bed hemmed in by a clothes rack against a wall. Peanut's crib was wedged between the clothes and the end of the bed.

"This is it." Lars grabbed a diaper from a shelf above the clothes rack and laid Peanut on the bed. "I gotta change him. I hope you don't mind. There's beer and water in the fridge."

"Sure. Looks like he's wide-awake now," she said as she rummaged around in the fridge.

"Peanut loves walking through the woods. Don't you?" He toyed with the baby's bare toes as the infant stretched out his legs. He always did that once diaper-free. Like, oh, yes, Daddy, let me dry out and be a nudist for a while. "Soon you'll be running through the woods and putting your daddy through the wringer of keeping up with you."

"What is his name?" Mireio asked as she sat before the kitchen table with a bottle of water.

"Peanut." He secured the diaper tapes and replaced his son's onesie snaps. He tossed the diaper into the bin, which he emptied every night, and then got a bottle of milk he'd poured this morning from the fridge. He set it in the pot on the stove half-filled with water and turned on the heat. It took only minutes to get a nice warmth to the milk.

"You named your son Peanut?" He could sense the dismay in her tone. "That's…unique."

Lars sat next to her before the table. "I don't know his real name. His mother didn't tell me it before she ran off. And the name on the birth certificate simply says 'baby boy.' I thought he sort of melded against me like a little peanut when I held him against my chest, so…it works for now."

"Peanut. Sure. But you are going to give him a name?"

Lars shrugged. "When the right one comes to me. I have up to a year to fill it in on the birth certificate."

"Sounds fair enough. Oh, don't get up. I'll check the milk." She tested the milk against her wrist, then sat down and handed it to him. "Cool, but just about right. So… do I get to ask you about Peanut's mom and where she is and why you're doing the single-daddy thing? Oh. Did she die?"

"No, she's not dead, and yes, ask me anything you like."

Because that meant she was open to the conversation, and maybe he might still have a chance with her.

"I want to know whatever you're comfortable telling me." She pointed to the baby sucking voraciously at the bottle. "Explain that little bundle of sweetness and wild rock-star hair."

She hadn't made an excuse to leave yet. And she wasn't standing by the door, eyeing the escape. So Lars marked himself as lucky. So far, so good.

"All right, here goes. I spent a few nights with Peanut's mom last year. It was a two-night stand kind of thing. We met in a nightclub in downtown Minneapolis. We weren't drunk, but you know how sometimes you just want to get close with another person?"

She nodded knowingly. "Oh, yeah."

"And the feeling was mutual," he continued. "So, you know, it happened. She stayed the day and a second night, then told me it had been fun, and she was moving on. She traveled a lot for her job as a photojournalist. Was hoping to get an assignment in Africa that would last for years. I marked it off as a fun couple of nights and life went on. Human women, you know…"

He shifted to tilt up Peanut a bit so the baby wouldn't get gassy from sucking in air from the bottle.

"What about human women?" Mireio asked.

"It's hard for we werewolves to have a relationship with someone who is going to freak out the minute she sees you shift. We can't trust that secret with just anyone."

"You can trust a witch."

"I know that." He winked at her and she smiled and wiggled on her chair. "Ten months after that hookup I get a knock on the door and the surprise of my life. She didn't want a baby. Didn't need one messing up her life. And she got the African assignment. So she said it was my choice. She could put the baby up for adoption, or I could take him."

Mireio's jaw dropped open. Then she closed it. "Wow. Tough choice for a young, single man."

"Not really. I took one look at this little peanut and knew I had to have him in my life."

"Really? Have you always liked kids? Babies? Usually men aren't so paternal."

"I have never been around kids much. Never even held a baby before this guy."

"How did you even trust that he was yours?"

"She does ask the questions, doesn't she?" Lars said to Peanut. "I just knew. But also, his mom said I should get a DNA test, and she even had the forms and details on how to do it, along with all the info she'd written down for Peanut's feeding schedule. She was an orderly woman. And she said she knew he was mine because she hadn't had sex with a guy after me for months."

"Did you do the test?"

"I did. Peanut is one hundred percent mine. But I knew that before I got the test results."

"How did you know?"

He beamed at her. "My heart told me he was mine. But also, could you imagine putting this little sweetie up for adoption?"

"He is a sweetie. But he might have made some other family happy too. Adoption isn't horrible."

"I know that."

"Oh, but wait. Is he werewolf?"

Lars shrugged. "Not sure. His mom is human, but human women can give birth to our babies, and they can be werewolf. But I won't know until Peanut hits puberty. Another good reason not to put him up for adoption. Could you imagine human parents discovering their adopted son, once he hits puberty, suddenly shifts to a wolf?"

"So his mom didn't know you were werewolf?"

"No need for me to tell her. You know it's not wise to share stuff like that with humans. How many people do you tell you're a witch?"

"Zero. Unless I get a feeling about them. Like you. Aw, look, he's sleeping. Sweet little Peanut. You really should give him a name, though."

"I'm working on it. I have to go to the county office and do a name change. I'm already on the birth certificate as the father. Peanut's mom had the foresight to do that, so he's got my last name."

"That was smart. Oh. Can I hold him?"

"Uh…" Lars set the bottle on the table and studied

her pleading yet smiling look. When he'd walked in at Dean's place to find her holding Peanut, he'd initially felt angry. What right had she to barge in and take hold of his child? But then he'd realized she hadn't even known who the baby was then.

Now? He was being foolish. Possessive. And with every right to be so.

"Oh, sorry." She sat back. "You're his daddy. I'm sure he needs you to tuck him in."

"He sleeps through most of the night after his final bottle. I'll put him down."

Once he'd tucked Peanut in, and left him uncovered because it was warm tonight, Lars then rinsed the bottle and dried it while Mireio got up to admire the lamp base on the table beside the couch.

"This is beautiful," she said of the carved pine column. "It's so intricate. I can see deer and squirrels and that looks like a swan. Did you do this?"

Lars shrugged and nodded. "There's a lot of wood out here. Sometimes I see something in the wood that needs to come out."

"Like Michelangelo and his marble sculptures. You're an artist."

"No, I'm just a regular guy who amuses himself with a hammer and chisel once in a while." He set the bottle on the rack above the sink and then approached her. He shoved his hands in his back pockets. "So, I know this is a lot of baggage I've unpacked here. And I'll understand if you don't want to see me anymore. I wasn't even in the market for dating, but then Sunday said I needed to get out, have some fun. And after that morning at your place, there were the lilacs. It was almost like I had to find you. Then I did. I think it's better you know right away."

"Lars, don't worry. There are a lot of single parents nowadays. And we're not serious. Just having fun, right?"

"Right."

"Oh, and if Sunday can't babysit, call me. I adore babies. Would love to have a couple, or twelve, of my own someday."

"I'll remember that." He sat on the couch and she sat next to him, which he took as a good sign that she didn't want to leave right away.

"That is, if you can trust me with Peanut. I have babysat a lot."

"Oh, I trust you."

"Yeah? But you didn't want me to hold him just now at the table."

"Sorry. He's my boy and…well, you're new."

"I get it." She clasped his hand. "You're a protective alpha wolf. Do not apologize for that. Ever. Now. I want to see this strange but interesting bathroom. Can we slip out with Peanut sleeping?"

"Yep. I've got a baby monitor in the bathroom so I can hear him if I'm taking a shower. But I promise you, it's nothing to get excited about."

"Any outhouse that isn't two holes in a slab of wood is exciting."

Through the crisp darkness, surrounded by cricket chatter, they followed a plank path back to the outhouse. The bathroom was indeed a small room with a toilet, shower and tub, and vanity. Plain but serviceable. But Mireio decided it would be a bitch in the winter if a person woke in the middle of the night needing to answer the call of nature.

"No holes dug in the ground," Lars offered as they stepped out into the night air.

He pointed out the wildflower field that backed onto his property behind the outhouse and the beehives he kept. He had eight stacks right now and would divide them in the fall and probably gain three more in the process. He'd promised to take some of Valor's bees when she divided the hives that she tended from the rooftop of her apartment building in Tangle Lake.

"So you're a keeper," Mireio commented, loving herself for the pun.

"I am? Oh. Uh, yes. A beekeeper."

She felt sure he blushed in the darkness. The man certainly was a keeper.

After the grand tour, Mireio suggested they call it a night. She'd felt bad he'd had to take Peanut out of his crib, but the infant had slept through being buckled into his car seat and the twenty-minute drive back to Anoka, and even her accidental slamming of the truck door when she got out at the sidewalk before her house.

"Can I call you?" Lars asked as he stepped down from the sidewalk to stand on the tarmac, which put their heights a little closer.

"I certainly hope so. Hey, how about an afternoon with Peanut tomorrow? I have to go in to work for a few hours in the morning. Valor and I are kegging the stout. But I'm free after one. We could go to a park and have a picnic?"

"I'd like that. You sure you're okay with this, Mireio?"

She shrugged. "I am right now. If I think about it awhile? Who knows? But I don't think I'll change my mind. I'm enjoying getting to know you. You are certainly an interesting man."

"Maybe a little too interesting, eh?"

"Better that than dull, right?" She laughed, but stopped abruptly. "So tomorrow it's a date."

"Should I pick you up at the brewery?"

"Yes." She tilted up on her tiptoes to meet the kiss that he did not pause to give her this time. His breath tasted like the wine they'd shared over supper, and his beard brushed her cheek softly. And when she started to pull away he dipped in for a firm press that won her completely. She sighed into the kiss and drew her fingers down the ends of his long hair. Mmm, he was some kind of all right. "I do enjoy these not-so-shy kisses."

"Me too. I would kiss you longer but…" He glanced over to the running truck.

"I'm glad you told me about Peanut. You two are adorable together. We're going to have fun, the three of us."

Lars turned and waved as he got in the truck. And Mireio hugged herself and recalled that the man had given her a choice to walk away now if she wanted to.

Did she want to walk away? Could she handle dating a man with a baby? Neither option felt easy. And she needed easy right now. Because that would counter the nightmares and her wariness over performing the immortality spell.

Chapter 6

Areas of the park were overgrown with wildflowers stretching as high as Lar's waist in some spots. They'd picnicked with egg salad sandwiches, fresh veggies and blueberry lemonade in mason jars. While Mireio packed up the basket, Lars wandered into the flowers with Peanut, pointing out the yellow sunflowers. He held out his hand and a bee buzzed closer, probably attracted to his movement. He never flinched. Bees would not sting a person unless they were given reason to do so. And he intended to teach Peanut to not fear the insect, and to also respect it.

"That's a dragonfly." He stood still as the insect hovered but four feet from him. Strapped to his chest in a baby sling, Peanut stretched out his arms and cooed. "Yes, you like bugs? Of course you do. But you mustn't squish them. Insects are good. Especially the bees. Like that one. See the fat sacks of pollen on her legs? She's going to make honey with that. And then we can eat it."

Though he'd read not to give an infant honey in his first year. Or had the pediatrician told him that? He needed to get a guide or book on all the things a parent should do and watch out for. This whole baby thing was new to him. He was walking a tightrope with Peanut, and didn't want to wobble off the line.

"We'll find a book or something," he said to Peanut.

"A book on what?" Having taken off her shoes, Mireio joined him. A camera dangled from around her neck. She took some shots of a bright purple coneflower. Bending, she plucked a few tiny white daisies.

"A baby book," he said. "I need something that'll tell me what I should and shouldn't do. I was telling Peanut about honey. I know that's a no-no for the first year."

"Right. There are great books out there for parents. Dr. Sears or the What to Expect books. They cover a baby's first year, telling you what changes they go through monthly and about their growth."

"Sounds like exactly what I need. Can we stop by a bookstore on the way back into town?"

"For sure! But only if you don't mind me checking out the books on beer. I'm looking for a new and interesting recipe."

"Deal." He turned and fist-bumped her. "You a photographer too?"

"Me? No. But I like to take pictures of flowers and bugs. I have a macro lenses that I usually use. Takes amazingly detailed shots, but I forgot it today. I do have one of my pictures hanging up behind my bed."

"I'll have to check it out sometime." Lars wandered forward then, with a wince, realized what he'd said. Check out the picture or her bed?

Well, he'd like to do both. In good time.

Spying a thick crop of wild grass, he sat on it and laid back with Peanut snuggling up to his chest. "Ah, this is the life. The sun is high and warm and I don't have a care."

Mireio leaned over him and snapped a few pictures. "Do you mind? You two look adorable lying there. He really is a little peanut all curled up on his daddy's chest."

"Go for it."

"Oh, wait. I forgot the daisies." She pushed a couple daisies into his beard. "I did tell you I'd have you in daisies, didn't I?"

"That you did." He even managed to smile, eyes closed against the sun, as she snapped the camera above him and Peanut.

After a few shots, she sat in the grass next to them and set down the camera. Tilting her head back to allow the sun to beam across her face, her hair tickled Lars's cheek. It was the color of overripe tomatoes, with a hint of golden sunshine within the strands. If her hair had a flavor, he decided it would be tangy cherry with a burst of lemon.

How had he gotten so lucky as to find a pretty girl who liked to spend time with him and his baby boy? While Dean Maverick had teasingly suggested that babies were chick bait, Lars had known that it wouldn't be so simple as strolling in to catch a woman's eye for more than a few oohs and aahs. But for some reason Mireio had stuck around after the initial reveal. So far.

He wouldn't count his blessings too soon. This thing they were doing was new and, as she'd pointed out, they were just having fun. So he had best stop worrying and get to the enjoying part.

"How about ice cream?" he suddenly said. "I don't think I've had any since I was a kid."

"Seriously?" Her blue eyes beamed above him. "There's a shop not far from here. And I'm pretty sure a bookstore sits a couple stores down from that. What do you think, Peanut?" She stroked his fuzzy crop of dark hair. "Aw, he's sleeping. All tuckered out from the sunshine. We'd better get him inside so he doesn't overheat."

"Overheat? Do babies do that?"

"Well, he's not going to blow his top, but yes, his tender newborn skin will burn much easier than ours does."

"Darn it, and here I thought the sunshine was good for him." Lars sat up and tugged the blanket over Peanut's head.

"Don't worry about it. He's not going to fry. Lars, you're a great dad. You've some amazing instincts about taking care of a baby. Don't question yourself so much."

"It's hard not to do so. I've never done this before. Sometimes I feel like I'm a little bug standing in the middle of this big field, trying to keep my baby bug alive."

"You're doing great." She kissed him then. A soft, slow kiss that tasted his mouth and dipped her tongue across his bottom lip. It was a sweet connection that promised more. When she pulled away, she plucked the flowers from his beard and tucked them into her hair over one ear. "Let's get ice cream."

When they stopped by the bookstore, Peanut was fussing, so Lars stayed in the truck to change him while Mireio dashed in for the baby book and then skipped a few stores down to grab ice cream to go. They headed to her house, and by the time they arrived, Peanut was giggling and blowing bubbles every time she shook her bright hair before him.

"You must have grown up with brothers and sisters," Lars commented as they strolled into her house.

"Nope. I was an only child. I started babysitting when I was ten. Every penny I made went toward spell stuff and crystals. And a really cool mermaid tail that I still have tucked away somewhere."

"A mermaid tail?" He dropped Peanut's bag of accoutrements on the floor near the sofa.

"Yes, it was rubber or something. I could pull it up like pants and there was room in the fin for my feet. It sparkled," she said, adding jazz hands because that was what one did when one talked about all things glittery.

"I'd swim out in the backyard pool for hours wearing it. But it only fit me for about a year. I was so bummed. I think I expected it to grow with me. So you are going to stay for supper, yes? I make a mean zucchini parmesan."

"I'm not even sure what that is, but I'm in."

"Great! Let me get it put together. It'll take about twenty minutes, and then I'll pop it in the oven."

"Me and Peanut will take a look through the book you got for us."

He headed into the living room. Mireio called out that he could take the yarn afghan off the back of the couch and lay it on the floor for Peanut to crawl around on. "Will do!"

Utterly pleased after an afternoon well spent, she floated about the kitchen, gathering and slicing zucchini and onions, grating parmesan, while on the stove top she stirred a tomato sauce with basil and shallots.

Around the corner in the living room she heard Lars reading the *What to Expect the First Year* book out loud. In a very dramatic tone. She peeked around the corner and spied the big werewolf lying on the violet-and-blue afghan on his back—he held the book overhead while he pointed out the pictures to Peanut. The baby, lying on his back beside his daddy, followed his gestures with burbling fascination.

"Did you know a four-month-old is supposed to get his first tooth?" Lars called as she slipped back into the kitchen. "Peanut has had a tooth for two months. Heh. You're ahead of your time, my boy. Also, he might start to roll over. Is that so? You want to give it a go, Peanut?"

Whispering thanks to Demeter, the goddess of harvest, and snapping her fingers over the sauce, Mireio imbued it with a touch of love and confidence. It was difficult not to create something to eat without adding a spell. She'd been doing it forever. Nothing intrusive. But Lars could probably use the boost to his confidence. Goddess knows he must have been going through heck these past few months. But to judge from the infant giggles in the next room he was managing remarkably well.

Peanut, eh? That was a horrible name for a child to grow up with. She'd have to work on Lars, help him come up with something before the kid got too attached to the name.

Assembling the dish with layers of zucchini, cheese and sauce, she then put the glass baking dish in the stove and set the timer. Pouring two goblets of honey IPA from the growler she always kept stocked in the fridge, she then strolled into the living room.

Lars lay on his side facing Peanut; the baby was sleeping. "Sometimes I can't get over how much I like staring at him." Wonder touched his tone as Lars said, "I made this little guy."

"That you did. Or at least, you helped. I'm pretty sure the woman had a lot to do with it too. Brewing the little tyke for nine months and all." She handed him a beer as he sat up and leaned against the couch. The open book lay near his leg. "Do you mind if I ask you a personal question?"

"I already told you how me and Peanut's mom got together."

"Right, but do you think she might come back for her boy? I mean, after a few years? What if she has a change of heart? Or if her biological clock starts ticking? Wouldn't that crush you?"

Lars ran his fingers back through his hair, pulling it into a ponytail behind him, then releasing it with a growl. "It would annihilate me."

The alpha wolf lived inside him. And she had felt his protective instincts in that growl.

"I'm already so attached to him I couldn't imagine not

having him around," he said. "But Peanut's mom won't come back. She had stars in her eyes. No desire to spend her days in a tiny cabin in the woods. She was pretty adamant about starting a new life in Africa."

"Did you offer to marry her?"

"Didn't have a chance. To be honest? I'm not sure I would have. We only knew each other two days. And we didn't share a lot of conversation in that time, if you know what I mean. But had she decided to give motherhood a go, I would have never backed down on my obligation to raise my son. I'm relieved, actually, that she thought to give me a chance to raise him instead of going the adoption route."

Mireio stroked the hair that spilled down his shoulders, then realized what she was doing and tugged her hand to her lap. He turned to look over his shoulder at her. "Whatever you're making, it smells great."

"Half an hour and you can test it. I hope you like oregano and garlic. How's the IPA?"

"Awesome. I can taste the honey."

"Got it from Valor's hives. So you've worked with her and her bees?"

He waggled his hand before him in an indecisive gesture. "I sold her some queens and suggested some good places to order equipment. Her honey is distinctively different from field honey. She lives in a city and has hives on the top of her building. That forces the bees to forage for flowers far and wide and they visit a greater variety of flowers, which makes for a robust honey."

"Do your bees produce a lot of honey?"

"Oh, yeah. I have to give most of it away because I'd never be able to go through it all. You want some?"

"I can always use honey, especially for baking. How do you do all that processing of honey in your little place? I didn't see any equipment."

"I keep it in storage at the pack compound over the winter. I'm hoping to build a room for storing my apiary and honey equipment with the addition. And an extra room for Peanut's bedroom."

"Do you know how lucky Peanut is to have a dad like you?"

He toggled the toe end of Peanut's sleeper. "You didn't see me that first month I had him. I was pretty crazed. And a walking zombie from lack of sleep. Wasn't sure which end was up on the poor kid and was pretty damn surprised how much stuff tends to come out of both ends. For the first time I truly believed a dirty diaper could kill a man."

She laughed and tucked her legs up onto the couch. Lars turned and she patted the cushion beside her so he moved up to sit beside her, making sure not to step on the sleeping baby.

"But by the end of the second month I'd gotten into a routine. I actually have one of those planner apps on my phone. I don't know how all the moms do it without a calendar and a personal secretary. Just call me Mr. Mom now."

"Mr. Dad more like it. You rock the single dad role. It's good for a kid to have a dad or mom."

"Or? You don't believe they need both?"

Mireio shrugged. "Not necessarily. I never knew my dad. And my mom…" She sighed, memories unexpectedly rushing to the fore. Though she'd long ago shed all the tears. A glance to the mantel over the hearth landed on the photo of her and her mom. Jessica Malory had auburn hair that hung to her waist and a smile that could have stopped wars. "She died when I was eight. I was raised by my grandma."

"Really? That's tough. Or was it?"

"Sometimes. I mean, it's been twenty years. But at the

time, I was old enough to miss my mom, and her death was very traumatic." And she'd avoid telling him about that for fear of being reduced to blubbering tears. "But grandma was awesome. And you know with witches, if we've performed an immortality spell, we can look young for a very long time. Grandma looks like a fashion model from the sixties with her long brown hair and she seriously still wears bell-bottoms."

"You mentioned something about focusing on a spell. Does that mean you've performed the immortality spell I've heard about? Or are planning to?"

"That means I'm at this very moment prepared to do it. I've been thinking about it a lot over the past few years, and I'm ready."

"I think I know that spell requires a vampire, right?"

"You got it. It's never pretty for the vampire. We witches call them a source."

Lars lifted a brow. "Yes, but the vamps call those vampires ash."

"There is that result. And before you think I intend to destroy another soul to extend my own life, I'll have you know that I've hired a witch to track down one of the meanest and vilest vampires. One who has killed and is a danger to society."

He shrugged. "Doesn't bother me. I mean, if you take out a bad one. Vamps who kill to get blood when they only need a little to survive? That's unconscionable. I had no idea there was an actual person, though, that tracks down vamps specifically for you witches and your spells."

"It's Raven Crosse. She used to be a vampire hunter until she married a vampire. Now she does the search on the side for a very select clientele. And she costs a fortune."

"How much?"

Mireio pressed the glass rim to her lips, then shook her

head. "I'd rather not say. Suffice it to say, it's something I want. Desperately. So it was worth the price."

"The idea of one lifetime doesn't sit well with you?"

"Nope." And could they change the subject please? If she had to tell him how traumatized she'd actually been by her mother's death she'd burst out in tears, and that was so not sexy or romantic. "I should check on supper. Be right back."

Lars followed Mireio into the kitchen, where the scents of oregano and roasted tomatoes made him hunger for a home-cooked meal. She'd sprung up from the couch to retreat so abruptly, he suspected he'd said something wrong.

"I'm sorry," he said to her as she bent before the open oven and tested the dish with a fork. "I think I went too far in there."

"No, you didn't." She popped up and set the fork aside. "I don't want to get into all the details about my mom. It'll make me cry. Okay?"

"Deal." At least she was honest. He could respect that. "How much longer? I could eat that whole pan if you let me."

"Let me have a little corner and you can go right ahead and attack the rest. Ten minutes. You want more beer?"

"No, I'm good. Gotta drive Peanut home later."

"Don't tell me you're a lightweight?"

"With beer? No. Takes a lot to get us wolves drunk. But I'm trying to do the responsible thing now. You know?"

"I get that. But if you ever want to not be responsible for a little while?" She pointed at her chest where her low-cut blousy shirt revealed ample cleavage. "You know where to find me."

"We do have a few minutes. Why don't you come on over and show me a little irresponsibility?"

She spun around the end of the kitchen counter and

leaned toward him where he sat on a barstool. With him sitting, they came face-to-face, and he was thankful for that when he saw the kiss coming. Pushing his fingers up through her soft, bright hair, Lars accepted her sweet offering and smiled against her mouth. "You taste like tomato sauce."

"That's a preview for supper. You like?"

"I do." He kissed her again and this time delved in deeper with his tongue, tasting her tomato sweetness and dashing the tip of his tongue along her teeth.

Mmm, she was hot and soft and when she put her hands on his knees to balance, he wished she'd landed that touch a little higher up. There, where his erection was teasing rigidity. It had been a while since he'd been with a woman. And truly, after the past few months of endless diapers and spit-up, he had forgotten how good it could be to kiss one. And touch her. And mmm, just to inhale her.

He coaxed her forward by sliding his hand over her hip, and she followed directions and leaned into him without breaking their connection. Yep, everything was hard now. Not going to be easy getting through this night.

Her fingers clutched his shirt and the connection zinged his every nerve ending, sending scintillating tingles all over his skin. It was as if together they created a sort of sensual electricity. And he couldn't get enough of her mouth, her tongue, her sighs.

Pressing a hand against her back, he coaxed her forward again and bowed to keep the kiss. Her moan said everything he was feeling: yes, yes and all the yeses in the world. This tiny witch felt so right in his arms; he had to thank the gods for putting him in her backyard even if it had been a strange night that had scared the hell out of him.

A buzzer dinged, startling them to part their lips, and Mireio laughed. "Supper's done!" She kissed him quick, then wiped her finger alongside his mouth. "Got a little lipstick on you there." She tilted her head at him. "Can I have a few more of those awesome kisses for dessert?"

"You can have as many as you like."

Another *ding* drew her away from him, and Lars adjusted his position and winced as he tried to adjust his hard-on in his tightened jeans.

"A water witch, eh?"

Mireio dished up another square of zucchini parmesan onto Lars's plate and then refilled his water goblet. She'd been telling him how she hadn't chosen the art of water magic but that it had chosen her.

"My grandmother could never get me out of the tub or the swimming pool. I used to tease her that I could make the water do things, so when she challenged me, I gave it a try. I cast my first water globe when I was ten." She held her hands apart but curved toward one another as if to hold a ball. "Then I threw it at my granny, soaking her. I had to clean the bathroom for a month after that."

Lars's laughter filled the quiet kitchen. Beside him on the counter, Peanut, asleep in his baby carrier, stirred but didn't wake.

She put a finger to her lips to shush them both. "So anyway, I mastered water magic by the time I was twenty. And that led to brewing beer. I like to change and control water. Add a few grains and some hops? Voilà!"

"So it's an innate thing with you witches? You're born able to do magic?"

"Some of it. As a baby I could swim underwater just like a seal. And I had a habit of curdling the milk before my mother could get it in the bottle. Or so I was told. But some magics we have to study and learn, and maybe never master. I'm trying to learn the healing arts. It should be easy for me. The body is made up of so much water, but I have real trouble invoking a healing spell."

"You'll master it. I know you will. You're so talented. And beautiful."

"You compliment me too much."

"What's wrong with that?"

"Nothing. I've got the Scandinavian gene, you see. We don't know how to take compliments."

"Uff da, you don't say?" he said with his best Minnesotan accent.

Mireio laughed. "Ya sure, you betcha. You've got the accent too!"

"Born and raised in Minnesota and damn proud to eat the lutefisk and lefse." He finished the food and pushed his plate forward. "I am stuffed. And relaxed."

She nodded toward his crotch. "I noticed earlier when we were kissing you were anything but relaxed."

He blushed.

"Oh, you're too cute. I'm going to keep you for a while. The baby too."

"Thanks?"

She stood up on the stool's bars and leaned over to kiss him quickly.

Peanut stirred in his carrier. "I should probably head out," Lars said. "I don't have any milk with me. Unless you can use your magic to turn water into milk?"

"Not quite that talented. And I'd hate to give the baby a tummy ache if something went wrong."

Lars packed up the baby's things and retrieved the book from the living room. Mireio walked with the two of them out to the truck parked in her driveway. After Peanut was fastened in and secured, Lars jumped back out and stood before her.

She waved at the baby and blew him a kiss. "See you later, Charlie!"

"Charlie?" He leaned against the truck door and gave her the eye.

"Yeah, thought I'd try out the name on him. You don't like it?"

He shrugged. "It's fine. I'll have to give it some thought."

"I've got a few more ideas rolling around in my brain. But I'll save them for another time. Give you a little time to try that one on a bit. So do I get to see you tomorrow? Uh, I have an appointment in the evening, but then…"

"What kind of appointment?"

"The one with the witch who hunts up vampires."

"Ah. Do you want me to go along with you?"

"Would you? She lives in Minneapolis. I know her but not well. I feel sort of weird about the whole thing…"

"I'll go along. For uh…" His gaze wandered over her head and took in the front of her house. The pause grew beyond a few seconds.

Mireio blinked, waiting for him to finish his thought. Did he do that often? Forget what he was talking about? He'd done it once before when she'd first met him.

"Wait," he said, focusing back on her. "What were we talking about?"

Strange. But she didn't want to draw attention to it. "Tomorrow night. Raven Crosse's place?"

"Oh, right! I can get Sunday to babysit tomorrow night. We'll stop by the witch's place, then do something after?"

"There's a new action movie I'd really like to see."

"I haven't been inside a movie theater in years. And action? Sounds like a plan."

He bent to kiss her and she wrapped her arms about his neck and bounced as she tried to get closer to him. So Lars lifted her by the hips and she wrapped her legs around his waist. That fit them together perfectly and made for a nice hold.

After a couple kisses he said, "You're so tiny."

"And you're like a basketball player. But I like a big strong alpha man."

Inside the cab Peanut giggled. Both looked to the baby, then back to each other and laughed.

"I think that's a hint," he said. "Time to stop kissing the girl and get the tyke home for his bedtime bottle. What time do you want me to stop by tomorrow?"

"Six!"

He kissed her again, quickly, then set her down and climbed into the truck. With a wave and a wink, he backed out and drove away.

And Mireio sighed one of those satisfied sighs that a girl reserved only for those moments she wanted to cherish. If she wasn't careful, she could fall in love. And she'd never been the queen of careful. Spontaneous, wild and free were her best attributes.

But what was wrong with the guy forgetting things midsentence? Hmm… Probably she had better not worry about it. She had a tendency to worry beyond the problem. There was no problem. Nope, none at all.

She had found herself a handsome werewolf. And a baby. Who would have thought?

Chapter 7

Raven Crosse lived in a downtown Minneapolis loft along with her husband of many decades, Nikolaus Drake. As a phoenix vampire, Nikolaus had survived a witch's blood attack (when witch's blood was once poisonous to vampires; that had been decades ago) and lived to tell the tale. The fact that it had been Raven's blood that had nearly killed him? That was a long story.

The witch, who had formerly been a vampire hunter, invited Mireio across the threshold, and drew her gaze up the long tall drink of werewolf who walked in behind her.

Only a little taller than Mireio, Raven scratched the back of her neck below the tight black ponytail and then pointed to Lars. "Who's he? I thought it was just going to be you?"

"Lars Gunderson." He offered his hand to shake, but Raven sneered at it. "I'm here for moral support."

Raven glanced to Mireio. "You're kidding me. If you need moral support, sweetheart, you're not ready for this."

"I'm ready. I would have come alone, but he offered, and…" Mireio shrugged. It was good to have him with her. She wasn't intimidated by a witch who drove a street chopper and could slay vampires with a single shot, but well, okay she was a little. "He's my partner. In this endeavor."

Again Raven drew a long discerning gaze down Lars. Not impressed at all. Then she shoved her hands in her front jeans pockets and nodded. "Fine. But this is between me and Malory, you got that, wolf? No talking."

Lars zipped his fingers across his lips and closed the door behind him. Raven led them to the long stretch of kitchen counter and gestured they sit on the stools.

"Nikolaus is out of town. I don't do this when he's around," she said as she pulled a black file folder out from a drawer and slapped it on the counter before Mireio. She placed her palm over the folder and leaned in. "You got the cash?"

"Oh, yes." Mireio opened her fish purse and pulled out the envelope that was an inch thick and filled with twenty-dollar bills. "All there. You can count it if you want."

Raven shoved the envelope in the drawer and closed it. She pushed the file toward Mireio, then stepped back with arms crossed over her chest, eyeing Lars cautiously.

Inside the file was a single sheet of paper with two color photos printed alongside the details. Neither photo showed a clear face shot of the man. "There's no name?" Mireio asked.

"Names are not important, and intrusively personal. You get a name and you'll never be able to go through with it. The pictures and the details of that vamp's MO should be more than enough to ensure you get the right guy. He's a monster. Feeds in a very contained area in north Minneapolis, so finding him shouldn't be a problem. There have been unexplained deaths in that neighborhood over the last two months. It's his doing, I know it."

"How can you know that?" Lars asked.

Raven tilted a sneer at the wolf, and both Lars and Mireio heard the unspoken, *I told you not to speak, wolf.*

Lars cleared his throat. "I'm sure you know, being a vampire hunter and all."

"Former," Raven corrected. "You ever play blood games with vamps, wolf?"

"No. That's barbaric."

Raven lifted her chin, still assessing Lars. "You're from the Northern Pack. Amandus Masterson used to lead the pack."

"He's long dead."

The witch sniffed. Masterson had engaged his pack in blood games that had tortured vampires mercilessly. It was likely a sticking point for a witch married to a vampire.

Trying to cut the tension, Mireio tapped the information sheet. "He's mostly out after midnight?"

"Yes, all the information you need is right there. Now, did you need anything else? You got the immortality spell?"

"Yes. My friend is still working on getting the dragon's exudation. Few sell it nowadays."

"Very necessary to make the blood go down smoothly," Raven said. "Trust me. I've done this six times. Did it one time without the exudation. Nearly fucking gagged myself to death."

Mireio swallowed. Drinking the blood from a vampire's heart was not tops on her list of things to do. But if those few moments of suffering would give her another century of life, then she could rally. As well, if it would give her the revenge she sought against her mother's murderer, then she was all in. But that detail was not something she intended to tell Lars.

"You going to be her wingman?" Raven asked Lars.

They hadn't discussed him helping her, but when Mireio started to answer, Lars draped an arm across her shoulders. "Yep."

"Good. Tiny witch like you will need someone strong to crack open the vampire's chest and pull out the heart."

Mireio gulped down a gag, but kept a stoic expression as she nodded in agreement.

"So we're good," Raven said. "Business is complete. You two will be on your merry way. I'd love to say it's been peachy, wolf, but I'm still not sure I like you. You trust him?" she asked Mireio as she collected the file folder and walked to the door.

"I do." But she was still thinking about watching a werewolf crack open a vampire's chest and then handing her a bloody heart. That was the stuff of nightmares. And man, did she have nightmares. "I think we should be going, then. Thanks!" And she shot out the door, not caring whether Lars followed.

Scrambling down two flights and out to the street, Mireio rushed along the side of the building and turned the corner. Catching a palm on the rough brick wall she bent forward and exhaled forcefully.

A gentle hand pulled away the hair from the side of her face. "You okay?"

She nodded. "It was really stuffy in there, don't you think?"

"Uh…yes, I think it was. Everything is going to be okay, Mireio. I'll be there to help you with this. I promise."

"I didn't even ask you. I'm sorry—she just assumed…"

"No need to ask. I'm volunteering. There's no way a tiny witch like you can accomplish…well, you know. Will you let me help you?"

Righting, she dropped her shoulders against the wall and looked up at him briefly, then away. She was still shaken from having reality so blatantly laid out for her like that. No wonder her mother had died. She must have faltered in that moment when she'd needed to be strong. She hadn't taken anyone along with her. Mireio knew because she had followed her and had witnessed the whole terrible thing.

"Do you think I can do this if I can't even listen to the details?" she asked. "I mean, what will I do when faced with having to consume the blood from a vampire's heart? I am so not that chick from *Game of Thrones*."

"Yeah? You don't have a hoard of dragons to protect either. But you do seem to have a fear that can only be abated by meeting this challenge. And while I'm still getting to know you, I feel confident that when the challenge presents itself, you'll do fine."

He held out his hand and she clasped it as if it were a life preserver tossed into the wild and wicked waves. "Thank you for having faith in me. I need that boost of confidence. And, obviously, a big strong wolf to do the dirty work. Oh." She bent again, clutching her palms on her knees.

"I was thinking we could drive through north Minneapolis, take a look around," Lars said. "But maybe we should call it a night?"

She shook her head. The last thing she wanted to do was go vampire hunting. But she didn't want this night to end so quickly either. Especially not when Lars had hired a babysitter. "No, I'm good. Just needed to breathe in the air."

"We passed a movie theater on the way here." He clasped her hand and bent to speak softly. "What say you and I go sit in the dark, drink lots of sugary pop and then make out during the boring parts."

She squeezed his hand. "Here's wishing for a lot of boring parts."

Mireio couldn't recall a time when she'd made out in a movie theater. They were the only two in the small theater. The red velvet seats creaked and smelled stale. The screen had a tear on the right side that tended to give actors scars in inappropriate places. And the action they'd come for had lasted all of thirty-seven seconds. Now the characters were trying to find themselves emotionally and heal past wounds through therapy. Ugh.

So the key to intense action in a movie theater was to create your own. She currently knelt on Lars's lap, kissing him. The man was always a little slow to warm to her, but now he let his hands roam over her hips and ass. His wide strong fingers curled, giving her a squeeze. And she let her hands roam up under his loose gray T-shirt to the hard landscape of muscle and hot skin and some surprisingly soft chest hair.

"Never done this before," he muttered between breaths as they tilted their heads to change up the kiss. "Like it." Her fingernail glanced across his nipple and the man hissed into their kiss. "Like that too."

"If I were more daring," she said, "I'd shove you down across the seats. But the arms don't move, and I'm not quite that adventurous."

"This works." He pulled her in closer so her knees hit the back of the seat to either side of him. "A little tight, but—"

"It's awkward." She flipped her hair over a shoulder and tugged at his shirt in frustration. "Let's ditch this place, yes? What time do you have to pick up Peanut?"

His slow smile beamed even in the darkness. "Not till morning."

"Nice. Let's go to my place and make out on the couch."

Lars felt like a randy teenager driving fast to get to the secret hideout so he could pull over, drag the clothes off his girlfriend and make out with her. Except, he wasn't sure if Mireio considered herself his girlfriend. Not that it mattered. They were adults. If they wanted to get their horny on, nothing would stop them.

And he didn't want to consider how hooking up could complicate things. What if they had sex and that was it? She didn't want to see him anymore? Could he handle that? He liked the witch. A lot. He didn't want to spoil the slow, sure connection they'd developed.

And yet, with Mireio snuggled up against his side, dragging her fingers along his thigh, he could not stop thinking about how quickly he could get her clothes off once the door to her house closed behind them.

He was a virile man. It had been months since he'd had sex because Peanut had occupied all his free time. He needed this. And he'd take the frenzied connection and worry about where the chips fell afterward.

Parking before the house, he shoved open the door, jumped out and offered a hand to help her out. Before she could step down, he took her in his arms and elbowed the door shut. He carried her up the walk and she punched in the digital code for the front door lock even as he held her in his arms.

"Set me down before we go in!" she said before he could step any farther. "No carrying over the threshold this night."

Uh. Okay. If she was implying some weird correlation to the whole carrying a wife over the threshold then, yes, he'd go with it. He set her down and followed her inside. After pulling the door closed, she turned and pushed her hands up under his shirt. He groaned at the sweet yet demanding touch against his tight muscles.

She shoved him none too gently and his shoulders landed against the foyer wall behind him. In the darkness, Lars raised a brow in question.

"Are we going to do this?" she asked, hugging her

breasts against him, which landed them about gut level because of her shortness. "I want to do this."

"We're doing this."

"Good."

"Couch?"

"No. The bedroom is up the stairs."

She jumped then and he caught her as she wrapped her legs about his waist. Bypassing the couch and going straight for the bed? Oh, yeah, this was happening.

Bowing to kiss her, he then turned to navigate the stairs, which were beyond the kitchen. She kissed his jaw and stroked his beard as he took the tight square turns upward. At the top, only two doors were open and when he spied the bed and the big picture of the yellow daisy on the wall behind it, he knew it was her bedroom.

Carrying her in, Lars set her on the edge of the high bed, but she didn't unwrap her legs from him. Seeking fingers pushed through his hair and tugged the wood stick out from the leather hair wrap he used to curtail his long hair. She pulled his hair forward, drawing it over her lips and cheeks. Then she nuzzled her nose and mouth into his beard. With a giggle, she fell backward and stretched out her arms across the frilly bed.

"Goddess, you're a sexy man. All dimples and beard. I have to admit, I'm a little nervous."

Crawling over her, but not resting his weight on her, he propped himself up on his elbows, meeting her eye to eye in the hazy light. "Why? Is something wrong? Shoot. This is too fast. I knew it."

"No, Lars. This is happening exactly as it should. That's how the universe works. Things happen when they are supposed to happen. I'm nervous because, like I said, you're sexy. You're handsome and kind. And you're so big and I feel like a little bird beside you. But that's a good thing. It's like you protect me. And—oh, my goddess, I'm chattering!"

He kissed her quickly, then nuzzled his nose against her cheek and sought the thick curly shelter of her bright hair. "You're the opposite of me. You like to talk. I'm a doer. A man of few words."

"You can do me, Lars. I want you to take off my clothes and kiss me everywhere."

Directions? The woman just made his life a whole lot easier.

Lars pushed up her shirt and she pulled it off and leaned back onto her elbows to reveal a lacy red bra that barely contained her lush, full breasts. He laid a hand over one and kissed the other through the sheer fabric, teasing at her hard nipple until her moans rose and her hips rocked against his torso.

Her fingers danced down his chest and abs and she couldn't quite reach his jeans. His erection pulsed within his jeans, which were normally comfy and loose. But not now.

Nuzzling his face between her breasts, he decided this pillow could hold his attention for a long sweet time. He glided his fingers over the red fabric, feeling as her nipple tightened even more. The red lace tickled his palm. He tugged down the bra and kissed her above the nipple.

"Do you have a condom?" she asked as he lashed teasingly at her nipple.

Lars looked up at her. Red hair splayed like goddess tresses across the bed. Lashes dusted over her blue eyes. Her mouth was plump and parted. A condom? Shit. Of all things he should be most vigilant about that was the one.

"No. I, uh…" Hadn't done this for a while, and—hell, he'd not planned this night very well. He'd never expected to bypass the couch and go straight to the bed. "Do you?"

he asked hopefully, assuming since she'd asked, she must not be on birth control.

"Shoot. No. And there's a spell I can do for birth control but I've been waiting for the right moon phase. It's required for efficacy. Oh, Lars, I'm sorry."

Like that, his heart dropped an inch and he rolled to his back to lie beside her, blowing out a frustrated breath. But when her hand glided over his erection he popped up his head to meet her winking gaze.

"There are other things we can do. Yes?"

All the side stuff but not the big event? He'd never done anything like that before. He was a man who always got to the point. And he never left a woman high and dry. Nor did he often walk away without the big bang.

Now she squeezed over his jeans, which made his cock grow harder, if that were possible. "Lars?"

Everything but actually putting himself inside her? That would prove a challenge, but he was always up for a test. And no way in hell did he want to walk away from lush red hair, plump lips and lickable nipples now.

She tugged at his zipper and he winced, anticipating some pain should she make a wrong move.

"Mmm, commando. I'll be careful," she said. And she was, sliding her hand inside his jeans and over his cock and curlies as she pulled down the zipper. "You got a name for this big guy?" she asked. "Or should I assume you've named it after a legume?" Her eyes twinkled from her position hovering over his newly sprung erection.

A legume? Oh, right. Peanut.

"Mireio," he chided and tangled his fingers in her hair. "You can call it anything you like. It'll come when you call."

She giggled at that. "All I have to do is call, eh?"

"Oh, yeah…"

Her fingers slipped around his hard length, squeezing

and setting off erotic shock waves that jolted through his system and made him hiss. A wanting utterance. Small as she was, the woman did possess a good firm grip. And she glided up and down his erection slow and easy, which he appreciated, because he hadn't any lube and wasn't all juiced up yet.

And thinking about that must have given her the idea to dash her tongue down the length of him. Lars gripped his fingers, then realized he still had them in her hair and didn't want to pull too roughly, so he swept them down her skin and dropped his hand to the bed, where he grabbed the coverlet as her lips closed over his swollen head.

"Oh, witch…"

Her mouth was a nice replacement for what he'd thought the lacking condoms had denied him. So hot, wet and… squeezing. She licked and stroked her tongue up and down the length of him. His entire body tingled and he felt a mad soaring sensation. And when she gently cupped his balls the darkness behind his closed eyelids took on color.

An animal growl came out, which stirred her head up.

"Mmm, my wolf. You like this."

"Oh, Mireio."

"You want to feel how wet I am?" He watched her slip her hand beneath her skirt, then she drew out her fingers and touched them to his cock. Sticky and hot with her wet dew.

Lars bit his lip and growled again. His body tremored and with a few more lashes from her tongue, he gave up the gold and came powerfully, hips bucking and breaths hissing.

Mireio's cell phone rang. She didn't stop stroking him. But he'd already come. He needed a few minutes.

"Get it," he said on a relaxing exhale.

"No, it's probably…" It continued to ring. With a heavy sigh, she said, "Sorry. Right, you need a little rest time, eh?" With a wink, she pushed aside her hair and retrieved the phone. "Hey, Valor…What? Seriously? That's the second time a keg has exploded this month…No, I can come in and help. I'll have it cleaned up with my water magic in two snaps. See you in a bit."

"You can't leave now." He sat up on the bed and pushed the hair from his face. Perspiration around his hairline made him swipe a hand across his brow. "It's my turn to make you come."

She sat on his lap, grinding her mons against his cock and moving up higher. "You can't imagine how powerful a girl feels when she brings a man to the edge like that."

"I might have some idea. I've done it a time or two to women."

"Only a time or two?"

"Aw, you know. I'm not going to detail my past conquests." He kissed her breast and suckled the nipple. His entire body was lax, yet humming with energy. "Five more minutes?"

"Lars, I know this is mean but the brewery basement is flooded. We've an old plastic fermenter that finally cracked open and gushed out eighty gallons of beer. Valor can clean it up with a mop and bucket, but I'm the one with water magic who can reduce cleanup time by hours." She kissed him as she pulled her bra back up. "Next time we'll both be prepared. Deal?"

"I'll add *condoms* to the list right above *diapers*."

She fist-bumped him then and slid off the bed, tugging her hair up and grabbing something off the vanity to pin it up as she sailed out of the bedroom. "I'm making a quick escape, because if I don't, I'll never be able to leave you. Don't be mad!"

Sitting up on the bed, feeling disoriented, satisfied, but also completely devastated that he'd not been able to do for her what she had done for him, Lars exhaled through his nose. What had become of his life of late? He couldn't please a woman. He had to be home by a curfew to feed his baby. He was waking up in the field naked, shifted out of werewolf shape, with no understanding of how he'd gotten there.

And...he pressed his fingertips together, wincing at the tingly pain that had begun a few minutes ago. It wasn't aftereffects from the orgasm. Soon the tingling would spread up to his elbow and he wouldn't be able to feel anything. He'd better get home quick before he wasn't able to drive. Wiping his T-shirt across his stomach to clean off the cum, he then headed downstairs.

They both rushed toward the front door, Mireio's fish purse bonking Lars on the knee as she made the dash.

"I'm so sorry the night ended this way," she said as they sailed down the front step and she angled toward the garage. "You must think me terribly insensitive to one minute have my hand on your cock and the next be thinking about work."

"No." Maybe a little. "I understand." If it had been a call about Peanut, he would have done the same thing and rushed off. "It sounds like an emergency. And you're right, we weren't prepared."

She spun and pulled him down for a quick kiss. "Call me tomorrow! And don't forget about your shopping list!"

The garage door opened and she disappeared into the dark garage. Lars waved and watched as the little red Volkswagen backed out and she cruised away. Off to help her sister witch clean up the disaster at the brewery.

He fired up the truck. They'd started the evening by securing information on a violent vampire that Mireio would ultimately destroy to gain immortality. Then the movie theater, which led to an awkward, but strangely satisfying roll on her bed. What a weird night.

He shook his hand, fighting the tingling that would not relent. His whole life felt unbalanced and not quite right. And it only promised to get weirder.

Chapter 8

The next day, Lars stopped into the brewery with Peanut in the baby carrier. Mireio stood over by the brew tanks. And when he noticed she wasn't stirring the contents of the first tank, but the big wooden stir paddle was moving around and around, he set the sleeping baby on the floor and approached cautiously.

"Hey!" She winked at him and then stepped down from the short step stool she'd been standing on. "I'm in the wort production part of the brewing process right now. Come over. Take a look."

Lars peered into the open stainless-steel tank. A big wood paddle stirred the grains in the water—on its own. A little magic? Cool. He inhaled the rich oat smell. "You really do make magic."

"Just call me the resident hopcromancer. I can do magical things with water and hops." She noticed his hand shaking at his side. "What's up?"

"Huh? Oh." He smoothed his fingers down a thigh, unaware he'd been moving his hand. "Nothing. Just some tingling I get every so often. Probably nerve damage from all the wood chopping I've been doing lately."

To distract her, he gave her a kiss, which she extended

by pulling him down and wrapping her arms about his shoulders.

"Everything go okay last night?" he asked.

"It took less than twenty minutes to rally the spilled beer back into some kegs, with magic, of course. Then we were able to dump it down the sink."

"Bummer."

"Yes, but beer from the floor would not have been a big seller. Losses are to be expected." She hugged up against him, pressing her stomach to his hips. "How are you today, big boy?"

If she pressed a little closer and longer, she'd know exactly how he was feeling. Hard and happy.

"Still riding the high of you," he said. "It smells great in here. And it's not just you and your lilacs." He peeked again into the stainless-steel brew tank and saw the grains spinning round as they were magically stirred. "You always do that?"

"Oh, yeah. Stirring grains takes a lot of muscle. Some days I like to take it easy. And it frees me up to watch the controls." She pointed to the control panel on the wall. "Lots involved in the brew process. The boil comes next." She tapped the second tank. "All that sugar from the grains is sluicing into this tank. Then I'll boil it and add the hops and the secret ingredients."

"And by secret does that mean magic?"

She crooked a sly smile at him. "You bet. So what are you two up to today?" She skirted around the end of the bar to check on Peanut. "Hey, Oliver, how are you? Sleeping like a baby, I see."

"Oliver?" Lars scratched his bearded jaw. "I don't know about that one."

"Too Dickensian?" She shrugged. "Had to give it a try. So what's up?"

"We're headed out to do some grocery shopping. I always drive up to the market in Maple Grove. And since that takes me right by The Decadent Dames…"

"And you'll have to return this way too. Hey, why don't you leave Peanut here with me? The boil is my time to generally futz around and do nothing. I'd love to do nothing with this little cutie-pie."

"He does need a bottle soon. Are you sure?"

"Sure? Are you kidding me? Some free time to hug and kiss and cuddle all this awesome baby?" She fluttered her lashes at him and her smile slipped into a seductive curl. "Don't you trust me yet, Lars?"

"I do. And if you keep looking at me like that I'll have to put you up on the bar and spread your legs."

"I'm game."

He glanced to the baby. "Not in front of the kid. Or…" He gestured toward the front windows of the brewery, not thirty feet away, where people walked by and peered in constantly.

"Sure, but can I take a rain check on that offer? Later? When you get back from shopping?"

"Hell yes. But as for leaving Peanut here, I don't want to impose. You are working."

"I'd never offer if I didn't want to and if I couldn't manage it. The boil begins soon. That'll give me some time to blow raspberries on Peanut's toes."

"I could make the grocery shopping quick."

"No. Take your time. I'll be here for hours yet. Go on."

"I might take a few minutes to run by the Jiffy Lube and have them top off the fluids in the truck."

"Yes, do that. Run all the errands you need to get done. We'll be good." She squatted near Peanut's carrier and ruffled the sleeping babe's hair.

Lars's cell phone buzzed. He tugged it out of his front pocket and checked the text. He frowned.

"Hot date cancel out on you?" she asked.

"What?" His face felt hot and his heart beat fast.

Mireio pointed to his phone.

"Oh, this? Uh, a text from my doctor."

"Really?"

He shrugged and shoved the phone back into his pocket.

"Is that normal? I mean, I've never heard of a doctor texting a patient."

"Oh, uh, I don't know. He's like a small-town doc. Not a lot of patients, and all of us are werewolves. He, uh… wants me to meet with him this afternoon for the test results. It's all good."

"How do you know? You could be dying."

Lars chuckled. "I'm going to live forever. And I don't have to eat a vampire heart to do so. We wolves tend to live three or four centuries."

"I know. Hardy genes." She bent and kissed Peanut's forehead. "So you go, and fit in your doc appointment while you're at it. We're good for an afternoon. And I promise I won't let the little guy drink too much beer."

"He's a teetotaler, that one. Thanks, Mireio."

As Lars started toward the door she called, "Don't forget the condoms!"

"Tops on my list!" With a wink and a wave, he wandered off.

Geneva Curtis, one of the four witches who owned the brewery, clicked over to the far end of the bar in the highest of red crocodile leather heels. Likely bought for her by a billionaire. In Dubai or some other fabulous vacation getaway that Mireio could only dream about. Geneva swept off her Chanel sunglasses, then startled at the sight of what sat on the floor near the bags of rye grains.

"What the hell is that?"

Mireio laughed and took her friend by the arm, hugging up alongside her. "Oh, Geneva. This. Is a baby."

"I know that, joker. I mean, what are you doing with one of those? Did you have a baby and not tell me about it?"

"Dear, sweet Geneva. You would know if I had a baby. Though you have been pretty scarce around here lately."

"Our shifts never overlap. You're the morning bird. I'm a midnight raven. So what? Did you think a baby would draw in customers during happy hour?"

"I'm watching him for Lars."

"The man you're dating?"

"Yep."

"Ugh. How can you? I mean, it's a baby. They're just so…"

"Adorable?"

"Sticky." Geneva cringed and took a step back from Peanut's setup on the blanket below the plastic play gym. Lars packed the baby bag like a pro. "What's its name?"

"It is a boy. And his name is Peanut."

The witch flashed Mireio a disdainful pout of her deep red vamp lips. "Seriously?"

"He doesn't have a name yet. Lars has been calling him Peanut. So what are you here for? You're not scheduled until tomorrow night. And I'm almost finished. Was waiting around for Lars to pick us up."

"Where is the guy? You just start dating and already he's using you as a babysitting service? Sounds sketchy."

"He's gone out for groceries and a doctor's appointment. And you know I'll babysit anytime, anywhere."

"What's wrong with him? I thought he was a werewolf? Werewolves don't get sick."

True. Huh. Mireio should have asked him to explain.

"It's nothing. Lately he's been experiencing some weird

tingling in his fingers and toes. He thinks it's from cutting wood."

"Sounds not at all sexy to me."

"The man has a beard and a baby, Geneva. My ovaries can't handle all that sexy."

"A beard?" Geneva mocked a shudder.

"Oh, sweetie, you've obviously never been on the receiving end of *the beard*. It has some amazing powers, let me tell you."

"Like catching food and being smelly?"

"Lars's beard smells like him. Sort of like a forest after the rain. Mmm..." Mireio wiggled her shoulders appreciatively.

"Ah-huh." Geneva slid onto a barstool and patted the stool next to her. "Well, leave Cashew to his baby stuff, and come sit with me. I need your advice about a man."

"Really? This is new. You know I can't begin to comprehend the level of financial status you require from all your men?"

"I'm not dating a rich guy at the moment. And it's driving me mad. Mad, I tell you. The man is positively..."

"Rustic?"

"Yes." Geneva followed with a drawn-out moan. "At least he doesn't have one of those." She thumbed a gesture toward Peanut, who giggled and kicked his feet as he eyed the spinning objects above him.

"As far as you know." Mireio climbed onto a barstool. "So what's up? Why did you even go after a man with no money?"

"I thought it would be a lark, you know? Sort of a reassurance that I really do enjoy dating rich guys and being treated like a princess and getting jewels and cars and stuff all the time."

"If there's a *but* to follow that statement, I will stab you in the heart. Do you know how lucky you are, Geneva?"

"I thought I did. But." She caught her chin in hand and flashed her million-carat sapphire gaze at Mireio. "I think I like this man. But he's a grocer." She squeezed her eyelids shut and put up a palm before her. "I can't believe I told you that. Argh! He works at a grocery store putting food in bags, Mireio. That is so…"

"Beneath you?" Mireio tried, but hoped her friend wouldn't nod in agreement.

"No. It's…different. We don't do big fabulous things like yachting or shopping in Dubai or even renting the penthouse of a New York apartment for a week. We just… talk a lot. And last night was the first time in ages I actually sat in a dank old dark movie theater."

"Hey, me and Lars were in a theater last night too."

Geneva shuddered. "The horrid popcorn smell and those lumpy seats. But do you know I enjoyed myself?"

"Oh, sweetie, you're in love."

"I can't be." Geneva actually cast her arm across her forehead in the classic tortured-heroine move. "What am I going to do?"

"Just let it happen, I guess. Seems to be the thing lately with us Dames and our men. And with Scorpio rising…"

"Oh, goddess, that means our sexual energy is so high right now. And me and Mr. Rustic haven't slept together yet."

Mireio almost said, "I don't believe that," because she knew Geneva went at her men fast, furious and with a mission, but she stopped herself. It had to be tough dating a man so out of her planetary orbit.

Thinking of which, she'd taken a bold, brave step by dating a man with a baby. Wasn't so bold. Wasn't even brave. It actually felt right.

"It's a good thing," she said, about her and Lars, but then Geneva hugged her suddenly.

"Thanks for the chat, Mireio. It means a lot. I know I

spend a lot of time away from The Decadent Dames because I travel so much. So I appreciate you dropping everything and giving me some time. I really like this man. He might be the one. Even if his checkbook is flatter than Valor's chest."

Valor was the resident tomboy who had a body like a boy, but she'd caught herself a sexy faery man—one of the Saint-Pierre brothers—who appreciated her exactly as she'd been designed.

Geneva pulled on her scarf and sunglasses. She stepped down from the stool and gave Mireio air kisses to both cheeks. "Thanks, sweetie. I'll be in tomorrow night," she called as she walked toward the door. "Bye, Hazelnut!"

Mireio sat on the blanket beside Peanut and tapped the mobile so it spun. "Don't listen to her, Peanut Butter. We'll get you a name soon. How about…Horatio?"

"Nope."

She hadn't heard Lars walk in. He must have entered as Geneva had walked out.

"Hey! Get all the necessaries?"

"You know it." He winked, indicating he knew exactly which necessity she was most concerned about.

"How did it go with the doctor?"

"Uh, fine. Just some routine stuff."

"Routine? Then why did he make you go in? I mean he sent you a text. That was so weirdly urgent."

"Huh? Oh. Uh…" He shrugged and shoved his hands in his front pockets. "He wanted to do one more test. I had to give some more blood. It's nothing. So I'm going to take Peanut home and try to get some work done this evening before the sun sets. And I need to check the hives. It's swarming season. I don't want to lose my queens."

"Okay." The man seemed…not right. Nervous? Definitely not telling her something. But he was also a shy guy so she'd give him that. For now. "I do have some inventory to do in the basement. I could continue to watch Peanut if you have things to do today?"

"No, we're good." He bent to disassemble the baby gym and shoved it in the diaper bag. Pulling out the soft flannel baby sling, he wrapped it around his neck, then picked up Peanut and tucked him against his chest. "He need to be changed?"

"Just did it. Are you sure, Lars? Because Horatio and I were starting to get into a groove."

"Not Horatio." He shoved the blanket into the bag and stood. "I'll talk to you later. Thanks!" And he strode out of the brewery.

And Mireio could but sit there on the floor, wondering what she'd said to make him act so curt and abrupt with her. He hadn't even kissed her before leaving.

No, it wasn't anything she'd said. Something had gone down between the time he'd left her with kisses and smiles earlier to visit the doctor and now.

"But werewolves don't get sick," she repeated Geneva's statement. "Do they? Hmm…"

Wood chips flew furiously about him as Lars slammed the ax down. Again, and again. He split the oak log, tossed the cut piece aside. Again. Split. Toss. Slam.

He'd been working for an hour and the sweat spilled down his face and bare chest. The overalls he'd shoved down to his hips were soaked about the waist with more sweat.

He glanced to the baby monitor but the red light that would indicate sound remained green. Peanut tended to nap in the early evening for almost two hours.

Swinging his arms up he brought down the ax with another forceful show of brute strength.

Yes, damn it, he was strong. He wasn't… Fuck!

He was not. He couldn't be.

He hadn't been able to get out of the damn doctor's office fast enough. What the doctor had told him had made no sense at all. And the man had been so sure, even though he'd suggested one more test. As a confirmation. But really? Werewolves didn't...

Lars let out a guttural shout as again he swung down the ax and the chips flew. At his feet a heavy pile of wood shavings had formed and he shook them off his work boots and grabbed another oak log. The air was thick with dry wood scent but he didn't enjoy that spring perfume this day.

He hadn't been able to walk away from Mireio fast enough when he'd picked up his boy. He hadn't wanted to stand in the brewery and try to act normal and happy to see her when...

"Fuck!"

The ax found its mark. He kicked the cut wood aside to the stack, which was turning into a haphazard pile. Picking up another piece, he slammed it on the wood stump before him.

The doctor was wrong. Had to be. Whatever the heck was going on with him right now? It would pass. Yet the doc had treated his dad in the months before he had passed so long ago. He'd kept those records and had nodded sadly as he told Lars he was confident he'd the same thing his dad had. But to alleviate any worries, he'd do one more test.

But seriously? Why take *more* blood from him after he'd announced such a dire diagnosis?

Swinging down the ax, he winced as his biceps stretched and a sudden piercing pain radiated from his left wrist toward his elbow. He flung the ax to the ground and gripped his wrist. To his side, the monitor flashed red. He heard the gurgling sounds of Peanut coming awake.

Bowing over the wood stump he caught his palms on

it and shook his head. Never in his life had he cried. And he wouldn't let that happen now. He was strong. He was a man. He could handle this shit.

He glanced to the monitor. Heaven help him, what was he going to do with Peanut?

Chapter 9

The next day Mireio glanced at the clock above the stove. It was late afternoon. Lars had not called. She hadn't spoken to him since yesterday afternoon when he'd picked up Peanut from the brewery.

She licked the buttercream icing from a finger and pulled the bowl of fresh-washed blueberries and raspberries closer. She was making a lemon poppy seed cake and the topping would be an artfully arranged assortment of fresh fruit. Lars would love it.

Or would he? Why the silence?

She'd called him a few hours earlier. His phone had forwarded her to messages. She'd left a quick one: "Call me. Thinking of you." But she couldn't help feeling unsettled. Worried for him.

What had the doctor told him?

On the other hand, she did have a tendency to think too far ahead, as Eryss often said. She had to stop worrying about a future that generally never turned out as she thought it would. Lars was fine. He was probably busy doing whatever it was the guy did. Maybe he'd started a big project yesterday and hadn't time to chat?

She wondered about the baby. Did the poor thing sit in

the baby seat all day while his dad worked away? No. Lars would probably stop what he was doing every so often to entertain the boy. She knew that he must. He and his boy were like two peas in a pod.

"Peanut." She sighed and toggled a blueberry under her finger. "Who would have thought I'd fall for a man with a baby. A baby who has the most handsome, irresistible dad, a dad who kisses like I'm the only woman in the world. And oh, that beard."

She shivered to recall it brushing her skin as he'd kissed her breasts. Indeed, it had some kind of sensual power.

She picked up the cell phone, smearing it with frosting. Tapping the voice messages app, there were no return calls from Lars. "I'll send him a text."

That way he wouldn't feel the need to call her, if that was the problem. Though why he wouldn't want to talk to her—the man had to have gotten over his shyness with her—argh! She was freaking out over nothing. Women had this terrible time schedule in their brains about how long people should go between conversations, yet she well knew men were not like that. They could go for days without talking, and then arrive at a girl's doorstep eager for fun, like no time had passed at all.

She typed in a message: You must be busy. I can make supper if you're interested. Thought maybe one day we could drive and look for vamp...

Yeah, give him a reason to want to see her. Like helping her out with looking for the big bad vampire. Unless he'd decided he didn't want to see her anymore and this was the dreaded "I'm ignoring you because I don't like you anymore" kiss-off?

"Oh!" She caught her forehead in her hands, smearing frosting across an eyelid in the process.

At that moment her phone buzzed. A message!

It was from Lars.

Sorry, she read. Been busy. Tonight's not good. Vamp hunt sounds necessary. Try me tomorrow?

She set the phone down and nodded reassuringly. "Okay. That's cool. He's busy. So chill, Mireio. Maybe tomorrow night. This cake will still be good by then. Of course it will be. I'll...put the berries on tomorrow so they don't get mushy. Right. I have to work on my water spells anyway."

The following afternoon, Mireio called Lars but again he did not answer, so she texted him. This time she didn't know what to say. Was he really that busy?

"Just checking in," she whispered as she typed. "Call me."

What was up with her chasing a man? She did not phone-stalk men. Until now. Mireio dropped her head and sighed again. "I guess that means more spell practice."

The afternoon crept toward evening while she managed to wrangle a water elemental to help her in the garden. The elemental would tend her flowers and alert her when they needed a squirt from the hose. The tiny liquid creature slid down Mireio's finger and landed on a wide peony leaf, hugging it gently. She liked to keep her elementals happy.

A text reply did not come until around six that evening when she was staring in the fridge at the frosted cake, wondering if it would look odd if she presented her lover with a cake missing a slice. The bowl of berries sitting beside it was getting mushy. They needed to be eaten today.

Mireio spun around and grabbed her phone. Lars had texted her. Sunday can watch Peanut after ten. Will swing by, pick you up. Vamp hunt!

Letting out her held breath, she nodded. Then performed a triumphant fist pump. Then, she caught a hand at her throat. Why did she feel as if tonight could be the last time she saw the man?

"I need some rhodonite and…rose quartz."

She wasn't going into the unknown without some sexy backup crystals. And with the new moon she could also finally work a birth control spell. Might be best, just in case the condoms were forgotten again.

"So much to do before he stops by." She closed the fridge door. The cake could wait.

As far as dates went, this one ranked as strange and unusual. But it afforded Lars time with Mireio, and he hadn't seen her for two days, so he was in for the ride. And what a weird ride.

Before leaving her place, the witch had insisted he eat cake. Lots of it. He'd finished half the cake and more than enough berries to make his skin turn blue (yes, he was a fan of *Charlie and the Chocolate Factory*), and then she'd grabbed him and made a dash for the truck.

Once in northern Minneapolis, they'd decided to park in a four-level open parking ramp. Upon exiting the truck Mireio pointed out a dark shadow pursuing a woman below in an alleyway. Lars could smell the blood and violence on the man. Definitely vampire. They could observe from the ramp, so he suggested they remain there, near the truck because he didn't want Mireio to get too close to a dangerous vamp.

And they were just scoping things out tonight. She had said there was a necessary spell ingredient she'd ordered. Dragon's blood or piss. Something disgusting like that. So tonight was simply to see if they could locate the vamp, get an ID on him, then return to his turf when Mireio was ready.

And besides, if they were both focused on the vampire,

then they didn't have to make small talk. And he wasn't sure he was ready for that.

"My grandmother never let me go in this area of the city," Mireio said. "Too dangerous."

"Your grandma?"

"She raised me. My mom died when I was eight."

"Oh, right, sorry about that. That's rough. My dad died when I was young, as well. I was raised by the pack leader and his wife." He pressed a hand over his stomach.

"Still hungry?" she asked eagerly.

"Oh, no," he said too quickly. "I mean, it was great cake. But that was a lot of cake. Whew!" A movement drew his attention. "There's something down there."

Both of them leaned over the concrete balustrade and followed the action below that wound deeper into the dark suburban landscape. A man pursued a woman, whose frantic breathing Lars could hear. He could also sense her heartbeat thundering madly.

Suddenly Mireio clutched his hand and he sensed her intense fear. "He's moving in on her. He'll bite her."

"That is what vampires do," he said.

"Yes, but he's a known killer. What if he kills her? Oh, I can't watch this. Lars?"

The witch was squeamish, which he decided was a good thing. But not if she intended to ultimately eat a vampire heart. Blood drinking only seemed palatable if you were a vampire. Well, it was what vamps did. And if a guy was going to accept that the world was filled with all species that sometimes destroyed others to survive, then he had to allow each their own survival methods. But Lars knew vampires didn't have to kill to survive. They committed homicide because they wanted to. Raven Crosse had reported this vampire had killed many. And that made all the difference to Lars.

"Nobody is going to die tonight," he said, trying to

hide the resignation in his voice. He'd hoped to remain a bystander. But there was obviously a price to pay for such voyeurism. "Stay here."

He climbed over the cement balustrade and stood at the lip of the fourth-floor level. Pushing off into a free fall, he landed on the tarmac crouched in a solid stance, his boots stirring up earthy dust. He turned up to Mireio and winked at her, then took off in the direction where the vampire stalked his victim. The fear scent was stronger down on the ground. As was the acrid tang of blood. Lars quickened his pace.

The woman struggled against her captor when Lars came upon them; the vampire had her pinned to the wall by both wrists. The blood scent teasing the air sickened him. He growled, alerting the vampire.

The longtooth turned to him, fangs dripping with blood. The vamp hissed, and took off.

Taking chase after the fleeing vamp, Lars followed him at a leisurely lope for three blocks. He wasn't about to go full-out assault werewolf. Not in the middle of a neighborhood populated by humans. And besides, Mireio needed this vampire to live for the night she would return.

When he decided he'd scared off the flesh pricker, he quickly veered back toward the victim, who wasn't there when he returned.

He sniffed and cast a glance around the dark alley, peering into nearby shrubs and between trash cans and parked cars. The human scent trailed west.

To follow her or not?

He glanced upward, his gaze meeting Mireio's. Even at a distance he could see her give him the thumbs-up signal. The victim must have wandered off to safety.

He returned the thumbs-up, then wandered back to the parking garage. When he reached the truck, Mireio ran up to embrace him. Wrapping her legs about his hips, she held him in a long hug. That connection brought him down from the adrenaline high of the chase. It was a sweet landing in the arms of a soft and sexy witch.

"I saw her wobble off," she said. "A car pulled up and two women got out to help her into the back seat. I hope they're taking her to the emergency room." Her body shivered against his. "It's been so long since I've seen a vampire attack a person. It kind of freaked me out. I wish I could have gotten a better look at his face."

"I saw him. It was dark, but I'm sure he's the one Raven Crosse told us about. This must be his territory. We'll return when you're ready to do the spell. Okay?"

She nodded, and he helped her up inside the truck. As he drove to her place, Mireio remained quiet and Lars sensed she'd been more shaken by watching the attack than he'd first thought. How desperately did a person have to want immortality to commit such an act?

Immortality. If only werewolves were immortal. Hell. He'd better not go there. He'd never get through this night if he allowed the doctor's diagnosis to do battle with paying attention to the girl.

Arriving at her place, he walked her into the living room and helped her to sit. "I'll make you some tea. It'll settle your nerves."

"Thanks," she whispered.

"She's going to be okay," he offered. "The victim."

Fortunately, he'd gotten to the vampire and his victim before the bastard could drink too much. The woman would survive. With luck the vamp had used persuasion to make her forget what had happened, but Lars guessed his showing up might have prevented that. That woman was going to have some hellacious nightmares.

In the kitchen, he found a cup and some tea, then filled it with water and set it in the microwave for a minute and a half. While he waited, he stared into the living room, spying Mireio, who had put her bare feet up on the end of the couch. Her reaction prodded at his own morals.

Raven Crosse had assured them this vamp was the baddest of the bad. That he had killed. Many times. He probably deserved a cruel and painful death. But how could Lars be the man to deliver that death? No matter how horrible the vampire was, he should not place judgment on him and decide it was okay to end his life.

Should he?

Mireio had asked for his help. He'd said he would. He was a man of his word. But now…

Shit. Things had changed. And it had been two days that he'd stayed away from Mireio, knowing when next he saw her he'd have to tell her all. He didn't want to. How could he? Could a guy get a rope to pull himself to shore?

Feeling a dizzy wave wash through his head, Lars slapped a palm to the counter. A weird feeling of dread crowded his thoughts. And then…his legs gave out and he went down.

Chapter 10

Hearing a clatter in the kitchen, Mireio sat up. Lars didn't answer when she called out, so she raced into the kitchen to find him lying on the tile floor between the counter and the fridge. Unconscious.

He still held a tea bag in hand. He couldn't have bumped his head. She didn't see any blood. Had he…fainted?

Giving his shoulder a shake, she jostled him awake. The big, muscular man sat upright with a sudden movement and a groan.

"What happened?" he asked.

"I think you fainted." Saying it out loud ratcheted up the anxiety she hadn't realized had tensed her fingers into claws. She shook out her hands. "Let me help you up so you can sit on the chair." She grabbed his arm but he roughly tugged away.

Turning onto his knees, he used the stove to heft himself up, and wobbled over to the barstool before the counter, where he collapsed in a huff. Hands shaking, Mireio filled a glass of water and brought it to him. When he refused it, she insisted. Finally he took a few sips, then he drank the whole thing and handed it back to her.

"Your tea water is ready," he said curtly.

"I don't need tea. I feel better now. But you are not fine. Lars, you fainted!"

"It was nothing."

She exhaled, hands to her hips. Grown men who were as strapping as Lars, and seemingly healthy, did not all of a sudden faint.

"It is something. Something you're not telling me. What is it? It's about the tests the doctor did, isn't it? You've had the blackouts and the shifting without volition. And you forget things in the middle of conversations. And you said something about your fingers getting numb."

"Mireio," he said warningly. He pressed a fist to his forehead and winced.

She wasn't going to be chided. The man was not okay. And she needed him to let her in, trust her and tell her what was up. She needed that for her own sense of well-being.

She placed both hands on his shoulders. "Lars, you can trust me. And I worry about you. Is it your health? What's going on?"

He exploded up from the stool, shoving her aside. Pacing between the counter and the front door, he paused in the center of the room. He eyed her sternly. His breaths were heavy. He glanced to the tea bag, still lying on the kitchen floor.

Then he turned and marched out the front door, leaving the screen door to slam in his wake.

Mireio gaped at his fuming exit. "Did I say something wrong?"

Just when she felt a tear wobble at the corner of her eye, the burly wolf marched back over the threshold and again paced a few times in the center of the room before her.

What was going on with the man? And why did men have such a hard time—

"You're right," he said. "It's—" he squeezed a fist before him "—something."

Of course it was. And it was a big something, to judge how upset he was. By the goddess, she didn't know how to keep doing this. The man had a way of dropping surprises on her left and right. What more had he to hide?

No. She would not accuse or berate him for keeping things to himself. Lars was a private man, never one to boast about himself. Or, obviously, bring up his problems. So she'd be open and prepare herself for whatever he had to say. "Tell me?"

"Mireio, I—" He swung a fist through the air in defeat, then stopped his pacing. "Fuck!"

"Lars, please, you're scaring me."

Turning to face her, his arm swaying out in helpless abandon, he looked at her as if for the first time. For a moment his mouth compressed and he blinked his eyes, as if tears might fall. But then he nodded and pressed his palms together before him as if in prayer. "Sorry. I thought taking a few days to think this over would make it easier to tell you. It's not. And it never will be. But you need to know." He scrubbed a hand over his hair, gripping it, then releasing it with another forceful swing of his arm. "I've got…this thing. A disease. The doc says it's rare and exclusive to werewolves."

She stood there, arms down and open to listen. Because any wrong move would surely send him fleeing. But already Mireio felt her stomach clench and tears began to well.

"I've been having symptoms. Involuntary shifting. Memory loss. Disorientation. And now this? Blasted fainting? I hate this! It makes me feel so weak. But I'm not, Mireio. I feel good still. I'm strong. I feel…" He sighed.

"What is it called, that the doctor says you have?"

"It's some fancy medical name. Lycanthorpus…" He

searched for the words, then punched a fist into his palm. "I can't remember the full term, something crazy. All I know is it's degenerative." He glanced to her for reaction.

Mireio touched her breast over the thudding heartbeats as the definition of that word coalesced in her thoughts. "Doesn't that mean...?"

"It means I won't ever get better. I'll only get worse. And then?" He spread out his arms in what seemed surrender, and stated, "I'll die."

Her mouth dropped open at that statement. Issued forcefully and finally. She didn't know what to say. She'd never... Feeling light-headed herself, she steered around the counter and climbed onto the stool. "That's..." Heartbeats thundering and skin prickling, she looked to him.

The big, strong werewolf whom she had come to care for. Pine for. Think about constantly. He was her boyfriend. They hadn't come out and stated their relationship status, but he was. He was hers. And she was his. And... The world faded in and out on muffled vibrations that at once made her heart pound loudly, and then she could not hear a thing.

Degenerative? He was going to die?

She sought his gaze and he initially looked away, but then, he met her eyes straight on. Shoulders rounded and hands still spread loosely beside him, he said softly, "The doc gave me a few months."

Mireio stood. "A few? But that's... Seriously?"

"I've been having symptoms for over a year. I didn't want to go to the doctor." He sighed. "But after shifting without volition one too many times, I finally figured I'd better check it out."

Oh, damn. Her heart dropped to her toes. She couldn't move. Her hands shook.

And she noticed Lars subtly shook too from shoulders to hands. And that was all she needed to break out of her shock and plunge against him and wrap her arms about him. At first he stood there, caged within her arms. But she hugged him tighter until he put his arms across her back and then bowed his head over hers and pressed his forehead against the crown of it.

Blessed goddess, she never wanted to let go of him.

They stood there for long moments. She could feel his heartbeat against her throat, could almost hear it. His heavy breaths that rose and fell with a world-weary exhale… Death?

"You need to get a second opinion," she suddenly said.

"Yes?"

"There's only one werewolf doc in this part of the States, sweetie. He's been taking care of the Northern Pack for much longer than I've been around. I trust him. He did all sorts of tests. Brought out books and explained things to me. He believes it was inherited."

"Inherited? But your…family?"

"My dad died when I was little. Not sure where my mom is. She left me alone with the pack after dad's death. It was hard on her. Ridge Addison and his wife, Abigail— a witch—raised me."

"But if the doctor has been looking after your pack? Didn't he take care of your dad?"

"He did. My father had the same thing. And—" he swallowed and dropped his hand down her shoulder and back "—he said he went quickly."

Compelled to give comfort, she hugged him even tighter, wanting to draw out whatever it was inside him that was making him sick. To cleanse him of it. To renew him.

"Maybe there's a spell?" she suggested. "There must be."

He stroked her hair and tilted her chin up so she would look at him.

"You won't die. We won't let it happen. I'll search my spell books. We'll figure something out."

He hugged her against his chest, so broad and strong. The deception of his outer appearance had surely fooled her. Her mighty werewolf was dying. There were simply no words to put that into proper focus right now.

"I want to make sure Peanut is taken care of," he said. "Thought about that a lot the past few days. I just get that sweet little piece of heaven and now he's going to be taken away from me. Or rather, I'll be taken from his life. Just like with my dad. Something's wrong with that."

She clung to his shirt, squeezing too tightly, but to let go of him might see him fade away. And then she'd never get him back. Because he was skittish in a way that always surprised her. Except earlier...

"Oh, my goddess." She pushed from him, turning away because she didn't want him to see her. "You went with me this evening. And the whole time you knew you were going to..." That he would die. And so quickly. Two months? "I can't believe I could have been so cruel."

"You're the least cruel person on this planet. What are you talking about?"

"Me!" She stabbed her chest with her fingers. "I've been seeking immortality, and I drag you along to make it happen. There you are standing with a death sentence on your head. How dare I?"

"Mireio, you didn't know. And this has nothing to do with the spell you want to cast. You need that immortality. You said you've been thinking about this for years. And I will help you get it."

She shook her head and spun her shoulders to face him. That he could suggest such a thing now revealed the capacity of his wide and giving heart. She truly was a monster to even think to ask him for such help.

"Can we sit and hold hands?" he asked softly. "I need that right now, Mireio. I... Please?"

His hand slipped into hers and she led him into the living room, where they sat on the couch. Tilting her head against his shoulder, they cuddled in the darkness, quiet, yet their minds racing. Two hearts who had found one another under the strangest circumstances.

Perhaps a half an hour had passed when Lars glided his hand along her arm and tilted up her chin to kiss her. Slow and easy, he tasted her mouth, taking his time and lingering on the sensitive inner dip behind her lower lip. It was such an erotic touch. She sighed into him as his hand cupped the back of her head and his thumb stroked her cheek.

He bowed his forehead to hers and asked quietly, "Make love with me?"

"Yes" fell out in a gasp. "Take me upstairs."

Standing, he took her hand and she followed the stoic werewolf up the creaky stairs and into her clove-perfumed bedroom. The pale mint walls glinted with sparkle dust she'd blown on while the paint had still been wet. Moonlight shimmered everywhere, as if in an enchanted haven.

A pop art portrait of Marie Antoinette stuffing cake into her mouth hung beside the window. A sunflower burst above the high bed. It was covered with a patchwork quilt comprised of shades of green, mint and violet. Her grandmother had sown it for her. The stitches wove wards and protective sigils and blessings for love into the fabric. Draped over the canopy, a sheer blue scarf with violet and yellow flowers dangled its long betasseled hem over all four sides. It was her mermaid's escape from the world.

Lars sat on the bed and pulled her to stand before him. The side of his face was illuminated by moonlight and his big brown eyes took her in as if she were magic.

Now was no time for thinking dire thoughts or discussing a dreaded future. Now…this man needed her.

He pulled her hand to his mouth and kissed the palm, burying his face there as if to imprint the lines that told her life story, past, present and future, upon his soul. Keeping her hand in his he glided her palm over his cheek and she tickled her fingers down and into his soft beard. He wore his wild on his face, but his tender, gentle soul revealed itself in the curve of his smile and the perk of his dimples as he cradled Peanut in the crook of an arm.

"Touch me everywhere," he whispered. "Make me yours."

For a moment she thought of his confession down in the kitchen. Her heart dropped. But mining bravery, she pushed that feeling aside. Didn't want to think about it. Not now. Now was for the two of them, getting to know one another on a deeper level. And she needed that desperately from this lovely yet broken werewolf.

Stepping up to stand closer to him with one of his legs between hers, she leaned forward and slid her hands down the back of his head, finding the wood stick and pulling it from the leather hair clasp. Tossing that over a shoulder onto the floor, she ran her palms over his thick, wavy hair and drew it up to press against her cheek, lips and nose. He smelled like wood and wild and salty, musky masculinity. His beard was thick and soft and so…fun to run her fingers through. He purred as she stroked it. Mmm…

And when he looked up into her eyes, she got lost. Her hands slipped away from him. Such deep memories of earth and ancient things in his irises. His soul was old, steeped with ages, perhaps millennia, of experience. He may not realize it. And Mireio was not a soul reader, but she sensed that they may have walked into one another's lives once or twice previously. It was possible. All things were possible.

She traced both his eyebrows with her forefingers, drawing that touch out and along his cheeks to stop at his dimples. His smile warmed her belly and spun that rush of heat to her toes and back up to her ears. So she touched his mouth, framed by a thick mustache and beard that was so dark it was almost black. He parted his lips, and she tickled across his lower lip. His tongue tasted the whorls on her fingertips and curled an erotic vibe all the way to her belly, where it coiled in anticipation.

Wetting her finger by allowing him to dash his tongue about the tip of it, Mireio then touched her own lips and tasted him. His eyes followed her motions intently. Outside this enchanted sanctuary's windows, a crow cawed and the maple trees that spread their leaf-frothed limbs over her entire backyard rustled. Inside, her heartbeats were calm and steady, but desire warmly flooded her skin and opened her pores to every sensation.

She leaned in and barely touched her mouth to his. Gliding her wet lips across his she didn't so much tease as leave a promise to return. And then she kissed down his bearded chin and neck to the top of his shirt where so much more dark hair tufted out.

"Take this off," she said quietly, and he obeyed, pulling off the T-shirt and tossing it to the floor.

His chest was a mastery of muscle and steel shaded with a manly brush of dark hair that grew sparser as it neared his belly. Mireio pushed her fingers through the silky hairs and shoved him backward to lie on the bed. She crawled up onto the bed, lying on a hip beside him and leaned over to brush her cheek over his chest hair. Following the hard line of a pectoral that pulsed under her touch, she made a slow journey to the tiny hard nipple that looked from her side vantage point a boulder standing in a clearing in the forest.

He hissed as she toggled her fingernail over it and then

teased around the areola that tightened and textured under her touch. Leaning over him, she cast a glance toward his face. His eyes were closed, one hand rested over his forehead. Under her palm, his chest rose and fell in anticipation. And as she touched her tongue to his nipple, he groaned. Like a quiet animal. Like a man in need of touch.

The tiny bead she toggled in her mouth, dashing it, licking it, sucking it and then giving it a pinch between her fingers. Slickened with her saliva, it reacted to every lash, taste and hush of hot breath.

Not to give the other short shrift, she glided over and did the same, while dancing her fingers through the wild dark hairs, down around his belly button, and lower to slip under the waistband of his jeans.

"Mireio," he whispered as if he were invoking a blessing. Or a goddess.

"I need to touch you with all of me," she announced and tugged off her shirt.

Lars's eyes opened and he watched as she unsnapped her bra in the back and tugged it away. When he reached to touch one of her breasts, she caught his hand with hers, fully intent on touching him everywhere, as he had requested. "Close your eyes again. I like knowing you can only feel, hear and taste me, but not see me."

"But you're so beautiful." His words came out as another worshipful prayer.

"You can look and touch all you like soon enough." She bowed to kiss his eyelid, then the other, and he kept them closed as she lowered her breasts against his chest and delighted in the tickle of his chest hair against her tightening nipples.

The glide of her thick nipples across his tiny ones made him rock his hips. "Mine are bigger than yours," she said.

"Yeah, and they feel great."

She reveled in the tease of his hard maleness against

her heavy breasts as she moved lower. The musky salty scent of his arousal lured her to unbutton his jeans. Oh, mercy, the man was commando again. The head of his erection loomed right there, begging for attention, so she took care in unzipping him, gliding in her other hand to protect his skin. He was so hot and hard she wanted to get him in hand, but she cautioned her eagerness. For a little while anyway.

Tugging at his jeans, she bent and placed kisses at the ridges of muscles that arrowed down toward his groin. And while his penis bobbed against her chest and chin she paid discerning attention to those cut muscles because that was where the man's magic lay. Those muscles, on any man, were capable of drawing women's eyes. Of stopping them dead and making their jaws drop. Of inciting fantasies. Of making ovaries sing. Of inviting and luring to the real treasure.

He swore on another hiss and his fingers twisted into her hair, not pulling but instead holding on. Anchoring himself. He lifted his hips and she was able to shove down the jeans and forget about them as the heavy material slid over the edge of the bed and below his knees. Brushing her breasts over his cock stirred his hips to rock subtly, so she pressed the ample girls together and around his hardness. A boob hug.

"Mireio…" Another roughly whispered prayer.

Nestling beside him on an elbow and leaning in closer for better study, she drew her fingers lightly up his bobbing cock, mapping out the thickness, the pulsing veins that bulged and made him even harder. She'd not taken such time to linger on the night when it had seemed a second best option in the absence of condoms.

Up she moved, along the heat that must surely drive him to some kind of edge, and tucked her fingernail under the ridge of the plum-firm crown. Circumcised. And the head of him fit against her palm as if she were cupping a juicy fruit that filled her grasp. Down the backside, she lightly journeyed into the nest of his curls where she wandered lower to trace the tender yet tightly tucked testicles.

Every bit of him was a masterpiece. Designed for pleasure. For study. For creating and sensual adventure. And much as she wanted to straddle him right now, knowing he would fill her completely, she knew putting off that pleasure would prove a sweeter reward.

So she slid off the bed and tugged down his jeans. He'd left his shoes at the front door, so the pants dropped to the floor. His socks she discarded, left and right with a flip. His legs were taut with muscle and thick with dark hairs.

A wolf under her command. She imagined what it must be like to stand before him in fully shifted werewolf shape. And then she remembered that she had. And she had been fascinated. What an awesome creature, both man and wolf. Wild and tame. Aggressive when need be, yet so gentle he could quiet a baby's tears with but a touch of his lips to the child's forehead.

Mireio bowed before him, palms to his knees, gauging the race of her heartbeats and knowing beyond doubt that she had fallen. Plummeted into his arms and so happy to be there. No matter the darkness. Because he, the big strong werewolf, faced so many struggles. She wanted to be a soft place for him. A comfort when he needed it. And a lover when he required the world to slip away.

Licking up his length roused a deep and throaty moan from him. His penis bobbed in approval so she gripped it firmly to keep it at her mouth. The taste of him made her sigh, and with a secret inner giggle she thought that if she had the inclination to use a wand for magic, she'd very much like it to resemble this exquisite rod.

She looked up and found he'd propped himself up onto

his elbows and was looking at her. Waiting? No, just… being. There. Sharing. Knowing.

Hastily, she slipped off her skirt and panties. She crawled up over him and pressed her breasts against his hard chest, her stomach to his rigid abs, and her mons placed firmly against his erection.

"Kiss me," she pleaded. "Take what you want from me, wolf. I'm yours."

He bracketed her face and before he kissed her asked, "What is it you witches say about things coming around threefold?"

"For everything we put out into the universe it comes back threefold."

"Then everything I take from you, I will also give to you threefold."

He rolled her onto her back and hovered over her. The man's hair slipped from behind his shoulder and spilled across her breasts. Mireio took the ends of it and tickled it over her nipple. And he bowed to brush his beard gently over the other.

With a glance up to her, he winked, then kissed the top of her breast. "I've never had sex with a mermaid before."

"It could get slippery," she warned on a tease.

The man's hot kisses explored her breasts with licks and gentle nibbles and when he took a nipple in a suckling squeeze, she moaned and dug the fingers of one hand into the bedspread while tangling the other in his hair. His fingers clasped her other breast, containing her abundance with his sure touch.

"So much," he breathed against her skin. "Your tits are big and round. Makes me mad for you, Mireio."

He sucked in her nipple and at her other breast pinched gently, then none-too-gently, causing her to arch her back as she sought the intensity of him. The tickle of his beard heightened every touch, coursing exquisite shivers through her system. Mmm, beard. Behold the power.

Shoulders pressing into the bed, she sucked in her lower lip. Nuzzling her mons up against his stomach she rubbed her clitoris against his hard abdomen, heightening the coiling tightness that promised a luscious release in her belly and loins.

"You're so hard." She clutched his head, keeping him there at her breast, silently telling him that what he was doing was perfect. It teased her closer, made her pant, stirred in the clove scenting the room with his wanton musk and salt, and it dizzied her.

"Come for me, Mireio," he whispered. "I can feel you so close."

She was. Just. There. Waiting to spill over. The texture of his hot tongue easing and prodding and suckling drove her giddy mad. His lips closing over her nipples. The erection thrusting against her thigh...

Breaths gasped and caught in her throat. She moaned, twisting her fingers in his long hair. Drawing up a leg, she squeezed her inner muscles, tempting her to jump, to make the leap.

And when he slid a hand down her stomach, over her panting belly, and glided through the dark strands that didn't match those on her head, his finger slicked across her swollen clit and that set off a chain of explosions inside her.

Mireio shouted and jerked upright as the orgasm overwhelmed and commanded her limbs, shaking her, extending her moan into a luscious pleading. And when she felt the lash of Lars's tongue move across her clit she bellowed with joy and spread her arms out wide as her shoulders and head landed on the bed.

The wolf had truly given back threefold.

Chapter 11

Mireio's body quaked beneath his hands. At once Lars wanted to contain her, to hug her close and tend to her shivers. And then, he wanted to open her wide and allow her to soar. So he hovered over her, kneeling on the bed, knees to either side of her thighs, head above her breasts, and watched her expression. It moved from gasping glee to a wincing but satisfied ache and then to panting relaxation as he felt her limbs settle beneath him and the flush that colored her cheeks and neck softened.

"Oh, my goddess," she said on gasps, "you…you really know how to do me right…whew!"

He chuckled and kissed her breasts. Her nipples were so sensitive and he could suckle at them all night. Lose himself in her lush, bountiful breasts. He nuzzled his cheek between them, rubbing his beard softly against the underside. It wasn't so much a sexual move as one of possession. The wolf in him was marking his scent on her, but she didn't need to know that.

He pressed his hard cock against her thigh, working it to a rigidity that tempted him to get to the really good part where he lost himself inside her, but he knew all parts of this were good. And taking his time, as she had when she'd stroked him, was important to him.

The curls inviting him lower were darker, almost black. Not that he'd considered her bright red hair color natural, but one never knew with witches. He nuzzled his nose and beard into them, meshing their tresses and seeking her alluring perfume. It was a lush aroma that enticed him to drag his tongue over her heated skin.

"Oh, Lars, you made me come, it's..."

He reached up to tweak her nipple and that quieted her protest. "Let me do this my way, witch. I have to taste you. And if that makes you come again, then so be it."

"You are a wicked wolf." Her toes curled at his hip. "Oh, sweet mercy, when your beard brushes my skin..."

Smiling, he swished his beard softly over her. Heh. Instant pantie dropper, his beard. But he wasn't cocky about it. He only wanted one particular witch's panties to drop. And...they had.

He slid an arm under her leg and, gripping forward over her hip, pulled her closer as he nuzzled the lush folds of her and parted them with his tongue. She tasted like earth and woman and wild and salt. And magic.

He wondered briefly if she'd bewitched him, and then he knew that she had. But it hadn't required a spell or a snap of her fingers. He'd been bewitched since the night his werewolf had stood staring at her bathed by the porch light, naked and unashamed.

Skating his tongue upward, he circled it about her swollen clit. This was where all the magic happened, and perhaps it was the source of her true magic. A woman's strength lay in her core and in the womb. He sucked the tender bud and the moan that spilled from her pleased him immensely. Her hips rocked and her fingers clawed at the bedcover. He liked that he could make her squirm.

Tasting her deeply with his tongue, he pushed in a

finger to curl up and forward. There, she felt rigid and slick and his gentle strokes increased her moans to fervent yeses and panting pleas.

He reached down and cupped his balls, which were so tight against the base of his cock he knew he could explode any moment. And then he remembered...

"I have a condom out in the truck."

"No! You stay right here. After our last attempt, I worked a birth control spell. We're good, lover. Promise. Oh, do that more. Like that, please, Lars."

She rocked her hips and squiggled down on the bed to embed his finger deeper within her, so he took that as a good sign, and pushed another finger into her squeezing sweetness.

She swore, and such a word had never sounded more like a prayer, yet also demanding. He pumped his fingers as if they were his cock and licked her clit, teasing her to a shiver. Her thighs squeezed beside his cheeks and her heels slid and slipped over his tense delt muscles as she sought to steady herself. He wouldn't allow her to fall into anything but his arms.

Pulling out his fingers, he gripped his cock, wetting it with her lush heat and marking himself with her scent. Mercy, he wanted all of her.

"Come inside me," she begged. "Put that big, thick cock inside me, Lars. You want to. I'm right there, and so are you. Oh, come on!"

Edged as it was with a touch of annoyance, he would not ignore that insistent command. Pushing up her legs so her knees bent, he lowered himself onto her. He groaned deep in his throat, bowing his head to hers at the heady meeting of skin and skin. Heat melded the soft and hard of their anatomies.

She groped for a hold of his cock, but his torso was

long and her arms wouldn't quite give her the reach she required. It was a tease he'd prolong.

Gripping his shaft, he nudged the head against her, slicking it upward over her clit. Now she panted, gasping out oaths that he hoped weren't actual witchy curses. Maybe he should get to it or risk getting hexed?

Gliding into her was like entering a new world. Jaws tight and eyelids shut, Lars moaned forcefully as she enveloped him in a tight hug. He rocked slowly at first, testing and feeling every inch of her on every hard inch of his cock.

"So thick," she murmured. "Goddess, give me more."

Words a man loved to hear. He hilted himself, which shoved her up against the pillows, hands reaching behind and above her to clutch one of the frilly concoctions. He thrust deeply, slowly, gliding in and out of her. Learning her. Memorizing her. He could do this forever…

How much longer do you have?

He chased away that nasty, intrusive thought with a growl and a fist to the bed beside her shoulder. Pumping faster, he fed the beast that demanded satisfaction. He answered her cries to go faster and harder. To give her everything. She could have all of him. He needed to expose himself, open himself up and let it flow out.

And with a flick of his finger over her clitoris, he set her off, her hips ramming upward against his, and that squeezed her tightly about him and stole his last moment of control. The surrender rocketed through him, shaking him above her and dancing in his veins.

This night the witch had given him magic.

Lars woke to sunlight prodding at his eyelids. He winced at the brightness, then felt his body waver and lean to the right. He slapped out a hand to the right and caught it against a pinewood nightstand. Then he glanced down at his position on the bed. He was stretched length-wise from pillow to the end, but only had about eight inches of mattress for his big wide body.

And the reason for his lacking space was the diminutive red-haired witch who lay on her back, arms out-stretched and legs spread, to take up the entire bed.

He chuckled softly, then let his body answer gravity and slid off the bed without disturbing the queen of the mattress. Wandering out of the room, he glanced down the hallway to the only other door on the upper floor. No, he remembered she'd said the bathroom was on the main level. He took the stairs carefully because he'd heard them creak when coming up before and managed a nearly silent descent until the last step groaned loudly.

Flashing a look upward he listened but didn't hear her stir. Once in the bathroom he intended to veer toward the toilet but he had to stop and take it in. Had he stepped into a Moroccan palace? A princess's hideaway? Tiles painted in jewel tones danced under his bare feet and traveled halfway up the walls. The upper half of the walls was painted a deep maroon and stenciled with elaborate gold arabesques. Fixtures gleamed gold, and the morning sun-light danced in the cut-glass panes that hugged the back of the room and curved in a half hexagon. The room was nearly the size of the living room and a huge round mar-ble tub mastered the center of it all.

"Like something a mermaid would bathe in." He smiled at that thought, then wandered over and found the toilet behind a half wall.

While he did his business, he scanned the room. A shower was tucked into a cove behind him, and that was big too. Definitely made for two people. The entire bath-room ceiling was domed and a couple panels were stained glass. It was like a mini cathedral or something. So cool. He could imagine soaking in the tub under that ceiling.

Everything was brightly colored and there were fresh flowers everywhere. Totally Mireio. His bubbly, hippie witch.

His witch?

Sure felt like it. He wanted her to be his. But he didn't expect that one night of sex—amazing, mind-blowing sex—would make her his. Sure, they'd gotten to know one another well these past weeks.

She'd even accepted Peanut.

He flushed the toilet and then washed his hands, noting the tips of his fingers tingled. Stupid numbness. What was that about?

The news about his health was something he wasn't sure how Mireio would deal with. Hell, he wasn't dealing with it. He was avoiding it. But he was glad he'd told her about it. Gotten it out there. Now he could push it aside and think about other things. Better things. Because what man who's been given a death sentence wants to think about his life ending?

He pressed a palm to the doorframe and blew out a heavy breath. He was that man. How could he *not* think about such a thing? The sentence had been shackled to him with a heavy yoke and he could no more shuck it off than he could have put Peanut up for adoption. This disease lived inside him. And it was doing things to him. Things he couldn't control.

And it would only get worse.

He shouldn't do this to Mireio. This was his trail to walk. It would be cruel to spread the misery. But, besides Peanut, she was the best thing that had happened to him. Could he simply enjoy what time he had with her? Would that be fair to her?

It wouldn't be, but he couldn't walk away from her. Not now. The witch had gotten inside him. He couldn't imagine a day without her in his life.

Pushing his fingers back through his hair, he strolled out to the kitchen and poured and drank a glass of water. Then he refilled it and carried it upstairs, where he found a landlocked mermaid witch lying on the bed all smiles and yawns.

"I'm not sure how someone so tiny as you managed to commandeer the bed." He handed her the glass and she sat up against the pillows and drank. "I almost landed on the floor had I not caught myself."

"I like to use the whole area." She swished her legs back and forth over the wrinkled sheet. "What's the purpose of having a bed if you don't use it all?"

"I can get behind that." He sat beside her and flipped a curl of her hair between his fingers and held it to his nose as a mustache. "But didn't your grandma teach you how to share?"

She laughed. "Sorry. I don't often have a big strapping man wolf sleeping beside me."

"I'll count that as a good thing. No other werewolves before me?"

"Nope. Not that I'm a slouch in the dating department, but you don't need those details. Nor will I ask for yours. Though I'm guessing you've had some gorgeous lovers."

"What does their appearance have to do with anything?"

"Really? But you're so handsome."

He shrugged. "I like women in all shapes, personalities and, apparently, sizes. Tiny is my new favorite flavor."

"Good. Because I have mastered tiny with a side of curves."

"I want to devour your curves." He kissed her breast and sucked in the nipple.

"What time do you have to pick up Peanut?"

"I told Sunday I'd be there before noon. It's ten now."

"Then we have plenty of time for a shower and breakfast." She crawled to the edge of the bed, but he caught her around the waist and pulled her onto his lap. His cock was already hard and her thigh crushed it against his gut.

Pulling the hair from her face and tucking it over her ear, he kissed her. She tasted like him and her fierce magic. "Last night was the closest I've ever felt to a woman."

"Really? Not even with…"

"I told you that was just a couple nights."

"Yes, but this, between you and me, has only been one night. What made this different from…you know?" Lush lashes dusted over her bright blue eyes.

"Everything. And things I can't put into words. Do I have to put them into words?"

She shook her head.

"Wait. I can," he offered. "She was a good time. A good time that gave me my amazing little baby boy. But I didn't have the time to learn about her and care about her. Nor did I want to. But I believe that baby was meant to be, and I was meant to raise him without his mom. We came together for reasons neither of us may ever realize. A grand-scale kind of thing."

"The universe was at work, making sure Peanut arrived in this lifetime to be with you."

"Yeah, I like the way you put it." He kissed her cheek. "But me and you? I care about you, Mireio. You mean something to me. You are a part of something I can't really explain either, but I know we came together because we were meant to do something great."

"Like have fabulous sex?"

"Oh, yeah. So let's go with it and see where it takes us, yes?"

"I'm all in. It was amazing. And let's not let it stop. You and me. Shower. Race you!"

And with that, the naked witch took off and ran out of

the room. Lars followed close behind, only stopping when he turned to close the glass shower door behind them.

After a long hot shower and two orgasms—or had it been three?—Lars and Mireio finally dried off and got dressed. Standing before the bed, he kissed her and pulled on his shirt. "I have to rush off. Gotta stop by the compound to pick up Peanut. I don't like to leave him too long with Sunday. Don't want to take advantage of her kindness."

"That's cool. I'm brewing apple ale this afternoon, so I'm headed in to work. Can I bring you supper later?"

"I'd like that."

He kissed her again and winced as the muscles wrapping his torso tugged.

"How you feeling?" she asked.

"Never better. And I don't want to talk about it. Okay?"

She nodded and Lars made a quick exit. He didn't groan from the pain that had suddenly wrapped about his hips and torso until he was inside his truck.

Chapter 12

Lars stood before the door to Dean and Sunday's home, his palm pressed to the white wood siding. Yet he couldn't feel the warmth of the wall against his skin. His fingers felt dead, lifeless, and his wrist tingled. He shook out his hand fiercely, trying to force the feeling back into it, but he knew it wouldn't work. He could but ride it out.

Gripping his stomach with the hand he could feel, he winced at the creaking ache in his lower abdomen. When he'd found him on the property, Lars had barely had enough time to tell Dean he had to run up to the house before he'd dashed away to avoid his principal seeing him in pain.

He swore under his breath as he pressed a shoulder to the door and rode out the pain that shivered all over beneath his skin. Felt like a bad sunburn, on the inside.

"Damn it, this better not get worse," he muttered.

"What's getting worse?"

He twisted and there stood Sunday, Peanut propped on her hip and smiling at him. The sneaky cat shifter must have seen him groaning in pain as well as heard what he'd said.

"Nothing. Hey, Peanut."

"There's something wrong with you." Sunday stepped up closer and her blue eyes took him in as her nostrils flared. It was a cat thing. He'd gotten accustomed to her scent so no longer read it as offensive—cats and wolves, you know—but she always did the scenting thing around him. "Oh, great goddess Bastet. I can smell the disease in you. Lars?"

"It's nothing, Sunday. I don't know what you think you scent—"

"I have a thing for picking up disease and cancers in people, Lars. Oh, shit, do you have cancer? I didn't think werewolves—"

"Sunday, please. It's not cancer. Just…" He blew out a breath and shook his numb hand, thankful that some of the feeling was returning. "I told Dean I'd help him move some hay bales, and he's waiting for me. But let's go inside. I'll tell you what's up."

Mireio was finding it difficult to concentrate on the laundry spell. She'd put too much lavender in the potion and it overwhelmed the hyssop. It was a quick and easy spell to cast a white light over her whenever she wore the clothing. But at this rate, she'd have to start over.

Blowing out a breath, she dumped the mixture outside onto the lawn—right on the brown spot where she suspected the neighborhood rabbits liked to mark their territory—then wandered back inside to the kitchen and the assortment of spell items strewn about the counter.

Measuring out the black sea salt into a clear glass mixing bowl, she paused and leaned forward to catch her elbows on the counter and her chin in her hand.

She'd had amazing sex last night. More orgasms than she could count? Check. World? Rocked.

And her lover was dying.

What the hell?

How was a witch supposed to deal with that? Magic did not enable a witch to bring back the dead. Not unless the witch practiced dark magic and wanted to deal with zombies as a result. But could she heal the dying? Her healing skills were miserable. If she suggested to Lars she wanted to give it a go, would that push him away from her? He did not want to talk about his condition. And she got that.

Yet, they'd grown closer last night. The man was amazing. Like no man she'd ever shared her body with before. He looked at her like she was magic. And he treated her like a princess. And he was kind and so gentle with Peanut. What more could a girl want in a man? She had to keep him.

But if she managed to do so, for how long would that last?

Lars set aside his work gloves and sat on the bale of hay. The pack rented some acreage to a nearby farmer who used the land to grow wheat and barley, and in turn, all they asked was a few dozen bales of hay. A stack stood four bales high out behind the compound. Dean used it around the compound, and Sunday spread it over her garden in the fall to protect the plants from the harsh winter chill.

Dean had gone inside the house to grab them some water and he returned carrying a thermos. Yet the wolf walked purposely toward Lars, as if something urgent were up. Suddenly feeling as if he were a teen who had pissed off the principal and was waiting for a talking to, Lars stood, hands flexing nervously near his thighs. And Dean grabbed him and pulled him in for a crushing man hug.

Ah hell.

"Sunday told me," Dean said. He slapped Lars's back

a couple times. Stepping away, he studied Lars's face. "You're dying?"

"Don't make a big thing about this, man. It's—the doc says it's probably the same thing my father had. You weren't here when he died. It took him…quickly."

"Oh, man, that's rough. I'm so sorry. Whatever you need, you know you just have to ask. Sunday and I are here for you."

"Thanks, but uh, I'm good." And it felt too awkward between them right now. He wasn't a feeble thing. He was still strong and could toss around hay bales as if they were Lego blocks. "Don't tell the other pack members."

"I won't. I'll be cool. Just want you to know I got your back, man."

"I'll let you know if I need anything. I should get Peanut home. I have a lot to do this afternoon. You good here?"

"Of course! Next time tell me if you're not feeling well. I never should have asked—"

Lars gripped Dean by the shoulder, tightly. "I'm capable. I am not an invalid. So don't treat me like one. Okay?"

"Got it." Dean slapped his bicep. "Thanks for the help."

Lars wandered up to the house and made quick work of packing up Peanut. He sensed Sunday hung back, probably feeling as though she'd done something wrong by telling Dean. Good. He didn't want to talk to her. To have to fit himself into the mold of "dying."

He didn't plan to die. He planned to live every day until his last breath.

He wasn't as mad at the wood he was chopping today. Mostly. Still tracing a bit of anger over Sunday having told Dean he was dying, Lars brought down the ax on the head of a pine log and crisply split the column in two. He gripped one half and split it again.

Out of the corner of his vision he saw a flash of pink, and for a second Lars thought his vision was starting to blur. A problem that was showing up more often lately. Was blindness in his future? Had his father suffered such? He couldn't recall. He'd been young and had spent his days playing with the other pack wolves with no concern for how his father had actually felt.

He brought the ax down with a forceful grunt. The pink lingered in his peripheral vision. What next? Had Sunday returned to check on him? He should have been more clear with her regarding not treating him like an invalid, as he had been with Dean.

"Hey!"

At the shout, he startled and whipped around to find it was not failing vision but rather a particularly tasty witch dressed in a short pink skirt, white lacy ankle socks and black high heels, and a tight T-shirt that said Mermaids Like to Get Wet stretched across her ample bosom.

"Whew! You surprised me."

"I guessed that from the way you swung around with an ax aimed at me."

He looked at the weapon, still hoisted high in readiness for defense, then set it down by the tree stump.

"Sorry," she said. "I should have expected that. You were in the zone. The cutting zone, or whatever you call it. So what's that you're sporting today? A man bun?"

"A what?" Oh. He shrugged and bobbed his head to test that the hair was still secure and tight at the back of his head. "Keeps it out on my way when I'm working. Man bun?"

"You haven't heard that term before? You're working it, let me tell you. Add in the beard and the overalls and ax? Most definitely a lumbersexual."

"A...? I don't even want to know."

"It's a good thing!"

"Sounds...skanky."

Her giggle lured him over to kiss her, but she squirmed and swiped a hand down her cheek, which left a dirty streak in its wake. "You're all sweaty."

"You don't like me sweaty?" He rubbed at the dirt smudge he'd left on her cheek but he only managed to make it worse.

"I like you sweaty in my bed, but this is, hmm... You have wood dust all over you and dirt streaking down your chest."

"Yeah, I got some dirt on your cheek. Why don't you run in and wipe it off." He stepped back and picked up the ax, but the handle slipped through his grasp and the heavy metal blade landed right before Mireio's feet. The witch let out a peep. "Shit. Sorry. I didn't mean to..."

He grabbed the wood handle and again couldn't get a good grip around it. He flexed his fingers, working them in and out, but it was no use.

"Loss of feeling again?" she wondered. "Oh, Lars. What can I do? You should maybe quit for the day and get some—"

"No!" he shouted a little too loudly.

Mireio stepped back from him, clutching the fish purse to her gut. It wasn't quite fear in her eyes, but concern for sure.

"Don't do that," he said with a forceful sweep of his hand between them.

"Do what? I was worried—"

"That," he said. "I don't want that from you. None of that—" he waved his hand wildly before him "—feeling sorry crap. I'm fine. It comes and it goes. I need to walk it off. Kick some logs or something."

At that moment the baby monitor blinked and the rustle of a little body kicking in his crib could be heard.

"I'll get it!" Mireio rushed out. "You're right. I'll leave

you to finish up your man stuff here. I brought stew and some bread that needs to go in the oven. I set it on the step before looking for you out back. Come inside in about half an hour?"

He nodded and turned to face the woodpile while she wandered into the house. When he heard her coo over Peanut and pick him up, Lars held back an oath. He'd been mean to her just now. What was wrong with her being concerned for him?

"Everything," he muttered.

He did not want to be treated like an invalid. By anyone. Such treatment would only make his diagnosis all the more real.

He punched a weak fist into his opposite palm, hoping to feel the pain, but all he got was a brush of his knuckles against skin. He couldn't even feel the tingle in his fingers now. They felt…dead.

Setting aside Lars's anger as just that—a well-deserved reaction to the sudden awful circumstances he'd been forced to face—Mireio put the stewpot on the stove top to warm and slid a pan of dinner rolls in the oven. Soon the cabin smelled like bread, potatoes, rosemary and caramelized carrots.

"Mmm, wait until you can eat real food, Peanut." She bent before the infant she'd placed in the baby seat at the table and dangled her hair before him. He swiped at it and managed to grasp a hunk but his little fingers slipped easily because they were sticky with his saliva. The kid did like to suck on his thumb. "I wonder if you're teething? You think so? Is that right? I remember your daddy reading to you about getting your teeth right about now. You need something to chew on."

She sorted through the neat collection of toys kept in a box on the shelf next to the other baby supplies. A puppy rattle, a squeaky bunny… "Yes! A teething ring." She washed off the nubby blue silicon circle and helped the baby get a good grip on it. It went right to his mouth and he kicked his legs and cooed as a means of thanking her. "Do I know how to make my menfolk happy, or what?"

"That you do." Lars strolled in and tossed aside his work gloves. He'd kicked off his boots on the step. His chest was soaked and his face streaked with dirt. "Sorry about that out there."

"No problem. You got the feeling back in your fingers?"

"Yes. Just now. Sometimes it lingers all day. Other times it's a short while. Damn, that smells great. Do I have time for a shower?"

"You do. Me and Thor will get the table set and have everything ready for you when you get back in."

Towel in hand, he paused at the door and cast a look over his shoulder. "Thor?"

Mireio nodded encouragingly.

"Nope." He strode out, leaving the screen door swinging gently back to close.

"Yeah, I didn't think so. But it is a good Scandinavian name, don't you think?"

With great dramatics, and a devilish grin, Peanut emitted a disgusting sound that she knew signaled time for a diaper change. The kid had definitely spoken against that name.

When Lars returned, she had stew in bowls and the table was set with dinner rolls glossed with melting butter. Peanut sat with his bottle, eyelids drooping heavily and a drool of milk trickling out the corner of his mouth.

Lars kissed his son on the crop of bushy black hair, wiped the milk away and then swiped his fingers across the towel he wore wrapped about his hips.

"Do I need to get dressed for supper?" he asked as she poured them water into two mason jars.

"Well, it will be a distraction. And I haven't eaten all day."

"Just checking. Wouldn't want to distract you from nourishment. I'll pull on a shirt." He winked at her.

His mood had bounced from angry to cheery. It was because of Peanut, she knew. The man adored his son.

After putting back his second serving of stew, Lars reached for what was probably his sixth roll and spread butter across the still steaming insides. "You, witch, know how to cook."

"Why, thank you. I like conjuring up spectacular things in the kitchen and in the brewery."

"Is there anything you can't make?"

She shrugged and considered that a moment. "Tofu?"

"I'm glad about that. You know how to keep your men happy, that's for sure. Look."

Peanut was asleep in his chair, the bottle lolling out of his mouth yet still his tiny bite held the end of it.

"Aw, Connor was tired."

"Connor?"

She waited for his reaction but got merely a shrug. "Really?"

"I don't know. Sort of wussy sounding."

"Lars. You do realize if you let the poor boy keep *Peanut* that when he grows up the kids in school will call him Pee for short. And I'm not talking about the vegetable either. Do you want that?"

"Not exactly."

"And if not Pee, then he'll be Nuts. How does Nuts Gunderson sound to you?"

"I'll come up with a name. I appreciate you giving me suggestions. Keep them coming. Something will stick, sooner or later. His mom left that up to me."

"What if you ever marry?"

He paused with a chunk of dinner lodged in his cheek.

"I mean, will the mother's name always be on the birth certificate?"

"I'm pretty sure that's a given. But if I should marry someday my wife could adopt."

"That makes sense. Only you don't want her to have to adopt a Peanut."

"I'll take care of it. Just keep the suggestions coming. It's a quick change I can do with a visit to the county records office. Sunday told me that."

"So Sunday is like your secretary as well as babysitter?"

He stopped chewing again and narrowed his gaze at her. "Don't be jealous of her, Mireio. She's married to Dean."

"I know. I just…" She set the spoon down in her stew and pushed aside the hair from her face. "Maybe I am a little jealous. I mean…well, I'll just ask. What are we, Lars?"

"We? Uh…you mean like…"

She nodded eagerly.

His shy smile surfaced and those dimples were anything but coy. "Well, you're my girl. Right?"

"Yes," she said immediately. "I'm your girlfriend. And you're my boyfriend?"

He took another bite of the dinner roll and smiled around the chew. "I'm all in."

She couldn't prevent a gleeful clap and a wiggle on the chair. Sometimes it was hard to define whatever she had going on with a man. And men were often reluctant to commit to labels such as *boyfriend* and *girlfriend*. He really liked her. Yes! Lars Gunderson was her boyfriend.

"I never thought you'd be happy about that," Lars admitted.

"About being your girlfriend? Are you kidding me?"

He shrugged. "With all that's happened lately."

"You mean with you telling me…? Oh, Lars. Don't even go there. I'm glad we said it. I like to know what's up between us. You're mine. I'm yours. Like it or not. Do you like it?"

"More than anything."

"Good. Then no doubts. Promise?"

He nodded. "So that reminds me… Did you sleep okay last night?"

"Sure. Why?"

"I was lying awake for a bit, watching you." He dipped his head and smirked. "You're so pretty when you sleep. And your breasts were highlighted by the moon. But at one point you called out like you were having a nightmare."

"Oh." She shrugged. "Ah…it happens. I'm a witch. I've seen things that are bound to come back to haunt me. I don't remember having a nightmare last night."

"I was worried about you."

"Don't be."

Kissing him on the forehead, she took his empty bowl and cleared the rest of the dishes to the sink, where she'd already filled one side with warm soapy water. She'd had a nightmare again? Why hadn't she remembered that? Usually the nightmare woke her in a sweat and sometimes she even screamed. Always the same thing. A vampire holding a heart and grinning at her.

Shoot. She didn't want Lars to know what was up with that. The man lay awake watching her sleep? While it should seem creepy, she couldn't go there with her new adorable boyfriend. Time to look up a spell to silence the dark and disturbing dreams.

Across the room, Lars cleaned up Peanut's face and then lifted him to pat him on the back. The baby burped loudly, gave a little giggle, then promptly fell asleep.

The twosome chuckled at that, and Lars, bouncing as he walked with Peanut, kissed Mireio on the cheek. "He's my boy."

"I can't say I've seen that obnoxious side of you yet, but I am duly warned."

He strolled over to the crib, big hand smoothing across Peanut's back and stood there a while, bouncing gently. The setting sun illuminated his silhouette. Eyes closed, he looked a man at peace. Content in this world.

Sometimes he hid his emotions well, Mireio realized. And she brushed a wet hand across her eye to wipe away a nonexistent piece of fluff. Wasn't as if a tear had dropped down her cheek. Nonsense.

Rinsing the dishes while Lars tucked in Peanut, she stacked them in the rack and wiped down the counter. Lars snuck up behind her, his hands slipping up under her skirt and surprising her into a peep.

"Watching your ass wiggle while you work gets me horny." He squeezed the aforementioned body part and she pressed against his hands and wiggled slowly. "Did you have plans to eat and run or…you want to stick around and see what comes up?" He leaned into her and his erection nudged against her derriere.

"I think something is already up." She made to turn around but he caught her wrist and turned her back, placing his hand over hers on the counter. "Oh, yeah? Bring it, big boy."

He dropped the towel and flipped up the back of her skirt. His hair, still wet from the shower, fell across her back and shoulder as he fit himself between her legs and she squeezed tightly to hold him there. She wasn't quite wet, but it wasn't going to take too long…

His hand glided around to cup her breast and pinch the nipple through her shirt and bra as he dragged his erection between her clasped thighs. His wanting growl tightened her nipples and…that was all she needed. She was ready for him.

Drawing a heel along the side of his calf, she thrust up her ass, begging for his entry. His big wide hand slapped to her stomach, covering it completely, then moved down under her skirt, where he simultaneously guided himself inside her and toggled her clit at the same time.

He was so thick, a man of girth and talent with that remarkable magic wand of his. He pumped slow, allowing her to feel every inch of his entry and pull-out. Add to that the wet slickery dance of his finger over her clitoris.

Mireio grasped the faucet over the sink with one hand and pushed against the marble counter with the other, wanting to hilt him inside her. In this position she could feel him so deep. A few times he lifted her shoes from the floor as his thrusts moved her entire body, pairing them together in a bond of skin and lust and wanton need.

He bit the back of her top and tugged as he growled. "Not going to be able to hold off much longer."

"Go for it, lover. Take me hard and fast. Oh, yes!"

His hand slapped onto the counter beside hers. He held her pinned there on his cock as his body tremored and he pumped inside her. And then a gasp of relief and joy. He slipped both hands around and over her breasts and pulled her body back against his. "Inside you is where I always want to be."

Chapter 13

A few days later Lars brought in Mireio's mail when he stopped by her place. She opened a package to find the dragon exudation had arrived. Okay, so it was dragon sweat. But she couldn't imagine what it required to get such an item from the source. Did dragons sweat much? And who stood nearby to catch it? Didn't sound like a job that would offer a lengthy employment. But perhaps the death benefits for next of kin were included. Eek.

It was exciting to finally have all the ingredients that would allow her to perform the immortality spell. She tossed the bubble packing material in the garbage and before she could tuck away the vials in a drawer, Lars pointed to her closed fist that hid the ingredient.

"Is that what I think it is?" he asked.

"What do you think it is?"

"Dragon piss?"

"Eww. No, it's dragon sweat!"

"And that doesn't rate an eww? Huh. I'll never understand witches." He winked at her and the dimples joined in. "So now that you've got the secret ingredient, are you ready to go vamp hunting?"

Not as much now that she knew he was dying. "I need

to study the spell a bit more and do an inventory of all the ingredients."

"Well, what if we stalk the longtooth again? I want to get out. It's a beautiful evening. Sunday's got Peanut. And afterward we can get ice cream."

"I'm in!"

As they walked the alleyway following what Lars had called "his sniffer," Mireio could only think about what neither of them dared bring up. She wanted to live forever. Lars had been given two months to live. And that count was ticking down daily. That was completely and utterly insane.

She could not do this! Especially not with him—a dying man—helping her. No question about it, she had to call it off. Now. Before it got out of hand and they actually found the vampire. She picked up her pace and just as she opened her mouth to call to Lars, his body suddenly contorted.

That did not look comfortable. Or warranted.

"Shit." Mireio rushed up and grabbed him by the arm but he twisted it out of her grip. "What is it?" He bent and slapped a hand to the brick wall of a residential garage. "Lars?"

"Shifting," he ground through his teeth. "Need to… get out of here. Can't stop…it."

"Witch's tits, this is not cool. Can you relax and let the urge pass?"

He growled at her through gritted teeth. And his hand began to shift. The knuckles bulged and his fingers contorted.

"Right. Not in your control."

He shoved a hand in his front pocket and pulled out the keys, thrusting them at her. "Get the truck. Go home," he said. "I'll…"

"You can't run around in the city. I'll get the truck and come for you." She took off and, remembering where the truck was, veered left. "Don't howl!"

As she scampered down the alley, she heard him swear again. Turning, she saw him pull off his shirt and unzip his jeans even as his feet tore through his boots. The shift happened so quickly. He hadn't even time to undress? Pulling off one pant leg, he hissed when the other leg split down the seam. His chest expanded and his head changed. Drastically. Fur grew over his body as claws curled out from his fingers. No, not fingers...

"Paws," Mireio whispered in awe. She couldn't be afraid of him. She wasn't. He was beautiful.

But not in public. This was so bad.

Finally the fully shifted werewolf stood, slapped a paw against the wall, and sent crumbled bricks flying. Then it turned, scented her with a flare of its nostrils and took off the opposite direction.

"Oh, crap. He's on the run."

Scrambling over to gather up his clothes, Mireio then clicked down the alleyway, cursing her need to always wear high heels. Short girl problem number fifty-five. But she made it to the truck without stumbling. She climbed up into the cab and started the engine. She had no magic to stop him from shifting. Or to make him invisible to others.

Rolling down the window she heard the wolf's howl.

"No, no no. Don't do that, Lars. Someone will see you."

On second thought, the howl would help her to track him. Sliding forward and stretching on the seat so her foot could reach the gas pedal, she shifted into gear and rolled around the corner in the direction he had run. Passing half a dozen teenagers walking and biking she winced. They couldn't see him. She had to find him first.

Turning abruptly left, the tires squealed as she headed toward a dangerous shadow moving swiftly before a high hedgerow, plunked right before a row of two-story houses with their porch lights on.

"That's him!" She sped up and slammed on the brakes beside the wolf. Leaning over she opened the door. "Get in!" Please goddess, let him understand her.

The werewolf crept forward. Somewhere down the street she heard, "Hey! Look!"

And in the next instant, Lars jumped into the front seat, and she took off without worrying that the door swung wide and probably her boyfriend in shifted form had no clue or idea how to pull it closed. Turning left again, she made it a sharp fast turn, and the door slammed shut.

The wolf yipped. Its big furry head bowed forward to fit his bulk inside the cab. Its toothy maw opened, drool dripping, and it barked at her.

"Dude, do not give me the sassy bark. I'm your girl-friend! Mireio. Friend." She reached for him but when he snapped at her she retracted. "Okay, stay in the truck and I'll get you home as quickly as possible."

Ahead, a well-lit intersection advertised flashing red and blue lights and another set of bright headlights aimed skyward. A car accident? The last thing she needed was to pass the police with a werewolf sitting in the passenger seat.

"Duck," she said, but he obviously didn't understand her speech.

The wolf suddenly shoved the steering wheel with a paw and Mireio focused back on the road. She'd narrowly avoided colliding with a parked car. Had Lars not done what he had, they would have crashed.

"Shit. Stop panicking, Mireio. This is just another night out on the town with your big handsome wolf. Relax. Smile at the cops as you drive by."

She gave a little wave as an officer ducked his head and appeared to look through and to the opposite side where she sat. Passing slowly, when she cleared the scene she stopped at a light and turned to Lars.

A naked human man sat on the seat, his head bowed and caught against a palm. Werewolves shifted so quickly, but she wasn't startled.

"Lars?"

"Drive!"

"Yes. Drive. I am driving." The light turned green and she slid forward again to reach the accelerator and headed back to his place.

Reaching over and under the front of her seat, Lars adjusted the seat forward so she could reach the pedals without having to skooch up to get close enough.

He picked up the clothes she'd tossed on the floor and pressed them onto his lap but didn't move or speak to her again. When she pulled up to his cabin, he hopped out of the truck and slammed the door behind him. The naked man stalked up to the front door and disappeared inside.

Mireio turned off the ignition and the lights. Her car was parked beside a weeping willow tree. She could drive home and leave him to sulk. Was he embarrassed? Probably at a loss as to why he was shifting without volition. The man was in pain, and he needed someone to hold him.

Would he let her in?

Hopping out of the truck, she swung her purse over a shoulder and stepped up to the threshold before the cabin. No lights on inside. She lifted her hand to knock, but couldn't do it.

Moonlight glinted on her silver rings. She touched the larimar crystal entwined within a platinum wire-wrap, wishing she had a water spell to make him feel better. A bath always made her feel better after a rough day.

She wouldn't be so stupid as to suggest a bath to soak away his insurmountable worries. And Lars's days would only get worse. He had to be careful if the shift were to again attack without his volition. Perhaps stop going near humans.

Sighing, she turned away from the door. And then heard him call from inside, "Come in. Please."

She entered the cabin quietly, seeming to walk on the balls of her feet so her heels wouldn't click too loudly. She stood there, acclimating to the darkness.

Lars lay on the bed, curled in on himself. The shift had come on him so suddenly that he couldn't stop it. He'd felt so helpless. Yet, thankfully, even in werewolf shape he'd recognized the truck and known she'd wanted him to get in. He'd felt small and defeated as she'd driven him home. Shifting back to were shape beside her, he had felt more naked than when he stood before her when making love to her. Exposed and wretched.

He still didn't want to talk. But he did need to feel her against him. Mireio was his safe place.

He stretched out an arm and she walked over to take his hand. "Stay?" he asked.

She kicked off her shoes and climbed onto the bed and cuddled up against him. Kissing his forehead, she then pulled his hand up to her mouth and held it there, her lips sealing warmth onto his skin.

"Sleep," she said. "I'm here."

Chapter 14

Mireio stayed at the cabin to make breakfast for Lars while he went for a morning run to pick up Peanut from the compound and bring him home for Mireio to feed a bottle.

He immediately headed out again, feeling he'd not spent enough time outside and mostly because he still didn't know what to say to her about what had happened last night. He felt like a failure. A werewolf who couldn't control his own shifts? There were no curse words strong enough for that one.

Tracking through the woods on the path he'd beaten down over years of running—both in his were, or man, shape and wolf shape—he suddenly realized the moon had been very round last night. It must be close to the full moon. Well, he knew it was. He'd been horny as hell lately. Of course, he had good reason with such a gorgeous witch as his girlfriend.

He smiled at that. He had a girlfriend. And life was good when he was with her. But if the moon reached full-ness tonight or tomorrow, that meant he'd have to let out his werewolf, no matter what. Had it been full last night? Was that why he'd shifted? No, it hadn't felt like the moon pull shift. That moment in the alleyway he'd been completely out of control of his body. A passenger who hadn't signed up for the wild ride.

Stopping and bending forward to catch his hands on his knees, he panted. A lot. Normally his casual jog didn't wind him so much. He wasn't going to consider that he was growing weaker. It wasn't right.

"Screw this." He turned and raced down the path toward the cabin, pushing full speed and pumping his arms.

Five minutes later he wandered to the back of the cabin, wheezing and coughing. He sat on the log splitting stump and hung his head. If he was going to die, he wished for it to happen quickly. No long endless days of suffering. Or to be bedridden?

"No, please…no."

He'd never imagined that death could be humiliating, but if he were reduced to a feeble invalid, that would be the worst possible condition. He wasn't sure he could face that.

But he would. He had to. For Peanut. And his girlfriend.

Suddenly a bee landed on the ground right beside his bare foot. Its wings buzzed but its furred body was slick with wet.

"Poor guy." He bent to gently stroke the tips of the bee's wings. "All tuckered out after a morning dew bath? I know the feeling."

He turned his hand palm up and nudged it beside the bee. The insect climbed onto his hand and sat there, content to soak up Lars's innate warmth.

He lifted his hand and studied the bee. Its big black eyes took him in, antennae flickering. "You live such a short lifetime, and yet you accomplish so much. You, my sweet little worker bee, are remarkable." He closed his eyes and shook his head. "What have I accomplished?"

Nothing of significance came to mind.

Standing, he padded over to the hive, his passenger still in for the ride. He set his hand at the entrance and waited until the bee climbed off and into the hive. There she would be warmed by hundreds of her fellow worker bees and then could return to collecting pollen. Accomplishing so much.

Did he have to leave a mark on the world before he left? He wanted... He wanted so much for his son that he might never be able to give him. Mercy. What would become of Peanut when he was gone?

"Lars?"

Mireio walked around the side of the cabin. He sucked in his winded breaths and gave her a nod.

She carried a wide-eyed Peanut, who chewed on the teething ring. "I'm sorry, but I forgot to mention last night that I need to go in early this morning. I'm brewing some IPA. I left breakfast for you on the table. Peanut has had a bottle and he's burped. Loudly." She handed the baby to him and he reached for him, but knew he wouldn't be able to hold him securely. His fingers tingled, as did his feet.

"Could you bring him in and lay him in the crib for a nap?" he asked.

She assessed him momentarily, then nodded. "Of course. You going to be able to eat?" she called back as she made haste toward the cabin door.

"I sure hope so," he muttered, forcing himself to walk. The going was slow. With every step the sensation in his feet decreased. But he made it to the front door, where Mireio kissed him quickly. She was acting brisk and he sensed she was in a hurry.

"Your fingers again?" she asked.

"And my feet." He nodded. "I'll be fine."

"I know you will. Call me if you need anything. Can I come over after work?"

"I'd like that. Uh, but, Mireio, what day is it? I mean, do you know when the moon is full?"

"Tomorrow!" she offered gleefully. "I know you wolves shift on the night of the full moon."

"Sometimes the day before and after too. I'm going to shift tonight. Or I'd like to."

"Does that mean I get to watch Peanut? Because I'd love to."

"I'd appreciate that." He kissed her, but didn't lift his now completely numb hand to touch her.

"See you later. Remember to call if you need anything!" She wandered over to her car and turned it around and drove down the winding drive.

And Lars fell to sit on the threshold because he could no longer stand on feet he could not feel.

Around four in the afternoon Mireio popped her head up from cleaning the stainless-steel brew tank and waved as Valor strolled in. The brewery didn't open until five, and Valor had the night shift.

"Here to help," Valor called as she tossed her backpack behind the bar and leaned over the sink, plunging her hands into the soapy water.

"I appreciate it when you come in early to help clean. You know Geneva would never think of doing such a thing."

"Well, hey, my hands are covered in motor grease so I figured all this sanitizing solution will cut that and get me clean in the process."

"Just don't get it on the parts," Mireio warned as she decided the tank was clean, and she could now move on to disconnecting the remaining hoses that led from tank to tank and run those through the wash. She really should concoct a spell to automate the process, but she felt the equipment got cleaner when it was hand washed, not… spell washed.

Valor's long chestnut hair, streaked with blue of late, was queued back in a loose ponytail. She wore combat boots, short jeans cutoffs, a Decadent Dames T-shirt and strands of talismans hung from leather cords about her neck. She was the tomboy of the group and generally did the heavy lifting and liked to close.

Mireio joined her at the sinks and started rinsing the items Valor had washed. They were stainless-steel clamps and rings and assorted parts she broke down and cleaned after every brew. The cleaning part was the most tedious, but with a helping hand things went quick enough.

"So I hear you've got a new man," Valor said. "A wolf?"

"Yes, Lars Gunderson."

"Yeah, Sunday told me about you two. I've spoken to him a time or two when I needed help with my bees. Very quiet. But man, is he a big one, and sexy."

"He's almost twice the size of me, and I adore every inch of him."

"Cool. So you two getting serious? Because I know that Sunday babysits for him. A single father? That's gotta make for some interesting dates."

"The two of us serious? I hope so. I really like him, Valor. And the baby thing doesn't bother me at all. You know how much I love kids."

"You do, but that doesn't mean you have to become the kid's mom."

"I didn't say I was going to do that. But a man with a baby is not a deal breaker. You would be amazed at what a kind and gentle dad Lars is. So attentive to Peanut."

Valor chuckled. "I can't get over that name. Every time Sunday mentions him I laugh."

"The mother didn't give the baby a name."

"Crazy. You know how all this affects Sunday, don't you?"

Mireio held a dripping clamp over the water. Other than knowing the facts about cats and wolves mating, she hadn't thought beyond that. "Why? Did she and Lars have a thing? I thought she and Dean had been married awhile?"

"It's the baby thing. Cat shifters can't have werewolf babies. Just isn't possible."

"I know that."

"So Sunday will never be able to have Dean's children. And even though she acts like it's no big thing, she wants a baby. So while she loves babysitting, it also tears her apart having to hand that kid back over to Lars. And now you."

"Oh, no. Did she say something about me? Is she… jealous of me? I'm not trying to be the baby's mom. But, well, Sunday shouldn't be either."

"Yeah, I know. It's her little weirdness she needs to work out. So don't take it wrong if she acts strange around you, okay?"

"I won't. I'll try not to. But could they adopt?"

"They had considered asking Lars about adopting the boy. But Sunday quickly realized that would have been awkward to the nines. Both men in the same pack and someone else raising his kid?"

"Lars would have never let that happen. He's in love with Peanut. He'll raise him alone no matter what—oh, my goddess."

"What?"

"I hadn't given the baby's future a thought. Oh. What's he going to do now about Peanut?"

"Mireio, you're freaking me out. And you're shaking." She took a heavy steel ring from her and set it aside. "What's up?"

"Oh, Valor." Mireio turned and leaned her hips against

the sink, pushing the hair from her face. "Lars has this thing. A werewolf disease. It's rare. Hereditary. His dad died from it. The doctor gave him only a few months to live."

"Whoa. And you're getting involved in all this? I know you like to take care of people and are compassionate, but are you sure about this, sweetie?"

"I am." And she was. "But what will happen to Peanut if Lars were to die?"

"Then Sunday and Dean could adopt him."

"Oh, my goddess, what am I saying? I don't want him to die." She turned and gripped the edge of the sink.

"Oh...uh...hmm..." Valor spread an arm across Mireio's back. Of the witchy quartet, she was the least comfortable with hugging and had always claimed she didn't have much empathy.

"He's so young, you know? This isn't fair. And he's just gotten this beautiful little baby that makes him happy. I know it's what puts the smile on his face every day. Here I've been sad because he has to go through something like this. But I didn't consider the struggle he must be facing knowing he may not be around to watch his son grow up. He can't die, Valor. He can't!"

She turned and hugged her friend. Even as she sensed Valor's initial reluctance, Vaolr soon returned the hug and smoothed a wet hand across Mireio's back.

"What did the doctor say?" Valor asked. "Can he take something for it? Is it like cancer? Can he do chemo or radiation?"

"No, it's degenerative. No pills or chemicals can stop it. He's got neuropathy and he loses feeling in his hands and feet. And last night he shifted without volition. He can't control his werewolf. It scares him. It scares me. I want to be there for him. But I feel so helpless. This morning I wanted to wrap him in my arms and tell him it was going to be all right, but I could sense he didn't want that from me, so I tried to do the nonchalant thing. He puts on this stoic werewolf act. I'm tough. Don't treat me like an invalid. How can I help him?"

"Have you tried healing him?"

Mireio pulled away from Valor. "You know I'm not a healer. I wouldn't have the skill or the power."

"Well, neither am I. But I have been known to bring a drowned faery back to life with my pitiful healing skills. And what if we combined our powers? Geneva is a master healer. I know we witches can't give back life or raise the dead, but...he's not dead yet. Maybe we could infuse Lars with some life-sustaining magic?"

"Oh, my goddess, I think it would be worth a try. But Eryss is in California now."

"As long as we have a triad, we're good."

"Right! Oh, I wonder if Lars would let us try?"

"Ask him. I mean, sure he's putting up a front, trying to act all tough and cool. But you gotta think the man would be desperate to try anything to stay alive."

"I'll ask him. Oh, he has to agree to it. I'm not sure if it'll work, but we can't not try, right?"

"I'm in," Valor confirmed with a fist bump to Mireio's wet fist. "And I'll make sure Geneva won't say no. Just let us know when you need us."

Mireio hugged her again. "I love you. Thank you!"

"Sure, but chill on the hugs, will you? I think I got enough hugging to last me a year now."

Mireio hadn't had much time for baking lately, so after picking up some things for supper to make at Lars's place, she stopped into a local sweet shop near the brewery and, after much debating over the triple chocolate bomb and the cherry pistachio cream delight, she went with the chocolate. It was a small cake, but it would serve the two of them. Or rather, it would serve a big hungry wolf, and offer enough for a taste for his girlfriend.

When she arrived at Lars's cabin, he met her at the door and grabbed the bags she was carrying, only kissing her quickly. He set the bags on the counter and started unpacking them. "I didn't expect you this early."

It was after six. She couldn't determine if he was angry or busy. "I usually finish up at the brewery around three or four. Valor stopped in to help me clean today. Where's... oh, there you are, Peanut."

The baby lay on a blanket before the couch beneath the bright plastic toddler gym. He kicked his legs eagerly when she sat next to him and tugged one of his toes. "You look so happy! Were you and Daddy playing before I got here?"

"He just got up from a nap," Lars offered over his shoulder. He had unpacked all the groceries and now seemed a little too concerned over the food, remaining by the counter with his back to her.

Mireio kissed the baby's exposed belly. "You're a little tub, you know that? A little tub! What do you say to that, Loki?"

She waited for Lars to react, but he was studying the red pepper she'd brought for the enchiladas.

"So that's a good one?" she asked, again waiting for a reply. "Lars?"

"What's that?"

She got up and walked over to the counter and he grabbed the onion and opened the fridge door. "Do you like the name Loki? Lars? What's up with you? Is everything all right?"

"It's fine." He finally turned and, even with the hair falling over the side of his face, she noticed the red streak by his eye. "I'll maybe take Peanut out for a walk while you make supper."

"Wait." She stepped in front of him, forcing him to look at her. The red mark was actually a cut and it looked new. "When did you cut yourself? Right before I got here?" Because she knew werewolves healed quickly, sometimes almost instantaneously.

"Mireio, I said it was nothing."

She grabbed his hands and did not back down. Without saying a word, she peered behind the shadows in his gaze and coaxed up the truth.

"Fine. I…might have fainted right before you got here. I came to right away. So like I said. Nothing." He tugged out of her grip and stomped over to collect Peanut.

"Nothing? Lars, you fainted? What if you had been holding Peanut?"

"I wasn't." He turned with an air of anger darkening his expression. "It's happened twice now, and I know that right before it happens I get a weird feeling of dread. So if it ever happens when I'm holding Peanut, I'll set him in the crib."

She put a hand to her hip. That was an utterly ridiculous defense and he knew it. But if she pressed him, she would only push him away. So she forced herself to nod. "I get it. No big deal. You've got everything under control. Why don't you give me half an hour to get supper ready? Are the two of you going far?" She realized what he'd think of that question only after it had come out.

"Just out back." He grabbed the baby sling, fitted Peanut against his chest, and headed outside.

And Mireio finally let the teardrop fall that had been threatening since she'd realized Lars had fallen and hurt himself. Had he been holding Peanut at the time, the baby could have gotten hurt too. Was the man degenerating so quickly? Did he need someone around to watch him? A caregiver?

Heartbeats thumping, she pressed a fist over her chest

and shook her head. She would be that caregiver if he asked. But she knew he would never ask. And she didn't want to make the man feel more helpless than he likely already did.

Navigating Lars's right to privacy and need to ignore his disease was a tough situation. And it would only grow more difficult.

Could she do this?

After supper Lars helped Mireio wash the dishes then, after she'd folded the drying towels over the sink, he took her in his arms and hugged her. "Sorry," he said. "It's how I'm dealing with this…stuff. For now."

"I get it. But allow me to stumble as I'm dealing with it too?"

"Of course. I'll try not to be such an asshole from now on."

"No, you've every right. I mean, not to be an asshole, but to be as unsure about how to deal with your feelings as any man would be. I can take it. I'm a big girl."

He squeezed her hand, then smiled. Just a little. "A big girl?" His eyes focused on her chest. "That you are."

"Oh! I have a surprise for you. For us, actually. We'll need two forks." She grabbed the bag she'd left by the door because it hadn't needed to go in the fridge and pulled out the white bakery box. "I didn't make this, but I know it'll be good. It's called triple chocolate decadence."

He held up two forks. "Deal me in."

Mireio sat on the couch, before which Peanut lay on the floor on his stomach. She opened the box and the sides folded down to make a plate. Lars sat next to her and kept both forks.

"This looks like mine," he said taking the makeshift plate from her. "Where's yours?"

"I only want a few bites. I think there's enough sugar in there to keep me awake for two days."

He forked the first bite and then turned to feed the next bite to her. The soft chocolate frosting melted on her tongue and she groaned.

"That good?" he asked.

She nodded. "But not better than sex."

He tried a few more bites and nodded in agreement. "But very good."

On the floor, Peanut suddenly rolled to his back and kicked his legs and arms.

"Hey! He's getting good at that," Lars said. "He'll be crawling soon. Probably before the book says he will. My kid is smart."

Mireio dashed her finger through the frosting and leaned over the baby. "Let's see if he likes chocolate."

"Wait!" He grabbed her wrist. "I don't know. He's not on solid food yet."

"I'm just going to put a little on his tongue. Let him taste. Okay?"

He considered it and she almost sat up and licked it off herself, but then he said, "Sure. A taste can't hurt."

"You're very protective of him." She touched her finger to Peanut's mouth and the baby tongued at it. "I like that about you. So fierce in everything you do, be it chopping wood, helping me to track a vampire or taking care of your boy."

He tilted his head against her shoulder and gazed up at her. "You forgot sex."

"No, that was next on my list. You are a fierce lover." She bent to kiss him and he dashed out his tongue to touch hers, giving her the sweet lush chocolate heat. "Mmm... More of that, please."

He peeled off some frosting with his fork and when she thought he would feed it to her, he dashed it across her lips, smearing them with chocolate. And he quickly followed with a kiss that devoured her more thoroughly than cake.

But the baby cooing at their feet lured them both forward to find Peanut bright-eyed and giggling.

"I think he wants more," she said.

"You've created a monster."

"So he really does take after his dad?" She nudged him with a teasing elbow. "I mean that in the nicest way."

"I'd better get him a bottle. He might go down early tonight. We did a lot of work out back today."

"Is that so?" Mireio picked up the baby, bummed that Lars had taken the cake with him to the fridge. She wiped a smear of chocolate from Peanut's mouth. "What did you and Daddy do today? Did you build something?"

"I finally got a building permit for the plans I handed in to the city. Soon as I get materials, I can start on the addition to the back of the cabin." Lars forked in another bite of cake while he set the bottle in the pot on the stove. Then he picked up the last piece with his fingers and ate it all. "You're right. That cake will have me flying high. Good thing I plan to stay up tonight."

"So tell me what happens when you wolf out under the full moon? I know you wolves have to do it. It's innate. But what do you do? Where do you go? Is there a werewolf party I'm unaware of?"

He laughed and joined her on the couch. When he held out his arms for Peanut she handed him over, knowing she'd have another chance later before bed to sit and feed him. The baby fit against Lars as if there were no other place he belonged. Truly Daddy's boy.

Once Peanut started to drink, Lars flipped his long hair over his shoulder and sat back. Noticing his eye where the cut had been, she touched it. "It's almost gone. Just a faint line now."

"Normally that would have healed within minutes. I'm hoping getting my wolf on tonight will restore my fading strength. Maybe that's all I need? To wolf out and race toward the moon?"

"Or toward a party?"

"There's no party. We werewolves need to answer the call to the moon once a month or we get really fucked up inside. Our bodies need the shift. So we run and race and sometimes even catch small animals."

"Seriously? Oh, I don't want to know."

"Then I won't give you details. Once in a while Dean and I run into one another and we have a good tussle and then race along the hill. We can run for miles and miles without worry of getting close to humans. It's why the compound is way out here."

"You tussle? So you have a werewolf fight?"

"Yep. Sometimes I win, sometimes he does. It doesn't get too nasty. And we always see each other the next day and bump fists. It's our nature. We need that. Like what about you witches? You must have something that you absolutely need to do in order to live and exist?"

"Practicing our magic. Not letting it go stale. And..." She sighed.

"What? Tell me?"

"It's just... I can't."

"You want to live forever. Who doesn't?"

"I do, but some people aren't given that chance. I'm so selfish."

"Hey." He kissed her but with Peanut in his arms it was only a brush of his mouth over hers. Always delicious, though. "It's what you want. It's what you need. Don't apologize for that." In his arms the baby burped, and that ended the serious portion of their conversation.

And Mireio was thankful for that. "When are you going out?"

"In a couple hours. I like the sky to get really dark."

"Despite the moonlight?"

"Exactly." He stood and bounced as he patted Peanut's back, mining for another release of gas. "I'd ask if you want to watch some TV before I go out, but I don't have one. So that leaves sex."

"Hmm…" She tapped her lips, making a show of giving it some good thought. "I suppose I could manage that."

"You suppose?" He spun on her with a smiling gape on his face. "Well, if you're going to be that way." He turned and bounced Peanut over to the crib.

Mireio stood and pulled her shirt off as she walked over to the bed. She slipped off her skirt and climbed onto the bed before Lars had turned around. And when he did, she pushed up the girls in her bra and winked at him.

Chapter 15

Making love with a baby lying not six feet away from their embrace didn't bother Mireio. Why should it? Peanut was asleep. Parents across the world had been doing it forever. Not that she considered herself a parent, but it was hard not to feel parenty when around Peanut.

But right now, she felt like a lush, desirable woman as Lars, hands to the bed beside her shoulders and beard brushing her bare breasts, thrust inside her slowly. His eyes were closed in bliss. They'd both come once together. Now the slow and steady, stay together as long as possible, was happening.

His tense abs gleamed with the moonlight beaming through the window and onto the side of the bed, and she wondered if they might have had too much sex. Because on the night before and after the full moon, some werewolves chose not to shift. One day during the month was enough. But in order to keep back that urge to shift they had to have sex until they were sated. Lars seemed insatiable.

"What are you thinking about?" he asked. "You've got this curly smile on your face like you know more than everyone else."

She pulled his hips toward her, urging his motions to speed up. "I was thinking how much you love sex. And how much I love having sex with you. But is this too much? Will you be able to shift later?"

"I'm already feeling the pull to shift. Don't worry, it'll happen. Just a little longer, please?" He bowed his head and nuzzled his beard across her nipple. "I like being inside you."

"I like your big, thick cock making itself right at home. Stay there always?"

"As long as I can, lover. But I'm almost there..."

She put her hands to his forearms, which tensed and the veins bulged as he neared orgasm. Fashioned of steel and suede, this man. So sexy. And he smelled like chocolate and sex. Yet when he slammed his hips to hers and she awaited his climax, he suddenly pulled out.

He kissed her mouth and then rolled off the bed. "I gotta go. I'm feeling it."

"But you didn't come."

"Can't. Or rather, won't. Gotta save my energy for the shift."

"Do you want me to wait up?"

"No, I should be out all night. Make sure Peanut gets another nip in an hour?"

"I will." She watched him stroll to the door, naked. Of course, he didn't need clothes. "You don't even bring along a towel or something?"

"Why?" He spread his arms, giving her a good long view of his physique. The muscles were steel, and his hard cock jutted upright. "I usually keep extra towels out in the bathroom. I can get dirty loping through the woods. Promise to shower before I come back in. See you in the morning." He blew her a kiss, then left the cabin.

Mireio sat up on the bed and realized Peanut was lying

awake in the crib. "He's pretty awesome, your daddy. You're one lucky baby."

Peanut giggled and kicked his legs in response.

Lars leaned against the huge oak trunk where he had established a sort of base for his moonlight outings. He'd been standing here for—hell, he didn't know how much time had passed, but it felt like an hour. A raccoon family had wandered past him, casting him shifty looks with their night-mirrored eyes. He growled at them, and they scrambled off.

He panted and shook his fingers and stomped his feet. The neuropathy wasn't rearing up, but he couldn't shift. What the hell? Normally the process was a seamless, minimally painful flow from human shape into werewolf shape. He'd done it hundreds of times since that first shift when he'd been a thirteen-year-old boy living with his adopted parents, Ridge and Abigail, at the compound. Shifting wasn't even a second-nature thing. It *was* his nature.

So why couldn't he do it now?

Had Mireio been right? Had he had too much sex?

That had to be it.

"Shoot." He kicked the grassy forest floor with his bare foot.

He still had the night of the full moon. So tomorrow night he'd try again. And he'd have to keep his hands off Mireio to ensure nothing went wrong next time.

"That'll be a challenge," he said as he turned to march back to the cabin.

Ten minutes later, Mireio muttered a sleepy "Really?" She lay in bed, naked, the sheets not covering her beautiful breasts. Lars had checked on Peanut. Sleeping soundly in the crib. "You couldn't...?"

"You were right," he said as he slipped between the

sheets beside her. But he didn't snuggle up close. "I had too much sex. I'm going cold turkey until after the shift tomorrow night. You okay with that?"

"Sure."

He kissed her forehead quickly, cautious not to touch her tempting breasts, then turned his back to her. When her fingers teased at his hip, he wiggled and scooted closer to the edge of the bed.

"Right," she said on a yawn. "Touch not the wolf. See you—" Yawn… "—in the morning."

The next night Mireio handed off Peanut to Lars, who wanted to tuck his son in before he went out to howl at the moon. There was something about the sight of a big, burly man rocking a little nugget of baby hugged against his chest and clutching his beard with chubby little fingers that made her ovaries quiver. Oh, mercy, she had it bad for the man and the baby. And the beard.

After Peanut was down, Lars kissed her. "We going to make another date to do some vamp hunting soon?"

"Uh, sure. But I'm still working on memorizing the spell. No rush."

"I made a promise to you, Mireio. I will help you with the vampire. Just tell me when we're good to go."

She gave him a thumbs-up, and kissed him at the door. He'd not taken off his clothes in preparation to go out and shift. Because he didn't want getting naked to make him even hornier than he was.

"See you in the morning," he said and slipped out the door.

Tilting a hip against the doorframe, she watched him stride away and around the back of the cabin.

"The vampire," she muttered. "I don't think I can do it anymore. How can I? I can't be so selfish. To ask a dying man to help me gain immortality?" She shook her head and sniffed back a tear. "I can't do it. But I still want that vampire dead. By the goddess, what am I going to do?"

Around eleven, Mireio checked on Peanut. He'd been fussy after Lars had laid him down, but after carefully sliding her finger inside his mouth she'd felt the edge of a tooth he'd been working on for days. So the fuss had been well-earned. She hadn't minded rocking and walking with him a little longer. Now she fluttered her fingers over his wild crop of black hair. So soft. She wondered if that's how wolf cubs' fur felt when they were little? Natural wolves, that is.

Werewolves gave birth to a human and the child was never actually a cub. They didn't have their first shift until puberty. What if Lars's son only ever remained human? With a human mother it was possible. Would it be a disappointment to the man? She couldn't imagine anything about Peanut upsetting Lars. The two had already bonded. No matter what the future brought...

She winced, realizing how far she'd let her thoughts wander. Lars would never live to see his son experience his first shift. Maybe?

Could the doctor be wrong? So what if Lars did have some crazy mean disease. Maybe the degeneration part wouldn't happen so fast as the doc expected? A few months? She'd known him almost a month. Time was moving too quickly. He had to have longer than that. And by all appearances he looked healthy. A strapping, fine man. What man could ever know when another would breathe his last breath? People, no matter if they were human or paranormal, had no such powers. And to believe such a proclamation to death would only make it real.

"Bastard," she muttered about the doctor. "He shouldn't have given him an expiration date." She could only imagine it must occupy his thoughts constantly. And it clawed at her insides that her proud man had been given a dark ending to a story she had only begun to create with him.

Tiptoeing over to the sink so as not to wake the sleeping baby, she quietly rinsed out the bottle and set it on the drying rack. Lars lived such a stark, simple life. No modern conveniences like a television or microwave or even a computer. He did have a cell phone, but she wondered about the Wi-Fi reception up here.

Not feeling tired, she decided to sit out on the front stoop for a while and listen to the crickets chirp. A blessing for the insects, and Lars's bees, would cap off the night perfectly. But when she opened the screen door she found Lars sitting there, a towel wrapped about his hips, head bowed and hair concealing the side of his face.

She sat next to him and hugged up to his shoulder. "Did you have a good run? I thought you were going to be out all night?"

When he didn't answer, her mind jumped to what could be the only reason he was not racing through the woods free and wild right now. "Oh, goddess. Again? You couldn't…?"

She tilted her head against his shoulder and rubbed his forearm. And he reacted by wrapping an arm around her and pulling her in tightly against his bare torso.

"It's crazy," he said on a whisper. "I've never felt so… incapable. So small. This is not me, Mireio. How do I stop this? I don't want to…"

She tightened her lips as they wobbled. Tears heated the corners of her eyes. This big strong man was being reduced to something lesser, and he was struggling. He was trying to fight back, but how to defeat the inevitable?

"How's Peanut?"

"Sleeping like an angel," she said bravely.

"You don't have to stay if you don't want to."

Hurt that he'd suggest such a thing, she had to mark it off as his feeling badly for not having shifted. Again.

"I want to stay with you, lover. Always. I want to climb in bed beside you and feel your skin against mine." She leaned forward and caught his gaze. Moonlight gleamed in his pupils. Only there did the moon possess him.

"When you look at me like that," he said, "you make me feel like a man. Like you've never seen me with baby spittle on my shirt. Or raging because I'm frustrated. Or even down because of…this. You make me feel sexy, Mireio. And whole. You make me want to live."

She touched his mouth then, feeling the quiver of his struggle. Moving around in front of him on the step, she slid between his legs and gave him the gaze that made him feel like the world.

"You are a man," she said. "You are my man. You are strong and proud. You are so patient and flexible. Kind and wise. You make me feel protected."

"Will you…" He glanced aside, and she stroked his hair over an ear. But he couldn't look back up at her. "Will you stay with me…for all of this?"

Tears spilled down her cheek and she nodded, knowing exactly what he was asking of her. She would never abandon him. The idea was inconceivable to her. He needed her. He needed a hand to hold his. Someone by his side, for good and for ill.

"You don't have to ask," she said. "I'm here, Lars." She took his hand and placed it over her heart. "And you are here."

He bowed against her, cheek brushing hers and head landing on her shoulder. And she held him while the crickets chirped cautiously and the moon continued to taunt at its trick against the werewolf.

Chapter 16

The morning was no better to him than the night had been. Lars woke hugging his allotted eight inches of bed and rolled off, glancing over to spy on Mireio, who had claimed her usual queen's portion of the bed. He had to smile at that. But when he straightened to stand, his back tweaked. He winced. Wandering over to the stove to put on a pot of coffee, he even felt the arches of his feet ache. It was as if he'd climbed a mountain wearing poor equipment.

He stretched up his arms and did a few twists. Man, he felt exhausted.

Coffee. He needed plenty. He flicked on the burner and put on a kettle of water, then noticed that Peanut stirred in the crib. He walked over, feeling as if he were an old man struggling against aging muscles, and looked over his smiling son. The kid never woke grumpy. Always that bright smile. So happy to be found, even though Lars suspected his diaper was mush. Which, when he thought about it, was the likely reason for his glee at finally being noticed.

Grabbing a clean diaper, and lifting Peanut, he wandered over to the blanket still spread on the floor before the couch. When he bent, his back again tweaked and he stumbled forward. One hand slapped the couch and he just managed to tug up Peanut to his chest like a football and roll to his side before he hit the floor. The baby giggled, but Lars squeezed his eyelids tight. That could have been a nasty spill.

He glanced over to the bed. Still sleeping. She hadn't seen his mishap.

"Your old man is feeling his thirty years today, Peanut," he whispered as he changed the infant's diaper. "I sure hope whatever it is I have, I didn't pass it along to you. Whatever you do? Live life. Don't waste a moment, okay? Make memories and…"

He glanced over to the bed again. "And…yes. Make memories all the time. Don't let death beat you to the end. Race that fucker."

With a determined nod, he knelt, fighting the pull of his sore muscles as he arranged Peanut under the baby gym. "I'm going to tilt back some coffee, then we're going to make some memories today. What do you think of that?"

Peanut kicked his legs vigorously and his fist pumped.

"That's what I thought. Good idea, right? How are you taking your milk this morning? Fresh from the fridge or with a splash of warm water in it? You know that cold stuff puts the hair on your chest? It does."

He wandered to the stove to check the kettle, which was already at a low boil. All he had left was some instant coffee, but that would serve. Stirring up the brew, he sipped. Heat trickled down his throat and warmed his gut.

What to do today that he'd always wanted to do? He had never been a man of great and wild dreams. He lived a simple life; he took the days as they came to him.

But life as he knew it had changed. And he wasn't going to sit around and let his body fall apart and then suddenly drop dead. He needed to grab life and enjoy it.

"Kayaking," he decided. Dean had a couple yaks stored in the compound shed and he'd wanted Lars to try them out. "I'll give Sunday a call and ask her to watch the babe."

The lake was smooth as glass, for the wind had taken the day off. Mireio skimmed her fingers in the water, drawing up the energy and feeling it invigorate her entire system. As a water witch she drew her power from the wild vibrations humming in the lake. Felt like a jolt of vitamin B straight to the cortex.

She'd worn her swimsuit beneath a life vest and almost felt compelled to jump off the kayak and into the dark depths, but Lars was paddling quickly and it was all she could do to keep up with him.

"Slow down!" she shouted to the wolf, who stabbed an oar into the water to spin himself to face her. "I need to enjoy this," she said. "Or are we still participating in the race portion of the event?"

He chuckled and paddled up to her, gripping the edge of her kayak to hold them together. "Sorry. Got carried away. You going in for a swim, Miss Mermaid?"

"When we get closer to shore. I brought my phone along, so I don't want to lose it if I dive in." She clicked a few shots of him with the camera. The man's smile was easy. And those dimples were worth a thousand flashes. "This lake is beautiful. I've never been here before. And we have it all to ourselves!"

Lars laid the oar across his kayak and leaned in. She met him with a kiss. "Wow, that one zinged me."

"Yeah? I'm in my element here on the lake."

"So what would sex with you be like in the water?"

"I do have a very large tub at home that will fit two people."

"Challenge accepted," he said.

And then she remembered that maybe she could beat him at a race.

"Race you to the shore?" She pointed to the distant shore that must be a good three or four hundred yards away.

"So now you want to race?" He eyed her curiously. "No magic involved?"

She pouted.

"All right. Let's see what the witch can do. But I get a head start."

"Go for it."

As he turned around and began to paddle off, Mireio pressed her palms to the water's surface on each side of the kayak. Calling on the water elementals and summoning a swift wind from the depths of the forest edging the lake, the kayak soared forward. Quickly. It took only a few seconds to catch up to Lars, and pass him by.

She waved and blew him a kiss. Arms spread out she tilted back her head as the rush of air breezed over her face and blew back her hair. Headed straight for shore, behind her she heard Lars cheer for her.

The kayak docked softly in the sand and she pushed it up and set her phone on her bag, which contained a towel and dry clothes. Instead of getting dressed, she waded into the water and dove, swimming out to meet Lars, still fifty feet off. She surfaced near his kayak and treaded water.

"Sing to me, mermaid," he said, setting his oar aside.

"You know if I sing to you, you'll become enchanted and fall in. Then I'll kiss you and drag you to the depths."

"Sounds like a sweet way to go." He bent to kiss her.

But Mireio suddenly realized what she'd just implied. That she could drown him. Why had she said such a cruel thing? The last thing they should talk about was death.

Lars opened his eyes, still waiting for her kiss.

She tapped his lips with a wet fingertip, then pushed

away from the kayak, swimming on her back. "Race you to shore!"

He beat her this time, though only by a hair. But he was cheating, not even paddling very much. She met him in the sand as he dragged up the kayak and only then did she feel okay to kiss him. Away from the depths.

He lifted her and she wrapped her legs about his hips, keeping the kiss. Their connection always started easy, then picked up to a deep and delving intimacy that soared through her every nerve ending, brightening her soul as if with a million volts. Nowhere else did she feel as if she'd found her place but in Lars's kiss. His mouth. His soft, sexy beard. The skim of his mustache beside her cheek as he moved to whisper at her ear.

"Today has been a good day."

"Best day ever," she agreed. "Thank you for giving the mermaid a chance to swim."

"I haven't forgotten the bathtub challenge."

"I should hope not."

"You want to get something to eat?" he asked as he loaded the kayaks into the pickup bed. "Someplace fancy?"

"Fancy?" Mireio looked over their attire. Lars wore long swim trunks and a wrinkled T-shirt. And she wore a sheer swim cover-up and sand-covered flats. And she was pretty sure her hair would dry a disaster. "I'm dressed for McDonalds, though I crave steak and potatoes."

"We'll swing by your place and let you change. You think I'll pass muster?"

"Sweetheart, you've but to smile at the hostess with your pearly whites. Flash those dimples, and give a suave rub of your beard, and you're in. Anywhere."

"What if it's a host?"

"Same result. Trust me."

At her place, she slipped into a flowered sundress that

fell below her knees but fit her body like a hug. Flats felt appropriate with the dress, even though it would make her look as though she was a child standing next to Lars. She didn't care.

Skipping outside to where he waited by the truck, she saw Mrs. Henderson had discovered the hunk and was chatting him up.

When Mireio approached Lars, he said, "Your neighbor has been doing some research online about the Sasquatch. She thinks it only comes out on the night of the full moon."

"Oh. Did you see it again last night, Mrs. Henderson?"

"I did not see it. Exactly. But I did hear some mysterious rustling in the cornfield behind our houses. It was a very *particular* rustling."

Mireio and Lars exchanged winks.

"Particular rustling. Hmm," Mireio said. "You should be careful, Mrs. Henderson. I certainly hope you don't go outside after dark."

"I would never! But I do have my camera set up on a tripod now so I can take pictures from the window. Your Lars was telling me he didn't think Sasquatches were a danger to humans."

"Is that so?" She clasped hands with him and he squeezed her fingers quickly and added another wink. He was feeling fine today, and she loved that he'd been able to enjoy the day and not fall into a funk. So this teasing she encouraged. "I imagine they are more afraid of us than we them."

"Oh. Do you think so?" Mrs. Henderson's eyes widened as she peered beyond the houses toward the backyard. "I wonder what they like to eat? I might leave out some lettuce."

"Oh, Mrs. Henderson," Lars said. "You stay safe inside. Don't try to approach the beast if you see it again. In fact, give Mireio a call and I'll come over."

"You will?"

Again, he winked. "Promise."

"You don't know what a relief it is to hear that I've such a big strong man willing to protect me."

"Sure thing, Mrs. Henderson. We're on our way out for supper. See you later."

The neighbor stood curbside, watching them drive off, and only when they'd turned the corner did Mireio laugh. "She's got a crush on you."

"You think? But what would she do if she learned I was her Sasquatch?"

"That's not going to happen, is it?"

"Fingers crossed." He crossed his fingers and drove toward uptown Minneapolis for seafood on the rooftop at Stella's Fish Cafe.

After eating, they strolled, hand in hand, back to the truck in the parking ramp near the Lagoon movie theater. Mireio decided that since Lars was in such a good mood now might be the time to toss out what she'd wanted to suggest to him since seeing him so down about being unable to shift.

She turned and walked ahead of him, backward, and he slowed and grasped both her hands. "I'm going to say something to you," she said, "and I don't want you to react. Just think about it a little before you rush out with a quick no. Promise?"

"I'm not sure I should make a promise when a witch says something like that to me."

"Please?"

"What is it?"

They stopped before the parking ramp building. The moon was high, and neither had mentioned anything about the fact it was the day after the full moon and that Lars should want sex right now in order to stave off the irresistible urge to shift.

"What would you say about letting me and Valor and Geneva work a healing spell on you? Now listen. Valor and I are not expert healers. But Geneva has some amazing talents. And we witches simply cannot bring back the dead. But maybe our healing skills could help you. In some way? Would you be willing to give it a go?"

He tilted his head, fixing his gaze on hers. When his jaw tensed, she expected a definite no. So when he nodded and said, "Okay," she plunged into his arms for a hug.

"Thank you. I want to take care of you," she said.

"I know that. If a bunch of witches want to work their witchy magic on me, what's there to lose?"

"Maybe your pants."

"What?"

She led him into the building's shadows and walls of concrete cinder blocks. "The healing works best in water. We'll plop you in my tub and see what we can do."

"I thought *we* had a date to get it on in the tub?"

"It'll happen. But first let me try this? I'll give them a call and we can do it tonight."

"Tonight?"

"Well, Sunday's got Peanut until morning. I figure we should take advantage of the free time while we can."

Lars sighed and nodded again. "I'm in."

Chapter 17

Valor and Mireio were busy blessing the bathroom with sage and witchy chants, while Lars stood by the big round marble tub. He felt out of his element, and was a little freaked by the suggestive looks the third witch, Geneva, was giving him. Sleek black hair hung straight to chin level and she wore some kind of fitted yellow silk dress that gave her a cosmopolitan flair, yet Mireio had told him she was as Scandinavian as the rest of them. With a finger to her red-lacquered lips, her bright sapphire eyes took him in.

The tub had been filled with warm water and sprinkled with Epsom salts. Now Valor began to tap some sparkly dust into the water, which she explained to him was actual faery dust courtesy of her boyfriend, Kelyn Saint-Pierre. The Saint-Pierres were a family of wolves, a vamp and a couple faeries. Lars had never met them, but he was aware the eldest brother, Trouble, lived up to his name.

"You can get in now," Mireio said to him. She clasped his hand and hugged up against his side. Her blue eyes beamed up at him with such wonder and respect Lars always experienced a second of disbelief that he'd actually found a woman like her.

"Uh." He eyed Geneva and she winked at him. Whispering to Mireio, he said, "You know I go commando, sweetie. I'm not sure about this."

"You don't want to get in with your clothes on. And garments will only impede the magical energies. Go ahead. They won't watch you undress."

"Oh, I'm watching," Geneva said as she circled around to the vanity where the witches had set candles and incense and crystals and all sorts of mysterious magical accoutrements. "Strip, big boy."

"Geneva," Valor admonished. She finished the circle then walked to the doorway. "We'll stand out in the hallway, Lars. You two let us know when you're ready. Come on, Geneva!"

The witch pouted and slowly glided toward the door, yet when out in the hallway, she kept the door open and, even though Valor turned her to face away, she cast a thick-lashed wink over her shoulder.

"Ignore her," Mireio said. "She's not interested unless your bank account has a minimum of ten figures. Besides, she'd have to go through me to get to you, and she knows that's not worth the fight." She helped him tug up his shirt and then unbuttoned his jeans.

Lars caught her hand over his waistband. "I can do this."

"I know. But I'm always so eager to get your pants off, lover."

"Not around those two," he whispered.

"Are you going all Mr. Shy on me again? They've seen naked men before. And you have so much to flaunt."

"You're not making this any easier," he said as he shoved down his jeans and stepped out of them, now completely naked. A glance spied Geneva and she was looking right at him. Her brow arched and she dragged her tongue along her lips. Lars clasped his hands before his cock, which, despite his embarrassment, was quickly growing erect. "I knew there was something about witches that should creep me out."

"Not me?" Mireio pouted at him.

"Never you." He kissed the crown of her head, then stepped into the tub. It was warm and inviting. Sinking down, he noticed Geneva was the first in.

"Now that's something to be proud of," Geneva said as she clapped softly. "Bravo!"

Thoroughly embarrassed but not about to let her see that, Lars lifted his chin and winked at her. Hey, he could play this game too. Even if it did make him uncomfortable.

"All right, witches, so the man has an impressive dick," Valor said as she strolled by the tub and toward the altar. She glanced back at Lars and said, "Well, you do."

He could but lift his shoulders a little higher. Yeah, so he did have his talents.

"But let's focus, shall we?" Valor insisted. "The pre-show is over. Geneva has briefed us on the spell. It's time for the magic. Mireio, it's your game now."

"Let's perform the blessing," Mireio announced.

The three witches clasped hands over by the spell stuff and bowed their heads. Mireio recited a blessing that asked for their safety and his, and then she slipped into Latin, which Lars had no clue how to interpret. The tones of her voice were harmonized by her fellow witches with hums.

Lars swept his hair over a shoulder and, spying a pink hair clip by the tub used it to hold back his hair in a messy tangle. Not a man bun. He didn't do man buns. Nor did he soak in a tub like some kind of spoiled...

Eh. Well. So this day was turning out to be challenging in ways he'd never expected to face. But still. The soak was kind of relaxing. The water was not clear, thanks to the salts and some black specks floating on the surface—

he suspected it was ash and hoped it wasn't something like crushed frog brains. He tilted his head back against the curved headrest and stretched out his arms along the marble edges.

He quickly sat up as the women convened from their prayer and circled the tub.

"Everyone ready?" Mireio asked. "How about you. Lars?"

He shrugged. "What do you need me to do?"

"Just sit there. Maybe close your eyes. Take in everything that comes your way. We will touch you at certain points in the spell…"

He cast a look at Geneva, who winked at him.

"…but those touches will be to ground you and allow our magics to flow into you. So be open."

"Open. Got it."

"All right, witches." Geneva spread her arms wide and opened her palms faceup. "Let's do this!"

What followed was more chanting and humming, and it, at once, gave Lars the chills and then made him feel kind of dreamy. Almost as if he were falling into a hypnotic state. Realizing that, he shook himself back to alertness. Valor had leaned forward to touch his right shoulder. Eyes closed, the witch murmured something in a low, haunting voice. Geneva followed by touching his left shoulder. Her chant seemed to trickle up his spine and radiate out through his veins. She was the witch with the healing powers, so he certainly hoped she knew what she was doing.

And from behind him, Mireio placed both her hands to his head, spreading her fingers along the sides and whispering what sounded to him like nonsense syllables, but he felt her energy. He felt the energies from all of them. Vibrations hummed through his body, singing an ancient tune. So he closed his eyes and accepted it all, taking it in and daring to hope.

Five minutes might have passed. Or maybe a half an hour. But eventually the touches left his body and he felt the pulling away like a snapped connection. But he didn't startle. As the women filed out of the room, Lars floated there, peaceful and content. Someone blew out the final candle, leaving the room dark, but he felt the moon beam through the stained glass behind him dance across his exposed skin and glimmer on the water's surface. And if he went there, to that place where hope lived and witch magic really worked, he felt…lighter. Actually happy.

And he knew that Mireio had returned to the bathroom and stood in the doorway, quietly observing him. He didn't call out to her. He was content to share this moment and know that something had happened tonight. Whether or not their magic had cured him or simply delayed the process of his death didn't matter.

What mattered was that he was pretty sure he loved the woman who stood watching him. And that no matter what, he'd fight for her. Always.

Chapter 18

A day passed, and Mireio only received a text from Lars. But she wasn't down because his text consisted of hearts, flowers and a thumbs-up emoji. He wrote that he was working on the framework for the back of the house and was making headway.

As well, he was probably rising into the healing they'd performed on him, allowing it to enter him completely.

Everything was good. And after a day at work brewing cherry cream ale—one of her favorites—she had stopped by Target on the way home. Now she spilled the bag onto the kitchen counter and sorted through her booty. Because there were bootees. Little blue-and-purple socks with cats paws on the bottoms (she intended to tell Lars they were wolf socks), a baby T that said I'm Wild and some teething chews and another soft blanket because Peanut only had two and there were days when he spit up on both and Lars had to do laundry before bedtime.

And who could resist the beanie with the floppy gray bunny ears on it?

Mireio now understood why babies always had so much stuff. Buying the things had given her such a cute high t was even better than a slow sip of wine after a long day at work.

A knock on her front door surprised her. Suspecting Mrs. Henderson might have another Sasquatch sketch to show her, she pulled a white light of protection over herself as a means to not take on the craziness on the other side of the door.

Before she even touched the doorknob, the door opened and in burst Lars with Peanut clutched to his chest. He strode in and set the diaper bag down, along with the baby carrier, then turned and pulled her in for a kiss sandwich. Peanut cooed between the two of them as Lars made it very difficult to be in cute baby mode when all systems in Mireio were heading toward *please take me now* and *don't even bother to get undressed.*

"Wow. What was that for?"

"You don't like my kisses?" His dimples were irrepressible as he brushed a palm over the baby's bushy coif. "Peanut approved."

"I love your kisses. Anytime, any way. But why so happy today? Did you get a lot done at the cabin?"

"I finished framing in the back of the house. But—" he put up a finger to pause her from cheering for him "—I have even more exciting news." Smoothing a hand down Peanut's back the man burst out with "I shifted to wolf this afternoon! And it was because I wanted to, and not without volition. And I shifted back with the same ease. I feel renewed, Mireio. And I have you and your witchy friends to thank for that."

He bracketed her head and kissed her forehead, then spun and picked up the diaper bag. "Gotta change Peanut. He had a blowout on the way here."

"I noticed that," she said, waving her hand beneath her nose to disperse the rank air. "I'm so happy for you, Lars. Who was watching Peanut when you went out?"

"Sunday. Both Dean and I went for a run. Man, that felt so good." He laid the blanket out on the floor and starting changing the baby. "And I have so much energy today. But I think it's my normal energy. I didn't realize how run-down I've been lately. You got any coffee?"

"Uh, no coffee for you. I think you're flying high enough. Oh, please put that one outside in the garbage can. I'm thankful tomorrow is pickup day. Whew!"

"I gave him carrots this morning. We're starting to try some food."

"Awesome. You know, I could plant a garden for you on your land and make homemade, all-natural baby food for Peanut. It shouldn't be too late to plant."

"Would you really do that?" With Peanut all fresh and beaming, Lars walked over and handed the baby to her. "I'll be right back." He headed outside with the stink bomb.

"I would do anything for you, sweetie." She kissed Peanut's head, loving his soft sweet scent so much, and she nuzzled her cheek and nose into his silky hair.

When Lars returned he stopped halfway to the kitchen and stared at her.

Mireio felt as if she might have forgotten to comb her hair. Or maybe she had baby spit on her she hadn't noticed. "What?"

"You're so beautiful standing there in a beam of sunlight. Your hair is like fire and your eyes like ice. And I can feel you right here." He slapped a hand over his heart. "You and Peanut are my two favorite people. How'd I get so lucky?"

"We're not always beautiful. One of us has mastered the stink bombs. And the other can work the cranky vibe once a month. So watch out."

"I'll take the stink and the crank. I'm so blessed."

"The one that's truly blessed is this little guy. Erik."

"Hmm, not so sure about that one."

"Oh, come on, it's very Scandinavian."

"It is. I'll put it on my possibilities list."

"Do you have such a list?"

"Maybe." He tugged the baby book out of the diaper bag and sat on the couch but didn't open it. "I should have picked up something for us to eat. I wasn't thinking clearly after the stink bomb hit in the truck."

Mireio laughed. "Want me to order pizza? I could actually go for a big cheesy slice with lots of pepperoni and sausage and…"

"Mushrooms and onions?"

"Oh, yeah, your kisses are going to be very savory later."

"As will yours." He winked. "Order an extra-large. I'm starving."

After they'd made the pizza disappear, Lars fed Peanut a few spoonfuls of mashed peas, which the baby promptly spit up. The kid was developing a bubbly giggle, and even with peas splattered all over his face and beard, Lars could but laugh along with him.

"I'm going to run a tub," Mireio said as she breezed by them toward the bathroom.

"For you?"

"Aha-ha-ha!" She paused and gestured toward his beard in a circling manner. "You're starting to look like the swamp thing with all those peas in your beard."

"'Bout time we do the tub challenge!" he called after her.

After burping his son and changing his diaper, he laid Peanut down on the floor to read to him while Mireio was in the bathroom. It was after nine and while he wasn't at all tired, he didn't expect to sleep too much later. Not with a sexy woman in the house.

He really felt great. And while he wasn't so hopeful as to think the witches may have actually cured him, he was going to ride this good feeling for as long as he had it.

Finishing the chapter on what to expect during the fifth month, he closed the book and turned to find Peanut sleeping. The infant sucked in his sleep sometimes, his little lips pushing out repeatedly. Such dreams he must be having.

A crop of bright red hair popped around the corner. Then Mireio stuck out a bare foot, and followed by stepping into view. Lars propped himself up onto his elbows and whistled in appreciation for the woman wearing only a towel.

"You going to strip for me?"

"No, I'm going to take a bath." She disappeared behind the wall again, and then the towel landed on the floor.

Lars dug in the diaper bag for the baby monitor he never left home without and turned it on. Then he rolled a blanket and placed it on one side of Peanut, and took the roll cushion from the couch and placed it on the other side. Standing over the boy he decided there was no way, if he woke without a sound, he could roll himself into trouble. Check.

Tugging off his shirt, he headed down the hallway and into the bathroom. He set the monitor on the vanity by the sink.

A witch lounged in the vast marble tub, sipping a goblet of wine. She fluttered her lashes and blew a handful of iridescent bubbles into the air. "Ready to screw a mermaid?"

"Yep." He couldn't get his jeans off fast enough. But before Lars could dip a toe in the tub, he paused, looking over the vast, sparkling bubbles. It was very different from herbs and healing salts. "Uh…"

"What? Do you want to bring Peanut in here?"

"No, he's good. Got the monitor set. It's just…there's

so many bubbles. And it smells like fruit and flowers. It's all so…"

"Delicious?"

"Girlie," he decided.

"Oh, lover, I'll still want to have sex with you if you smell like a girl. Promise. And pomegranate is an aphrodisiac. The scent should drive you wild."

"I don't need anything to make me wild for you."

"Just give it a try." She slid her hand down a breast, wiping away the bubbles and her nipple peaked above the water's surface.

Lars stepped into the warm water and lowered himself cautiously. It was just bubbles. Nothing to freak about. And his woman looked so lickable, all wet and with bubbles in her hair. When her hand stroked up his thigh and found his cock, he forgot about the smell and the silliness of a grown man sitting in a bubble bath and glided up to kiss the nipples that teased at him.

Mireio cooed in response and hooked her legs over his hips. He caught his hands on the curve of marble behind her shoulders and suckled her breast until she squirmed so much the waves threatened to slosh over the edges.

"Steady on deck," he said while dancing his fingers down her body till they were between her legs. "Mmm, this mermaid doesn't have a tail. And I've found something interesting. I think it's treasure." He slid fingers inside her and circled her clit with his thumb.

"You'd make a terrible pirate," she said, gripping the sides of the tub to stay above water. "But I'd walk the plank for you any day. Oh, Lars, yes, just like that. Slow and firm." She bit her lower lip and groaned deeply in her throat.

He loved the sound of her unabashed pleasure. And he was the man who was so polite and respectful with a woman—until she begged him for more.

Pulling her toward him and kneeling on the bottom of the tub, he used the wave of water to glide her body against his torso and then fitted her neatly onto his jutting erection. Mercy. Nothing felt better. Not. A. Thing.

She began to rock upon him, sending water over the sides of the tub. He encouraged her motions, tensing his jaws as the exquisite tremor of orgasm rushed to his core and coalesced in one perfect blast of oblivion.

Lars howled and clutched the witch against his chest as he released inside her and sighed out a satisfied breath.

The bubbles had dissipated and the wine was gone. Mireio's body hugged his as if she were an exhausted mermaid clinging to her earthbound lover. The world was right. No matter the darkness that germinated within his body. As long as he had his two favorite people, Lars could face anything. And he would do anything for Mireio. Thinking of which…

"Did you want to go out again one of these days on a vampire hunt?"

"No. I uh…" She pulled from him and floated to the back of the tub, sliding her arms along the edges to anchor herself. "I think I'm going to put that search off for now. I don't need to rush into things."

"But you paid Raven Crosse a lot of money to locate a vamp for you."

"I know. But I feel differently about it now."

And he suspected the reason behind that change of heart. "Mireio, you have to do this for yourself."

"I will. Someday."

"It's because of me, isn't it?"

"What do you mean?"

Sitting up in the water, he bent his knees and propped his elbows on them. "I know what you're thinking. How can you seek immortality when I might drop dead any day?"

"Don't say that. You're feeling so good today."

"I am. And I intend to take it one day at a time. But it would make me feel better to know your future is secured."

"To be honest? I've decided not to do it. And that's that. So don't argue with me, okay?"

The staticky baby monitor alerted them both.

"Peanut's up," she said. "You go get him and I'll drain the tub. We can have midnight margaritas out on the patio if you want."

"Midnight margaritas?"

"It's a *Practical Magic* thing. I love the Owens witches, even if they are fictional." She sat up and flipped her wet hair over a shoulder. "Go get your son."

Lars reluctantly got out, wrapped towels around his hair and hips, then wandered off to claim the stirring baby.

Mireio propped her chin on the edge of the tub and tapped the wine bottle with a fingernail. "I'll figure some other way to get revenge on the vampire. When Lars isn't looking."

Chapter 19

The next day, Lars stopped into the brewery. Mireio had told him she'd be finished brewing around three, so he made a point of getting there at two. Just in case she'd let him help a bit, maybe even learn a few things. With Peanut in the baby carrier, he strolled inside the empty brewery to find no one behind the bar or back near the brew tanks.

"Mireio?"

Someone walked up behind him and hugged him fiercely. He set Peanut on the floor, letting the carrier rock, then turned and pulled his tiny witch into his arms. She wrapped her legs about his hips and dove in for a kiss.

Lush red hair spilled across his face and hands as he tasted beer and salt on her tongue. He leaned back and studied her. "You been drinking?"

"Ha! No. Maybe. Okay, yes. I had to test the stout. And all I've had all day to eat is a bag of stale pretzels. Did you bring me food?"

Estimating that she was a bit tipsy from her "beer testing," he offered to pick her up a sandwich from the deli down the street.

"Yes!" She pumped the air with a fist and did a little

shimmy before Peanut. It ended in a wobble and a spat of giggles.

"How much beer did you test, sweetie?"

"Half a pint? Of the stout. And then maybe a few tasters of the honey IPA and the pale ale. The Scottish ale has gotten rangy. That stuff never lasts for long with the happy spell on it."

"A happy spell." That explained a little. The woman was certainly in her happy place.

He hugged her to him and she made to jump for another kiss but landed awkwardly on her high heels and he had to catch her before she toppled backward.

"I'd better get you some food, stat." He glanced to Peanut, who gave him a wondering look. He'd be fine with the drunk witch for the ten minutes it would take him to find food to sober her up. "Be right back. Don't dance too suggestively for Peanut. The boy's an innocent!"

He left to a spill of giggles and quickened his steps down the street. The shop wasn't busy, and besides an all-veggie sandwich for Mireio, he grabbed a foot long with all the fixings for himself, as well. When he got back to the brewery, Mireio lay on the floor next to the baby seat, toggling the puppies hanging from the mobile. He'd wanted wolves but the closest thing had been blue plastic puppies.

"You finished brewing for the day?" he asked as he set out the food on the bar. "Everything all washed up? I could help."

"I didn't get to brew at all. Ended up kegging the stout with Valor earlier. Since then I've been doing some dusting, inventory and…"

"Beer testing?"

"You know it!" She slid onto a barstool and dove into the sandwich.

Surprised that a woman who actually brewed beer for

a living could get so tipsy from her own brews, Lars took it all in stride. But something about Mireio's actions bothered him. She was smart and had a good head on her shoulders. She knew better than to get drunk at work. Something must be bothering her. Had to be.

She finished the sandwich and twirled around behind the bar. She turned up the radio and grabbed an empty pint glass.

"Uh—" he gestured toward the fridge "—maybe you should have water?"

"What's up with you today?" She set the glass down with a clink. "You're harshin' my vibe."

"Harshin' your— Mireio, what's wrong? Is there something you want to talk about? You're not yourself today."

"Can't a girl indulge in a little beer therapy once in a while?"

He shrugged. "Sure, but during work hours? Is it about the immortality spell? I know you said you were going to set that aside, but, sweetie, if that's what you want…"

"It's not that." She waved him off, then turned to grab a bottle of water from the fridge. "Did Peanut eat yet?"

"Gave him a bottle and some peaches before coming here. I think he likes peaches."

"I volunteer to *not* change that diaper." With a giggle she glided around the bar and plucked a few chips from the bag he'd opened. "What are we going to do tonight? Have any plans?"

"What do you want to do?"

"I thought you were all about doing things that made you happy? Going for the adventure."

"How adventurous can we be with Peanut tagging along? Sunday can't sit for him tonight."

"You should find a backup babysitter."

"It's an idea. I haven't needed a babysitter so much until I met you."

She blanched.

"That's a good thing," he said to alleviate her pout. "I could spend every hour of every day with you and still want more time together. Even when you're drunk."

"I'm not that drunk. And I'm starting to sober up. The food is helping. Thanks. You're right. Something was probably bugging me earlier and…" She blew out a breath and dove to the floor to kneel before Peanut and toggle his toys.

So she didn't want to talk about it? He could respect that. She'd tell him when she felt like it. Or not. But if it was something about him, he'd like to know.

"I think he looks like a Vladimir today," she declared.

Lars turned to see if she was being serious or if that was still the beer talking. The witch leaned over Peanut's carrier, toggling his toes. She then lay on her stomach, knees bent and feet tapping in the air. She looked like the kid's mother, playing with him. And that thought put a catch in his throat.

Would he ever find a mother for Peanut? Before he died? And what about Dean's request the other day that he change his will? It felt right. Like the responsible thing to do. But something held him back from committing to such a drastic move. Because nowhere in that legacy would there be room for Mireio.

"I love this song!" She stood and traipsed to the other side of the brewery, where the speakers sounded best. Freddie Mercury crooned softly. The woman wrapped her arms across her chest, eyes closed, and swayed as she sang.

Lars wiped his mouth with a napkin and wandered over to her. Compelled by the magic of her being, he held out his hand for her to take, and she stared at it.

"But you don't dance," she said, brushing the hair from her face. "You made that clear the first night we met."

"I can dance to this slow stuff. It's just swaying back and forth, isn't it?"

She put her hand in his and hugged up to him, and Lars bowed his head over his tiny witch. Her melting up against him was the best feeling in the world. Holding her close. Feeling her heat mingle with his. The brush of her hair against his bicep tickled in the best way. The world was right.

Until he caught a few of the song's lyrics. It was about living forever. Or maybe not? Mercury asked him if he wanted to live forever.

Hell. This was her favorite song?

Sighing, Lars tuned out the words but the one stuck in his brain. *Forever.* So he put a positive spin on it.

"I want to hold you like this forever," he whispered.

Suddenly she pushed away from him, swiping at a surprising tear that rolled down her cheek. "Don't say that!"

"What? Mireio, what is wrong?"

"Don't you get it? I'd like to hold you forever too. But that can never happen because you're going to die! Oh, my goddess, this stupid song! I don't want you to die, Lars. I…don't…"

She dropped to her knees on the hardwood floor and bowed her head, the tears coming full force as the song ended and segued into something more upbeat.

Lars knelt before her and, unsure what exactly to do, he first bracketed her head with his hands, but didn't try to lift her face. She sobbed. And he felt her pain pulse in his heart. It was a wicked, relentless pain that promised to bring him down if he didn't defeat it. But there didn't seem any way to do that.

Suddenly she looked up, clutched his shirt and said, "I love you, Lars. I don't want to lose you. And I know there's no way to change that. That's the toughest part."

"You might have changed it. I still feel great from the spell you witches worked on me."

She smirked but her tears continued to spill. "M-maybe."

He pulled her in close and stretched his legs out before him so she could sit on his lap. Holding her there, he nuzzled his face against her hair. Nothing sweeter than his tiny witch. Yet the thought that he might lose her, and Peanut, cut through his heart like a blade.

"Why did you happen to me now?" he whispered, "When I've just learned that life isn't going to go the way I expected."

She brushed her hair away. "No one should ever expect life to go a certain way. We signed up for this. You and me? Our souls agreed to this before we were even born. But that still doesn't mean it won't hurt. A lot."

He kissed the back of her hand. "You said you love me."

"Because I do. How can I not? You're the most amazing man I've ever known. And how lucky is Peanut to have you as his daddy? I don't mean to be so forward, but if I'm going to let everything out, I have to be truthful. What are we going to do when you're gone?"

That blade that had cut into his heart? It now sawed it in half. And Lars knew that kind of wound could never heal so swiftly as he wished.

"Life always goes on," was all he could say.

"I love Peanut so much," she said. "I hate to think of this—of you dying—but should it happen, I want to adopt him."

Lars bowed his head to hers. He hadn't told her about the will change yet. And now, more than ever, he knew his decision to think about it had been a good one. But how could he deny a couple who could never have children of their own simply because another woman who had known Peanut a short time had fallen in love with him? Mireio could have kids someday.

How he wished he could have a family with her.

"What do you think about that?" she asked.

"It's a generous offer. But I also have a lot of thinking to do about a lot of tough things. And I'd kind of like to linger a bit on that part about you loving me."

She turned on his lap and met his gaze. "I do. I really do."

"I feel like if I say the same to you—and damn it, but I do believe I do—that I might only break your heart all the more. I don't want to do that to you, Mireio. I…" He choked down the rising pain. "I don't want to die…"

She wrapped her arms about him. The two sat there on the floor as the music continued, oblivious to their pain. Peanut had fallen asleep. And Lars's heart had broken open.

It felt good to have told Lars what had been hanging over her head lately. And the tears had helped, as well. Part of her witchy water magic.

And hearing him confess that he didn't want to die had reassured Mireio in ways she hadn't realized she'd needed. What man *did* want to die?

So she'd take it one day at a time. With the man she loved.

A man who was afraid to tell her he loved her because he didn't want to break her heart? She understood where he was coming from and was glad he'd put that into words for her. They were on the same page. Only, some days it seemed like he was slowly sliding away from her. She intended to grasp his hand and hold on tight.

They got up from the brewery floor and Lars checked on Peanut. Though the infant was sleeping soundly, he was smiling, which indicated a diaper change was necessary.

"Hate to wake him," Lars commented.

She waved her hand before her nose. "Oh, please, you have to or I will perish from the stink bomb."

He laughed and carried the baby into the bathroom, where the brewery provided a pull-down baby-changing table, which was installed on the wall.

"You still haven't suggested what you want to do tonight!" she called.

No answer from behind the closed door. She gathered the food wrappers and tossed them in the trash. It was close to suppertime, but she was full. And no longer tipsy. Okay, bad judgment letting her angst rule and her better senses take a vacation earlier. She should never have had that last half-pint of bad ale. Lesson learned.

On the other hand, her relaxed inhibitions had allowed her to make her confession to Lars. So she'd take the good with the bad. Even though some days it felt all bad. But she wasn't going to get down on herself anymore. She wasn't the one with the death sentence. She had to stay strong for Lars.

As for immortality? Nope. Not going to do it. Even if the one vampire she most wanted dead was out there stalking the streets.

"I know what I want to do tonight." Lars strolled out of the bathroom with a smiling Peanut and a small plastic bag that he held away from him as if it were labeled Hazardous Materials. "It could be a family date."

His choice of words warmed her very soul. "What?"

"Not sure how you'll feel about this, but uh… Would you like to go bowling?"

Mireio clapped her hands once and bounced. "Yes!"

He gave her a surprised dodge of his head.

"Sorry, was that too enthusiastic? You don't know how much I've always wanted to go bowling. The glossy lanes and the sparkly balls! And the shoes! Everyone gets their own special shoes!"

"Uh, okay? I've never seen a woman so excited about the prospect of wearing shoes someone else just got done sweating in, but let's do it!"

Chapter 20

Bowling was…complicated. And while Mireio had yet to knock down a single pin after six attempts at tossing that ugly pink sparkly ball down the lane, she didn't feel at all upset. How could she when watching Lars was like staring at a kid in the candy store? The man loved bowling.

He was talented with the bowling ball. And he had a style. The tall, hulking wolf approached the sacred line beyond which you shouldn't step—which she'd slid across four times already—and with a bend and a glide of his right leg behind his other, he released the ball in such a smooth, speedy throw she could but marvel. Even the lanes paralleling them stopped and watched as the ball crashed into the pins and, most of the time, knocked them all down. This time all went down.

Lars pumped an arm and did his little "strike dance" as she'd come to call it. Hips wiggling, he twisted on the toes of his shoes.

She glanced to Peanut, who seemed to watch eagerly, though it could also be the squishy teething ring that made him look so enthralled. "Your daddy is a rock star, Peanut Butter."

"What was that?" Lars cupped a hand to his ear as he

glided back over to the chairs behind the ball holder. "Did someone call me a rock star? Oh, yeah!" Another fist pump was well-earned. "You going to let me help you on the next one, sweetie? I think all you need to do is bring your swing back a bit more. Put a little more oomph in your delivery."

"I know what I'd like delivered with some oomph." She winked at him and stood to collect her ball. The thrill over sparkly balls and shoes had dissipated. Seriously? Who put on shoes that someone had just got done sweating in? Well, she did. Because it made her man happy. And that was all that mattered. Of course, she did have one trick up her sleeve. She glanced to him as she held up her ball. "I got this one."

He bowed grandly, gesturing she go for it, then bent to kiss Peanut on the head.

Cautiously she approached the do-not-cross line, eyed up the neighboring aisles—everyone was chattering or focused on their games—and with a whisper of Latin, Mireio then sent the ball flying. It traveled slowly, but this time it was almost straight.

With her back still to Lars, she lifted her hand near her stomach and directed the ball with a finger and another whisper. "To the right." The ball corrected and rolled right up to the pins and…knocked one down. "Yes!"

Lars ran for her, lifting her in his arms and spinning her around. "You did it!"

"I'm so close to being a rock star, I can feel it." She kissed him. "Maybe the rock star's groupie. It's fun watching him do his victory dance."

"I have a victory dance?"

"Seriously? You do that hip shake and toe twist thing every time you knock them all down."

"Huh."

He didn't realize he did that? That made it all the more sweet.

After four more attempts at hitting the pins, and with the use of magic, Mireio was able to add two and a half more pins to her tally. The half one wobbled, looked like it would almost fall, then decided not to. But she was going to count it anyway. Stupid, magic-resistant pin.

Wandering back to the chairs, she sat beside Lars. Peanut was fussing, kicking his feet like a sumo wrestler and twisting uncomfortably in his carrier. "You want me to pick him up?" she asked, surprised that Lars hadn't already done so.

"Would you?"

"Sure. You go knock 'em all down again. I got this."

"I think I'm going to sit the rest of them out. We've had a good game. But this rock star has taken his final bow for the night."

Mireio picked up Peanut and as she did she noticed Lars sat with his hands between his legs, and his fingers dangling, and, while it wasn't an odd pose, she immediately knew what was up.

"Fingers numb?" she asked as nonchalantly as possible. Making a big deal out of it would only make him feel weaker.

He nodded. "Feet too."

"Okay. I'm going to head into the bathroom to change Michael. I'll be right back. You good?"

"Yep. And...Michael isn't bad, but I once knew a bully by the same name."

"Ugh, Michael? What an awful name." She kissed Peanut's head and strolled off. "How about Mason?" she tried. "Or Morty, Maxwell or Mouse?"

The poor kid needed a name soon. He couldn't be named after a legume for the rest of his life. She then thought maybe she shouldn't have left Lars sitting alone, but with a glance over her shoulder she saw him conversing with a man on the seat behind him. He'd be good for a few minutes.

Thankfully, the bathroom had a changing station and she made swift work and then kissed Peanut's head. The woman at the sink eyed him and cooed. "Your son is adorable. Look at all that hair! Oh, I saw you and your husband out there. He's a big tall drink, isn't he?"

"He certainly is." No need to correct her mistake. Mireio left the bathroom, but her thoughts scurried toward a surprising future.

What if they got married? She could adopt Peanut, and if anything did happen to Lars—because who knew how long the healing spell would be effective—the baby would be taken care of. It wasn't a ridiculous notion to entertain. Sure, she'd only known him a short while, but what she knew of Lars was that he was honest, kind, hardworking and so true. And a good lover. What more did a girl need?

Not that she'd expected to get married so early in life. What she'd expected was to perform the immortality spell and gain a good hundred years. And then a hundred more. And a hundred more. And so on. Marriage? That could wait, because she'd have centuries to find the perfect man.

Who would have thought that without even searching she would have netted such a perfect catch?

When she returned to the chairs, the diaper bag sat on Lars's lap.

"You got the feeling back?"

"A little. I think we should head out, if that's okay with you. Everything aches. I want to get home so I don't have to face this in public."

"Deal." Hooking Peanut on her hip, she then dug into Lars's front jeans pocket and grabbed the truck keys. "I'll drive."

"I think you just shifted gears." He pressed up against

the back of her to show her that some part on him wasn't giving him problems. "Think you can manage the diaper bag too? I might have to use the ball shelves to lean on to get out of here."

"Not a problem. Hook it over my shoulder. You want me to help you?"

"Nope. Just give me some time."

"Fine. I'll walk ahead and get Peanut in the car seat. We'll drive back to pick you up." She turned to kiss him and he caught her head with both his hands and delivered her a long, deep, promising kiss. One she hadn't been expecting. It reminded her exactly what a hold he had on her heart.

"You're too good to me."

"You make it easy to want to be so good. Let's go."

She walked ahead, trying to act casual as she kept slipping looks over her shoulder. Lars walked a little hunched over, pressing his fist to the shelves for support, but he made it up the two steps to the carpeted landing and gave her a nod of reassurance. So she dashed outside and put Peanut in the car seat. She'd gotten good at climbing up into the monster truck and adjusting the seat. She made it to the front door as her lover wobbled out. At the door, he stepped up but his foot slipped. She saw his hands cling to the door and seat as he attempted another go at it. Jaws tight, he was in pain. She wanted to lean over and pull him up, but she didn't. She would allow him his pride.

Finally, he made it up and with a "Whew!" he gave her a wink and said, "Home, Jeeves."

Once at her place, Mireio suggested Lars go upstairs and lie down for a while. He didn't say a word, only crept slowly up the stairs as if an old man struggling in his twilight years. She hugged Peanut to her, wishing she could help the man, but she was at a loss as to how. The healing spell was apparently starting to fade.

There had to be something she could do.

Spinning Peanut about, she realized he would be staying the night if Lars wasn't feeling better, so she would give him a bottle now. He'd have to sleep in the baby carrier. It was better than laying him on the hard floor, even on a blanket. Although, she could make a little nest for him…

"Nah, the carrier should work for a night. It'll get you toughened up for those nights when you're in college and you have to couch surf, or when your girlfriend kicks you out of bed. You little rascal, you."

After giving Peanut a bottle, Mireio ran upstairs to check on Lars. He lay facedown on the bed, as if he'd fallen there, arms outstretched. Snoring filled the room.

"Oh, sweetie."

Carefully, she removed his boots and set them on the floor by the bed, then she kissed his cheek and went back down to find Peanut snoring, as well.

"I've got to do something for him." She glanced about the room, feeling helpless, and yet, when her gaze landed on the red witch ball she kept over the kitchen sink—not a charm against witches but to keep out demons—the most obvious answer struck her.

Chapter 21

Eggs and bacon bubbled in the frying pan, but the scent had yet to wake Lars from the coma sleep he'd fallen into last night. Mireio didn't mind.

Blowing raspberries on the bottoms of Peanut's feet was interrupted by a knock at the front door. She promised the baby more fun amid his delirious giggles and hastened to answer. It was Valor, on her way to work. Mireio had called her earlier, asking if she could drop off some grimoires.

Valor handed over a tote bag. "It's all I have and that I'm willing to loan you. And Geneva sent one along too. You think you can find a spell to reverse imminent death?"

"Not sure. Maybe delay the actual dying process? I mean, I know we witches can't bring back the dead. And I'm pretty sure we can't stop an inevitable death, but…" She sighed and clutched the tote bag to her chest. "I have to try, Valor. The healing we performed has weakened. Lars was feeling pretty awful last night."

"That's tough. Big guy like that must feel so…"

"Small, is how he puts it. Oh, it kills me, Valor." She hugged the tote bag to her stomach. "But thank you for this. It means a lot."

"Let me know if you need my help. I'm always willing to do what I can. But no dark stuff, got it?"

Mireio nodded, but couldn't quite get behind an enthusiastic agreement. She'd do what was necessary to help Lars. And if that required dark magic? She'd face that hurdle if it approached. "You waxing the floors at the brewery today?"

"Yes. I'm excited to use the buffer. Rented it from Home Depot. It's going to be a blast."

"Only you could get excited about stripping hardwood floors and waxing them. Thanks, Valor. I'll get these back to you as soon as I can."

After Valor shut the front door, Mireio laid out the books on the coffee table before the couch and browsed through them, keeping Peanut in peripheral view. She loved grimoires. Bound in leather, velvets and other fabrics, some were so old, having been preserved through centuries of family, or sometimes even belonging to the same witch for those many centuries. The pages always smelled of herbs and age, and some even came alive with the proper incantation or a knowing eye.

The stairs creaked, signaling the wolf had woken. Lars wandered into the kitchen, rubbing his beard. He wore only jeans and Mireio's eyes veered to his tight abs. Mercy.

He sat before the counter and the plate of breakfast she set out for him, but before lifting the fork, he apologized with a yawn for falling asleep last night.

"It's not your fault, lover. Besides, Peanut and I partied it up while you were sleeping."

"Oh, yeah?" He ruffled the infant's wild hair. "Did she get drunk again?"

The baby kicked his legs and cooed. It seemed like a very definite yes.

"Telling stories!" Mireio protested. "He's a sneaky one."

"So what's all that stuff on the coffee table?" He shoveled in eggs and growled a satisfied noise.

Mireio pulled out the ingredients for the cupcakes she intended to make after the breakfast dishes were cleared. But now that he'd asked, she had to tell him. "It occurred to me last night that I'm a witch."

He cocked a brow above a dimpled smirk.

"And that witches cast spells. All kinds of spells."

"Thus, the healing spell," he said.

"Right. But we can conjure so many other kinds of spells. Some, which are dark, ancient and very powerful, can even possibly save lives."

"Is that so? I thought there was something about witches not being able to bring back the dead?"

"Exactly! But you're not dead, are you? So there's hope. I called Valor and Geneva and asked them to gather all their grimoires and spell books. Valor dropped them off. There will be something in one of them. I know it."

"A spell to save my life? Didn't you just basically try that?"

"It was more a general healing spell. And after last night, I feel as though it wasn't as effective as I'd hoped. So what do you think? Can I give it another go?"

She squeezed his hands and bounced on her heels, hoping he'd get behind the idea, but preparing herself for an argument.

So when he nodded and kissed her mouth and said, "Go for it. I approve," she squealed and wrapped her arms about him.

"I love you," she said. "Thank you."

"I'm all for trying everything in our power. But that's a big stack of books."

"It is. But can you feel it?"

He shrugged.

"The magic emanating from all those sacred texts. It's in there, Lars. I know it!" Skipping around to collect his plate, she set it in the dishwasher. "Now, I'm going to make cupcakes because some guy gave me a lot of honey and I need to do something with it."

He smiled at her.

"You take Peanut in the other room and read to him, why don't you?"

"Are you suggesting I look through the witch books?"

"If you want to."

Glancing over the assortment of grimoires, he scratched his beard. "What am I looking for?"

"You'll know it when you read it." She tapped a finger to her lips. "Probably don't read anything too dark aloud. But me and my friends don't practice dark magic, so you should be safe. On the other hand…some of our relatives may have dabbled in the dark arts. Hmm…"

Lars glanced to Peanut. "She's a little nutty. But I like her. Come on, Charlie, let's do this."

"Charlie?" She beamed at him. "That was the first name I ever suggested."

"I know." He winked at her. "I like it. But I'm not committing to it yet. We'll see if it fits him, okay?"

She nodded eagerly.

Lars lay on the blanket on the floor next to Peanut-Maybe-Charlie. He'd paged through one of the grimoires that smelled musty and of lavender, but the writing was in some kind of hieroglyphs. Must be witch writing. He didn't know if that was a thing, but he knew he didn't need glasses.

Another book, from which he read a few pages out loud to Peanut, seemed to feature only love spells and those for womanly concerns. Women had a lot of issues.

Who would have thought softening freckles would require a spell?

Now he picked up a dusty book bound in scratched blue leather. The spine was laced with wide red silk stitches. He smoothed a hand over it and thought it felt warm, as if alive.

"What do you think of this one?" he asked his son. "Let's take a look inside."

As he opened to the first page, Peanut cooed as if in marvel. And there was quite a reason for such a reaction. The first page featured a kind of family crest or logo that seemed to leap off the page at him. Like a 3-D design or hologram. The stags clashing horns at the top of the crest turned to look at him and their blue eyes glowed.

"Now that's freaky. But cool, eh?"

Peanut blew spit bubbles, a sure sign that he was enjoying the book.

"So the first spell is…" Lars loved reading to his son and no matter what it was, from the morning paper to ads to nonfiction or fiction, he always tried to add some dramatic inflection. "Casting out transgressions of the heart. Ooo… Now isn't that interesting? And see here? The insects drawn along this page…" He moved the page slightly and the bugs seemed to turn fluorescent and glow. "Do you think they could fly off the page?"

Out in the kitchen Mireio called, "How you two doing? We'll have frosted cupcakes in about ten minutes."

"Great! We're reading about bugs in magic books."

"Sounds awesome. You want chocolate or vanilla buttercream frosting?"

Lars thought about it only a second. "Both!"

"Both it is."

He turned to meet Peanut's pale blue eyes. "She spoils us." The baby cooed.

"Okay, next page…"

He read through spells for opening the third eye, a charm for attracting health—hmm… No, he'd read the squiggly text wrong. It was for attracting *wealth*. But on the next page he was pretty sure it did say health. The words were written in blue and emerald ink, and the dark brown ink that depicted a raven in the corner he suspected could be dried blood. Scents of earth, ash and flowers emanated from the page. And something darker.

When he turned to the next page, which was blank save for some decorative scrollwork, all the pages fluttered and the corner of the upper page suddenly blackened, as if burned. He smelled sulfur and could taste blood at the back of his tongue. He traced a finger along the ink scrollwork that edged the left side against the spine and he pulled back with a flinch. A blood drop formed on the cut he'd gotten on his thumb. And before he could wipe it off it dripped onto the old stained paper.

"Oops." He glanced into the kitchen. Mireio was too busy to notice him damaging her book.

He tried to wipe off the blood but the droplet seeped into the toothy paper and crept outward, forming words in bright red. It was fascinating, but also a little scary. Lars looked to Peanut, who sucked his thumb with great intent.

Turning over to lie on his stomach, he set the book on the floor and watched as it filled with text. And within the text were tiny drawings of skeletons, hands pointing in various mudras and at the bottom crawled a snake. He flinched when he saw that. The snake lashed out its tongue at him, then rolled into a circle, biting its own tail.

And the final text formed a title across the top of the page. He read in a whisper, "To Dissuade Death."

Dissuade meant to deter something or to stop it. Had he found a spell that could save his life? This was remarkable. It was almost too good to be true. But maybe it only meant putting if off for a little while? Eventually death would come.

"Even a little while is better than what I have now," he muttered. "What do you think, Peanut?"

The baby rolled to his side and his chubby hand slid across the page. And behind the brush of his skin over the scrollwork, another tiny pinpoint of blood showed.

"Ah hell." Lars grabbed the boy's hand and saw he'd been cut. But he must not have felt it. The infant held his head up with some effort, grunting. Lars pressed his lips to the cut, then licked it. Then he rolled Peanut to his back and gave him the teething ring. "Such magic is not for you, Charlie."

Hmm, maybe that name would work. He did like it.

Turning back to the book, he watched his son's blood crawl over the page in a perfect bubble, not leaving a trail but seeking... The bubble stopped over a word. "Immortality," he read. Then the blood dispersed into the paper and left a faint pink stain.

Immortality?

Lars saw that the word was part of an ingredients list. Dragon's blood. A baby's cry. Pixie dust. Ashes of vampire. And... "A witch's immortality. She must ransom her borrowed years for thee one on whom thy spell is focused." Lars caught his forehead in hand. "Shit. That means..."

The witch performing the spell had to have already performed an immortality spell for herself. And what witch would give up such a precious thing?

Didn't matter because Mireio had told him she no longer wanted immortality. Which he didn't believe for a second. She would go after it. Someday. When she didn't have to stand alongside one who was dying. She shouldn't feel bad for having such a desire. She wouldn't have sought it if she hadn't genuinely desired it.

If Mireio read this spell she'd probably perform the immortality spell just to help him. He knew that she would.

Such a sacrifice was too much to ask of her. And he could never live knowing what she had given up to save him.

"Everything all right in here?"

He jerked around, slamming the book shut.

"It was so quiet I figured I'd better check to see if one or both of you were taking a nap."

Lars looked to Peanut, who was napping, arms splayed and teething ring lying on his chest. He twisted forward, effectively hiding the book behind him with a sweep of his hair.

"One of us is still awake. Cupcakes ready?"

"Yes! And they've cooled enough to frost. So, uh, did you find anything?"

"Nope." He sat up, wrapping his hands about his knees, and shrugged. "Nothing but some ways to cure monthly cramps or get a man to fall in love with you."

She narrowed her brows. Could she see the damn book behind him?

"Let me bolster Peanut in and I'll be right in to sample the goods," he said, shooing her off with a gesture.

"Okay." She spilled her gaze over the floor one last time. "You want some coffee too?"

"Yes!" he called.

Turning, he grabbed the blue leather-bound book. What to do with it? If he didn't draw attention to it, and slipped it back in the pile... No, she was going to look through them all, surely. Panicking, he shoved it under the couch. Then he stood, made sure he couldn't see any part of the book from where he stood. Grabbing the bolster pillows from the couch, he set them on either side of Peanut. Good for a few minutes.

And he swung around the corner, following the delicious aroma of chocolate and sugar.

After Lars's fifth cupcake, Mireio refilled his coffee. If he wanted to eat a dozen she wouldn't be happier. She would like nothing more than to cook and bake for this man every day.

"What's that?" he asked.

Standing across the counter from him, she straightened and looked about. "What's what?"

"That look on your face. Like strange stories of romance and adventure are taking place behind your eyes. I'd love to know your thoughts."

"Honestly? I was thinking how happy it makes me to watch you eat the stuff I bake. I've always considered food a form of love. You eat my food, that shows me how much you love me."

"Then I'm not leaving until all these cupcakes are gone." He winked at her. "Though I probably should slow down a bit, eh? Whew! These are sweet."

"I promised Valor a couple. Going to drop them off tonight as thanks for her hard work at the brewery today. It's supposed to rain tonight and tomorrow. Are you going to take Peanut home?"

"Yeah, we should hit the road. I used the last diaper in the bag."

"You can keep some diapers here if you like. And I wouldn't mind if you kept a bassinet or something for him to sleep in here, as well."

"That might be a good idea." He leaned over the counter and met her lips with a kiss that tasted like chocolate frosting. "Sorry I didn't find anything for you in the spell books. We paged through most of them. You'll have to bring them back to your friends. Or I could drop them off on the way home."

"No, I can keep them awhile. I want to look through the one Geneva brought. It's one of the oldest and is filled with ancient magic."

"Which one was that?"

"It's got a red cover and gold foiling. Very elaborate. Did you look in any of the living grimoires?"

"Are those the ones that have pictures that move and put out scents? Yes. A little creepy, but kind of cool too. I couldn't activate any of those spells by reading them to Peanut, could I?"

"Definitely not. I hope we find something."

"Mireio." He clasped her hand and pulled her around the counter to stand between his legs. Bowing his forehead to the crown of her head, he swallowed, then bracketed her jaws with his hands and tilted her gaze to meet his. "I'm dying, sweetie. You and I both have to accept that. It could be in a few months like the doctor predicted. It could be years. No man ever really knows when he'll take his last breath. Let's live in the now, okay?"

Chin wobbling, she staunchly defeated the need to break out into a wail. "But you said I could try another spell. Have you changed your mind?"

"No. But I don't want you getting upset if you can't find anything in those dusty old books."

She stepped back and said defiantly, "And what would Peanut say if he could speak?"

"What do you mean?"

"He'd say he wants his daddy around for a long time and that no matter what he should never stop trying."

Lars swiped his hands over his face. The nervous beard swipe ended in a squeeze of his fist. "You can't change what nature intended."

"I will!"

"I'm not going to let you sacrifice—" Lars grabbed the

diaper bag sitting on the floor behind him. "I should get going. When Peanut wakes, he'll need a diaper change."

"Sacrifice what?" she asked as he tromped into the living room to gather up the baby things, along with the baby.

"It's nothing. You do too much for me, is all. You make sacrifices."

"Nothing I don't want to do. You know I would do anything for you, Lars."

Baby and supplies in hand, he hustled toward the front door.

"Why are you in such a hurry to leave? Are you mad at me?"

He stopped on the threshold and turned with Peanut clutched to his chest and the diaper bag over a shoulder. The baby's face skewed into a pre-cry twist.

The man's jaw tensed but he shook his head. "Sorry. I'm…having a weird moment, I guess. I'm not mad at you. But I don't like to talk about…this. You know?"

She nodded, understanding. The man was dying. He knew that. No need to constantly remind him. "Can I still come over tomorrow? For the rain?"

"Just for the rain?" He managed a wobbly smile.

"And you, of course. But mostly the rain. I need to recharge."

"I can't wait to find out what that means. Come here." He nodded because his arms were full. "I'll see you soon. And bring me the rest of the cupcakes, yes?"

"Of course." She tilted herself up on her tiptoes and barely managed to brush his lips with a kiss because he didn't want to bend too far and crush Peanut. She kissed the infant's head, which stopped what could have become a loud wail. "See you later, Charlie."

"The name is growing on me," he said.

"Me too. See you later, lover!"

As soon as Lars was out of the driveway, Mireio

dodged into the living room and scanned the stack of books. He'd been trying to hide one with a blue leather cover. And he'd done it so obviously, as if he were up to something. What was in that book he hadn't wanted her to see?

Chapter 22

Mireio laid her hands on the various grimoires stacked on the floor, trying to sense a lingering remnant of Lars's touch. On one, she immediately felt his gentle warmth, and she opened it and paged through. It was the grimoire dedicated specifically to women. This one he must have explored with more than a little discomfort.

Setting that volume aside, she sat on the floor, legs stretched before her, and caught her weight on her palms behind her. "What is he trying to hide from me?"

She lay back and decided it had been months since she'd dusted the ceiling lamp that dangled with purple crystals. Sighing, she turned her head to the side. A book under the couch? And so far under.

"Well, well, well, what's that?" Something like that couldn't have possibly been an accident. It had to have been pushed under there.

Reaching under, she slid out the thin volume bound in blue. "Valor's great-grandma Hector's grimoire."

She knew it from the family crest on the inside front page. That witch was still alive. Mireio had no idea what she was up to lately, but she and Valor had been close because she'd raised her granddaughter. So many witches had been raised by their grandmothers. It almost seemed the norm as opposed to an exception. Hector Hearst had also practiced dark magic on occasion, so what was compressed between the covers of this grimoire gave Mireio a warning tingle.

Had that same warning frightened Lars, someone unfamiliar with the intricacies and dangers of magic? That would have been enough to make him skittish and try to shove the book as far away as possible.

Hmm, that didn't convince her that he hadn't read something inside, which could have also freaked him.

Paging through, she marveled at the ornamental designs and elaborate writings. Some pages were blank. She knew those spells could only be activated with blood magic. That was definitely dark magic.

"Oh." She turned a page and her finger came away sticky. It was… "Blood? But how…?"

How had he known to activate a page with his blood? Impossible. He must have cut himself on the paper. But the spell title took her breath away: "To Dissuade Death."

"Oh, my goddess, this could be it. The spell that could save his life."

She quickly read the incantation and the ingredients. All of it was easily obtainable, and it promised to dissuade death. And to her, dissuade meant to stop it.

"Did he read this spell? Is this really his blood? Why wouldn't he say something to me?"

And then she tapped one of the words on the ingredient list that was stained pink: *immortality*. The witch performing the spell was required to sacrifice her immortality as the final ingredient.

If she went through with the spell she'd been angsting about lately, she'd have to give up that newly won immortality to save her lover. And she knew damn well the last thing Lars would ever ask of her was such a sacrifice.

She closed the book. What to do? The answer was simple.

"It's not a sacrifice for someone you love."

With Peanut-Maybe-Charlie down for an afternoon nap, Lars set the baby monitor on top of the outdoor closet that contained his beekeeping equipment and then approached the hives. He wasn't going to check them today. He'd done that three days ago. Disturbing the bees overmuch wasn't good for their productivity.

Since ancient times people had been telling the bees their good news, their bad news, about their celebrations and also about their family deaths. It was a tradition that Lars had started a few years ago when he'd needed someone to talk to. He always landed in a different place by putting his thoughts, fears, dreams and emotions out there by telling the bees.

And he needed to do that now.

Wildflowers and grass freshened the air. The sun hung high. And a gentle breeze listed through his hair. Spreading out his arms, he tilted back his head and took in the gentle hum from the hives. Their busy noise seemed to vibrate in his veins. The sensation felt like a symphony, and he was humbled by it. A few bees buzzed about his head. Bees wouldn't sting unless threatened. His bees had yet to sting him.

"Bless you for your hard, endless work and for the gifts you've given to me" was always how he began.

Standing straight and putting his hands down, palms facing the hives, he mentally reached in and put his heart out before him. "My life has been filled with some ups and downs lately. Some really awesome ups." Thinking about the past weeks with Mireio put a huge smile on his face. "You may have noticed the witch who comes here all the time. I love her."

It was the first time he'd said that out loud other than suggesting he couldn't say it, even though he wanted to, to Mireio. Because to give it to her in words? He didn't want to break that vow when he died.

"And she loves me, which is some kind of awesome. She also loves Peanut. I'm thinking his name should be Charlie. It's a good name. I have to remember to run down to city hall next week to fill out a change for the birth record. So there's the up. Love is indescribable. It's like I can't breathe without thinking about her. She keeps me alive."

He caught a palm over his chest. If only it were so easy to stay alive.

"And then there's the down." He rubbed his jaw, stroking his beard tentatively. "I've been struggling with this stupid death sentence. Damn! Why did this have to happen now when I've found the one I want to spend every day with for the rest of my life? A life that is supposed to end soon, rather than later. I can feel it in my bones. I haven't told Mireio. I ache all the time. My fingers and toes always tingle. But I can function and hide it most of the time. It's as if I'm being eaten up from the inside out. And I don't want to get to a point where I'm frail and incapable. I…couldn't bear that. Me. The big guy who's always been strong enough to push a tree over with but a shove."

He knelt then because it felt right to honor the bees that way, and telling all this was difficult and his voice subtly shook. "And my wolf. I feel as if I've lost that part of me. Yet when it comes on me without my volition it feels like a punishment for not being able to control myself. I wish… I wish I could understand this. I wish my father was here so I could talk to him. Ask him questions. Learn from him. Why do we die like this?"

He'd not known at the time what had taken his father from him. Only that it had hurt his child's heart like no physical injury ever had. And when he'd most needed his mother to wrap him in her arms and tell him the world would not end and life would go on, she had fled the pack, never to be seen again. It had taken years for Lars to forgive her. He knew she hadn't known any other way to handle her grief. Or at least, he hoped that was what had allowed her to abandon her son without a look back over her shoulder.

"What should I do? I need guidance. I want… I think I want to leap. To take life and rip it to shreds and live every moment. But then I've a little boy to take care of. I want the best for him. And Mireio. Do I dare? Can I? What should I do?"

Catching his palms in the grass before the hives, he listened as the bees flew out en masse and formed a swirling cloud above his head.

Straightening, Lars lifted his arms and closed his eyes, taking in the flutter of thousands of wings against his hair and skin. They had never responded this way before. And he sensed what they wanted him to know.

He needed to leap. Be damned, the fall.

Chapter 23

Mireio set the plate of cupcakes on the table, which caught Lars's eye. He had been making the bed when she wandered into the cabin with a cheery "Hello!" She had no intention of discussing the spell she'd discovered in Hector Hearst's grimoire. It could wait. Until she had a solid plan.

It had started raining as she'd driven the winding tree-lined road up to the cabin, and her skin absolutely tingled in anticipation of her plans.

"A dozen left for you," she said, licking a smear of chocolate buttercream from her thumb. "Where's Peanut?"

"Sunday has him. I wanted it to be just us tonight." He winked, then shoved a pillow into the case. "So what's up with your plans for the rain?"

"I've come to renew. I am a water witch," she said as she unbuttoned her red short-sleeved blouse. Drawing her fingers down to her cleavage, she eyed him through her lashes. Darting her tongue along her upper lip seemed an appropriate tease. "I have needs."

"Needs?" He tossed the pillow behind him without a care. The man could work the overalls and wrinkled T-shirt. And talk about dimple overload. Goddess, he looked sexy tonight. His gaze aimed for her bust, barely contained by the red lace bra. "Any sort of needs I might be able to assist you with?"

"Not really." She draped the blouse over the back of a chair before the kitchen table, then shimmied down her skirt to land about her four-inch plaid heels.

"Then you've really got me confused." He pulled her closer by her hips and bent to dust the ends of his hair over the tops of her breasts.

She cooed with desire and stroked his beard. "Mmm, hold that thought for a bit, will you? I intend to go out in the rain and draw in its power. Revive and reinvigorate my water magic. I can't do it so often at my place because, while my backyard is private, you know Mrs. Henderson and her sketch pad."

"That I do. You think she's ever sketched a naked witch?"

"I hope not!" She giggled as he moved up and licked under her chin. His hair was what tickled, and yet it also set her skin on fire with desire. "Give me an hour to take it all in."

"An hour out in the rain? And…in your underthings?"

"Not exactly."

She reached behind her back and unhooked her bra, then let it slide off. When she stuck her fingers under the waistband of her panties, Lars put his hands over hers and helped her slide them down, slowly, his face moving over her stomach, his breaths drawing up the goose bumps on her skin. He knelt before her, breathing heavily at her mons.

"I said you have to wait. Can you manage that, wolf? I don't want to miss the rain. It's only supposed to fall for a couple hours."

He pouted up at her.

She stepped out of her shoes and bent to kiss the top of

his head. He cupped her breasts as she did so. A squeeze of both her nipples did not make her want to step outside into the rain, especially since the night was beginning to cool off.

"You're cheating," she said with an admonishing wave of her finger. She snapped upright and marched to the door. "Maybe all I need is half an hour. Eat some cupcakes, why don't you?"

"Can I watch?" he called as she stepped outside.

"I can't stop you, but it'll be weird if you do. You'll know when it's cool to come outside and find me."

Still kneeling on the floor, he saluted her, then reached for a cupcake.

Arms spread, head tilted back and eyes closed, Mireio called on the rain to embrace, baptize and renew her. She whispered an ancient chant that her grandmother had taught her. One that spoke to the water elementals that clung to the raindrops and that flittered among the soaked grasses. The water skittered over her skin, gliding and teasing and infusing its wild and vibrant energies into her.

Her body hummed with power. And she felt her smile grow as she flicked her fingers and snapped away the rain droplets. And with each bend and flick of her fingers she controlled the drops, sending them spraying out in a fan, and then an arc that coiled above her head and performed a rain dance for her, the master.

She liked to think of rain as a direct infusion of star stuff. Because that's what everything was anyway. Ancient and ever alive, the soul never faded as it journeyed through the ages. And perhaps this rain was the same that had fallen on her bare skin centuries earlier as she'd performed much the same spell. It was a nice thought, and she truly believed it.

Her ritual ended by crafting a water cage sphere around

her. It was her way of sealing her commitment to water magic. Out of the corner of her eye, she noticed Lars standing close.

"Sorry," he offered. "I couldn't resist watching. You're more beautiful than anything I can put to words. And your magic is incredible."

She swept her hand through a swath of the water cage before her, which opened a door. Then she crooked her finger at him, welcoming him inside her haven.

"Really?" he asked.

She nodded. "But you gotta get naked first."

"I can do that."

She was pretty sure no man had ever shucked off his clothing so quickly. Never would she tire of admiring his muscles and long sculpted body. The rain misted his skin, tightening her nipples as she thought about how fun it was going to be to lick the moisture from his hard lines. Padding through the squishy wet grass, he looked over the rain cage first before carefully stepping inside.

"Don't worry—it's strong. Only I can break it," she said.

"You're more than a witch." He pulled her slick body against his. "You're a goddess."

"Flattery will get you anything you desire, lover. Mmm… I think we need a bed to lie on." She swept her hand and produced a knee-high flat surface fashioned from water.

Testing it with a palm, Lars flashed her a look of awe. "Can we really sit on this?"

"Lie down and try it out."

He did, and his body almost stretched to both sides of the cage, so, in complete control of her magic, Mireio teased the sphere a bit wider with a push of her hands outward.

She climbed onto the bed. Straddling Lars, she lifted

her wet hair and splayed it out, commanding it to dry, so by the time it fell the red coiled curls brushed her cheeks softly. Inside the sphere they would be protected from the rain, which had picked up again. Not that she minded a lot of wet.

Reaching down, she gripped Lars's penis and slicked her hand up and down, drawing up a hiss of pleasure from him. He propped himself up on his elbows. "I'm still worried we're going to drop through this funky bench."

"Trust me." She leaned down, almost touching his erection with her lips. "You do trust me, don't you?"

"Yes?"

Smirking, she licked the head of him, then took him in deeply and sucked him until he orgasmed.

Sitting naked on the edge of the framed wall behind the cabin, Mireio fluffed her bright hair, which did not seem to get any more than a few droplets on it, even though it was still misting.

Lars was soaked. And he hadn't felt this good in days. His muscles were stretched and lax and his heartbeats still thundered from his orgasm. The moment felt enormously promising. The air was fresh and, even though there was no moon in sight, the night was bright.

"So you want to go in and snuggle under a blanket?" she asked coyly and added a flutter of her lashes.

The woman owned him with that sexy lash-fluttering smile. Every part of him belonged to her. Wanted to be inside and out with her. Forever and always.

"I have to say something to you first," he said. "And I need to apologize because I said before I wouldn't say it, but now I don't care. Or rather, I do care. A lot. I have to put it out there. For you to know."

"Sounds ominous."

"It could be. Mireio..." He knelt on the ground before

her and threaded his fingers with hers. Eyes meeting hers he felt her power in the blue irises, and her compassion and kindness. "I love you. And…uh…I was wondering if you'd marry me."

Her mouth dropped open as she pressed a hand over it. "Really? You're not on a sex high right now and will regret this later?"

"No, lover, I thought about this after I got home yesterday and talked to the bees. I don't want to spend a day without you. And nothing would make me happier than if you'd become my wife. Oh, and…that includes accepting Peanut into your life, as well. I know it's a lot to ask—"

"Yes!" She plunged into his arms. Not expecting that reaction, Lars toppled backward. They landed on the slick ground with kisses and squeals from Mireio. "Oh, yes, yes, yes! I've been thinking the same thing lately. I love you so much, Lars. And I want to be with you always. No matter what the future brings."

"And Peanut?"

"I adore Peanut, you know that. I would be honored to be his stepmother."

"I think he'd like having you as his mom. You have a way with him. Just like you have a way with me. You've bewitched us both. And I'm happy for it. Can we get married soon? Like this weekend? I know you women like a big fancy to-do, but—"

Her kiss stopped his protest. "I don't need a to-do. I just need you. But can we have my girlfriends there? And you might have some friends you'll want there?"

"Dean and Sunday for sure. And Peanut can be my best man."

"Yay! Let's do it this Saturday. That'll give me a few days to find a dress. I do need to find the perfect dress, even if we go to the courthouse. I guess I need a little to-do after all."

"Pretty yourself up. Do what you want to. Do I need to get a suit?"

"You can wear whatever you like. Oh, Lars, we're getting married?"

"We are."

Chapter 24

Mireio turned before the mirror in the tiny department store dressing room. Geneva sat on the bench observing with the practiced eye of a seasoned fashion designer. Mireio had found a sequined pale pink dress that stopped at her thighs and whose back plunged to above her waistline. In front it draped to reveal her cleavage. Add to that the five-inch silver Pradas and she was in love with her bad self right now.

"I'm not sure." Geneva tilted her head against the wall where half a dozen rejected dresses hung.

"Oh, come on, Geneva, this one is perfect. And I am so not going to wear white. I'll spill beer or drop a cupcake on it. I think Lars will love this one."

"The dress is gorgeous. Your bright hair falling over the pink sequins makes it all rock. But I'd wear red shoes with it."

"Good call. Back to the shoe department! But uh, what are you not sure about?"

Geneva stood and unzipped Mireio down the side. "You're getting married in two days. You've dated the guy for what?"

"Long enough. I love him, Geneva. And he loves me."

She crossed her arms, unconvinced. The perfect cat's-eyes black liner she always wore gave her a majestic demeanor, even though she was shooting daggers at Mireio right now. "You sure this isn't some freaky rushed thing so when he dies his kid will have a mom?"

She gaped at Geneva, but the woman merely shrugged and waited for a reply.

"No. It's not like that." Mireio slipped the dress from her shoulders and spied her lying eyes in the mirror. "Okay, so part of it might be me wanting to have as much time with him as I can. And I love Peanut. I would much rather he comes to me than become a ward of the state, or whatever happens if Lars should die." She slipped down the dress to puddle around the high heels. "Which he's not going to do."

"I thought the doc gave him a couple months? Seems like his expiration date should be coming up pretty fast."

"You're rude, Geneva."

"I'm playing devil's advocate here."

Yes, and she couldn't blame her for that. But Mireio had thought about all this. She couldn't change any of it. Well, not without one last attempt.

"What's so wrong about me wanting to grab a little happiness? For wanting to make Lars happy?"

"Nothing. But you're trying to convince yourself he's not going to die. What do you know that the universe doesn't?"

"Let me tell you."

Two days later, Lars drove to Anoka with his bride at his side. They decided to hold the wedding ceremony down by the Rum River, behind The Decadent Dames so that afterward the party could move to the brewery. Lars had picked up Mireio, who had bounded out of her house in sweats and a T-shirt. Strange attire for her. Was this her idea of a casual affair? He was feeling itchy in the dress slacks and white shirt. He'd even rented a tie, which clipped on, thank the gods. He'd mess with that later.

He cast Mireio another glance. She twisted to make faces at Peanut, who sat strapped in on the back seat. Before he'd left this afternoon, Sunday had stopped by to give Peanut a present. It was a onesie that looked like a tuxedo with a little black tie at the neck. That was one smart-looking boy.

"What?" Mireio asked as he cast her yet another glance.

"Just never seen you so dressed down before."

She patted the plastic dress bag. "I'm not going to let you see me in all my stunning beauty before the ceremony. I'm changing at the brewery."

"You're going to make my heart stop. But then, you do that every time I see you." He winked at her and turned from the highway and into town. "You know, I realize that by marrying you I'm agreeing to wake every morning clinging desperately to my eight inches of the bed?"

She waggled her shoulders. "Got a problem with that?"

"Nope. I'd fall on the floor every morning just to be near you, and I have a few times already."

"We could get a king-size bed. It would fit at my place. Where are we going to live? Your place is awesome with all the woods and quiet. And there's the bees. You couldn't leave them or move them. But…it's one room."

"I'm working on that."

"Right. Doubling the size would be nice. And then Peanut could have his own room. Could we keep my place until that happens? I'm not attached to living in my neighborhood but there is my bathroom."

"The mermaid's throne. I wouldn't dream of asking you to give that up. We'll figure something out. But I don't ever want to spend a night without you."

She clasped his hand. "It'll never happen. Promise."

"So uh, I need to tell you something."

"That sounds ominous. You mean you still have more secrets? I can't imagine what they could be."

"Not a secret, just…facts you need to have before signing on the dotted line. About me. When I'm werewolf."

She tapped a finger on her lower lip. "Like what?"

"When we werewolves take a mate, it's for life."

"I know that. I wouldn't agree to marry you if I wasn't in it for forever."

"As short as that might be," he said, then shook his head. "Sorry. I have to stop thinking like that. Take one day at a time."

"That's the way I intend to do it. So it's me and you. For life."

"Right, but we wolves? We like to also take our mates when in werewolf form."

"Oh? Hmm, I think I knew about that. So you, all shifted to werewolf shape and, uh…little ole me?"

He nodded. If he thought she looked like a teenager standing next to him now, she'd be positively dwarfed by his werewolf. "I would never harm you, Mireio. You know that. But my werewolf will want in on the action."

"I love all of you, Lars. And I would never deny you a thing. But can we take it slow? Work up to that experience?"

"Of course. Just the fact you're open to it is all I need to hear. We can go really slow. Like months. Years." He cleared his throat and swallowed. He didn't have that long, but he wasn't going to be a downer. Not today. Not on the best day of his life.

"Since we're doing the confession thing here…" She twisted on the seat to face him. "There's something I have to tell you. You need to know this before you marry me."

"Is it worse than anything the two of us have already been through together?"

"I don't know. Depends on your perspective."

"Tell me, Mireio."

"I've had a change of heart about the immortality spell."

Lars's jaws tensed. "You want to do it now?"

"Yes."

"I see."

"You're not cool with that? I thought you were."

He was. Until he'd found that spell. And really? He shrugged. "I might have had second thoughts about taking the life of an innocent vampire."

"He's not innocent, and you know it."

"I only know what Raven Crosse has said about him."

"Lars, I had Raven search for a very specific vampire. Which is the part I need to confess to you."

"And this specific vampire? Why would he make you change your mind about performing the spell?"

"He was the vampire my mother went after when she had plans to invoke the immortality spell. Except before she could rip out his heart, he ripped out hers."

Lars slammed the truck to a stop at a stop sign at a four-way in a quiet neighborhood. Both of them shot a look into the back seat. Peanut slept.

"Sweetie. Really?"

She nodded. "Mother left me alone that night. I knew she was going out to invoke the spell to live forever. So I followed her. I was eight. And…" She sniffed. "I instead watched the vampire murder my mother. Thank the goddess, my grandmother had followed us, as well, and was able to get me away before the vamp came for me. You'd think that would have scared me away from casting the spell. But all my life I've wanted immortality so that I'd be protected against a vampire attack."

He nodded, understanding.

"But, as well, I've wanted revenge against the bastard

who took my mother's life. Those nightmares I told you I didn't remember? I do. They are about my mom dying. I always see that bastard vampire standing there, holding her bloody heart."

"I had no idea." He clasped her hand and met her teary gaze. "Then I'm in. All the way. You want revenge?"

"I—I want immortality."

"Truth, Mireio."

She nodded decisively. "I want revenge too. To stop the nightmares."

"Don't say another word. It's done. Just let me know when we need to go out on the hunt."

"Thank you. For understanding."

"I'd do anything for you, my love. Anything."

He wished she'd told him sooner. He would have never said anything against going after the vamp. So long as she didn't find the spell, he could be okay with helping her to track down a vampire and kill it. A vampire who had haunted her since she was eight. A bastard longtooth who had murdered her mother while Mireio had watched. Hell, what a thing to have experienced.

He'd take away her nightmares. If it was the last thing he did.

A goddess in pink spangles walked down the sidewalk toward him. The small gathering of friends stood on a shaded path alongside the river. The day was bright and warm and ducks swam in the river. Maple, elm and oak leaves performed a cancan in the breeze. To his right stood Dean Maverick. And Sunday held Peanut. Charlie. The best man.

Lars watched with awe and a reverence that pushed up tears at the corners of his eyes as Mireio approached, led by Geneva, who was dressed to the nines in a long black sheath dress and who held white roses.

Mireio's bright hair spilled in luscious coils over her shoulders and down her back, and…did her shoes match her hair? What a fiery bundle of witch and mermaid-wannabe he'd gotten for himself.

Lars adjusted his stance and swallowed a lump in his throat. Yeah, so he was getting emotional. That this woman wanted to marry him did not cease to amaze him. Did they deserve one another? Maybe. Would she be better off finding a man who would live long enough to take care of her and have a family with her? Yes.

But he wasn't going to question his luck. She had said yes because she loved him. And her love was what kept him going.

One of her hands slipped out from under the bouquet of red roses. Fingers beringed in silver and crystals, she took his hand and beamed a smile up at him. "You ready for this?"

"Let's get hitched, sweetie."

The ceremony took ten minutes. It was a long ten minutes. Lars didn't hear much of it because his focus was on the part where he finally got to kiss his bride. And when prompted, he tilted his new wife back and bent over her for a long, binding kiss. Their friends cheered. Peanut giggled as a flutter of rose petals was tossed in the air. Then they all convened at the brewery where the DJ had already set up, and word had spread. Dozens of friends were already partying it up inside.

"You know we have to do the first dance." Mireio said as she kissed him. "I'll request something slow."

"I'm good with that. Where's Charlie?"

"I love that you're keeping that name! He's…" Both of them scanned the taproom. They spotted the baby in the midst of a half dozen women cooing over him and arguing who would get to give him his bottle. "I think he'll be fine for a while. You want to check on him?"

"No, let him party it up. See? He's already a ladies' man. He's got more chicks surrounding him than I've dated in my lifetime."

"Ha! And now you're mine so you are off the table. Come on, husband, let's dance."

Two hours later, Mireio sensed Lars was tired. He didn't say anything, and he was very good at hiding it, but she saw him flicking his fingers behind his back as if trying to work the circulation back into them. And he took mincing steps. His joints must be bothering him. When he found a moment to himself, his smile dropped and his jaw tightened. Then a friend would congratulate him and he'd force on a cheery demeanor.

It was time to call it a night. But first, she'd collect Charlie. Who was currently sleeping in his carrier on the bar with Sunday dutifully watching over him.

"Has he been sleeping awhile?" Mireio asked as she gathered his blanket and looked around for the diaper bag.

"Ten minutes. Oh, Mireio, don't worry. Dean and I will take Peanut home tonight. You and Lars go on—have your wedding night."

"Really?" Though she expected her new husband would probably crash as soon as he saw the bed. And he deserved it.

"Yes. I've got this," Sunday said. "I stocked up on diapers and even bought a crib for the house, so we're all good to go."

"That's quite a commitment. We won't be needing a babysitter so much now. Well, I'd still like to go out with my new hubby once in a while."

"Mireio." Sunday placed a hand over her wrist. "You are aware that Dean and I will get legal custody of Peanut should Lars die?"

"What?"

Chapter 25

In the morning, Mireio brushed the hair from her face and rolled over to find her new husband clinging to the edge of the bed. One leg hung over the side of the bed, and so did one arm. But somehow he managed to snore through it all. The guy *had* stated that he'd known exactly what he was getting into by marrying her.

But had she known everything? What Sunday had said to her last night still bothered her. She'd wanted to ask her to explain, but Lars had come up to her and put his arms around her waist from behind, nuzzling his face into her hair. It had been a silent signal that he wanted to leave, so she'd left the baby with Sunday and driven him to her place. Lars had almost fallen asleep on the ten-minute ride, but he had made it upstairs and to the bed. By the time she'd showered and anticipated a little wedding-night snuggling? Snores.

Good thing he wasn't a loud snorer. More of a gentle whispering type. And to be fair, there were times she'd woken herself with her own snoring. Not proud of it either. Maybe a little proud.

She stroked his hair along his arm, and that touch startled him awake. He lifted his head, snorted, then wobbled and fell off the bed.

Mireio leaned over the side of the bed. "Good morning, husband!"

After a groan, he gave her a thumbs-up from the floor.

"It's actually closer to noon," she said. "So what will we do with ourselves on our first official day as husband and wife?"

He exhaled and rubbed a hand over his abs, blinking as he came fully awake. "Sorry about denying you wedding night sex last night. I was beat."

"I understand. We can still have 'morning after the wedding' sex."

"That we can."

And with an energy that surprised her, he lunged up onto the bed and crawled on top of her. She, of course, had slept naked, but he still had on his dress trousers. So she unzipped him and he swiftly kicked the pants to the floor.

"How's it feel to be married?" he asked, then lashed his tongue over her nipple and sucked it deeply.

"Oh…goddess, yes."

"That good, eh?"

She raked her fingers into his hair and held him there at her breast. Her body reacted to his intense motions by arching and squirming and…every nerve ending sang.

When his fingers slicked between her legs and pressed firmly against the edges of her opening she gasped. The man knew she liked pressure there, that sometimes he didn't even have to enter her to coax her song to a wild, rocking anthem.

"I think I found the right spot," he murmured against her ear, then tugged the lobe with his teeth. "Like this?" He glided his fingers firmly along the opening, contacting her clitoris, and occasionally slipped his thumb over her swollen pearl. "Oh, yeah, my witch is so happy she can't even speak."

Clinging to the sheets, she threw her head backward and it slid off the edge of the bed. He kissed her throat, laving her skin with his hot tongue. And his fingers increased pressure as he slowly stroked her to a long and moaning climax.

"I love to listen to you come," he said. A shift of his thigh pressed his erection against her leg. "So loud and proud."

Panting and laughing at his admiration for her, she gripped his hair and tugged him down to kiss her. Hard and messy and delving for the deepness of him. Heartbeats still thudding and the high fluttering away, she pushed up from him and gripped his cock. "My turn."

"I've got a better idea." He stood and pulled her into his arms, standing and swinging her over his shoulder in a smooth move. "Let's take a shower."

Half an hour later, wrapped in a towel and with wet hair tickling her shoulders, Mireio felt ever so satisfied. She brewed tea and fried up some vanilla cream French toast. She stirred honey into some mascarpone cheese to make a topping, sprinkled it with cinnamon and set the plate before Lars, who also wore but a towel.

"You spoil me," he said, as he dug in with fork and knife. "Mercy, this is amazing. I don't think I've ever eaten so good as when I'm being fed by you."

"Food is love," she said. "And I love you lots. More toast?"

He put up three fingers and she happily dipped more bread into the mix and fried the slices up for him while she ate one herself, standing before the stove.

Domesticity came easily to her. And now knowing she'd wake every morning next to the man she loved, well, life couldn't be better. Add to that a sweet baby boy?

"So, uh…Sunday said something to me last night that confused me."

"What's that? I suppose I should head over and pick up Charlie. Hate to leave him there too long."

"I'm so glad you're going with Charlie. It fits him. But Sunday said that she and Dean would get custody of Charlie if anything should happen to you. Why would she think that?"

Lars set down his fork and looked aside. After a long draft of water he stood to walk around and lean against the counter opposite from the stove where she stood. "That's not completely true."

"But partially true?" Her heart thudded loudly.

"The pack has been pressuring me to change my will. They want to make sure they get Charlie when I die."

"But why would you do that? Lars, I'm your wife. When I agreed to marry you I knew what I was doing. I knew that I was becoming Charlie's stepmom. I adore him. I can take care of him if…well… Don't you trust me?"

"You're the best mom Charlie could ever have. I've had the will sitting out. But I've delayed calling a lawyer to make changes because of exactly this. Us. I know you would make an excellent mother to my boy. But…"

"But? But you're still going to change the will?"

"I don't know." He raked his fingers through his wet hair. "Have you ever raised a werewolf?"

"No, but I'm sure I can learn."

"Mireio, my boy could be an entirely different species from you. Don't you think it best he be raised by a pack? His own kind?"

She eyed the browning toast in the frying pan, knowing it needed to be flipped. Sweet vanilla could not coax her from the sudden anxiety she felt tightening her jaws. "Is that what you want?"

"I honestly don't know. It's why I still haven't made changes to the will. I need to think about it. Is that okay with you? I want to do what's best for my Peanut."

Affronted that he didn't immediately fall in favor of her, Mireio cautioned her anger. He only wanted the best for his son. And a werewolf would thrive if brought up in a pack, living and learning among others of his kind. What could she, a witch, offer him?

On the other hand, no one knew if Charlie was actually werewolf. He could be human. And she could handle that fine.

But he was right. She needed to give him some space on this. Some time.

Lars reached around and grabbed the spatula and flipped the toast. The top side was burned. He bowed and kissed her softly, slowly. His mouth melted against hers, giving her the sweetness the vanilla promised. Had she been angry about something? And then he met her gaze, seeking, searching, asking without words.

She nodded. And he kissed her forehead and scooped the toast out to toss in the garbage. "Let me make the last few. You sit down and eat."

So she did, because she was unsettled at learning she wasn't her husband's first choice to raise his son.

That night they sat out on the back porch. Fireflies fluttered in the garden above the jasmine and primrose. Cicadas droned in a nearby oak tree. And relaxing on the hammock with Charlie tucked between his arm and chest, Lars read the only thing he could find that wasn't a spell book or a cookbook.

"Sign up now to receive your free toaster when you open an account," he narrated to his son.

"I promise tomorrow I am getting some kid books," Mireio said as she returned to the porch from the kitchen with apple ale for both of them. She set Lars's on the wood floor beside the hammock, then curled into the big wicker chair that swallowed her with its wide white wings. "You just like to read, don't you? Anything and everything."

"I do. Finally found someone who will listen to me, so I'm going to take advantage of that." He sat up and, gripping Charlie's torso, dangled him over the summer grass so the infant could test his legs. He was in a bouncing phase. "I'm sorry about our talk earlier. I didn't give you a chance. And I've been thinking about it. I'm swaying toward you for adopting Charlie. In fact, I called the county records department today, and there's a form that needs to be signed for you to become his official parent."

"Really?"

"Yeah, one issue, though. It needs the real mother's signature."

"Oh." He read her pout and suspected she thought all hope was lost.

"I know she'll do it. It's just tracking her down and getting the paperwork to her and back to me that could be the challenge. I only know that she headed off to Africa."

"What about her family?"

"We didn't talk family trees or contact information during those two days we had our fling. And while she left me with a stack of legal documents, there wasn't an address to contact her because, well, at the time, she was on the move."

"Right."

"But the birth certificate lists an address in Minneapolis."

"Maybe you could start there to find a family member?"

"It's an idea. But how do I do that? Show up at her mother's door. Hey, I'm the guy who fathered your daughter's son, whom you probably don't even know about, and I want her to give me complete custody."

"I'm sure her mother must know about it. Kinda hard to hide a pregnancy from your mom."

"If she has a mom."

"True. Do you have any computer hacker friends? They might be able to track her down somehow."

"Computer hacker friends." He chuckled. "Do I look like a guy who has friends like that?"

"No. Maybe Valor could give it a go. She's always the one who fixes our computers when something goes wrong. She's handy with a wrench and hammer, as well."

"I could hire a skip tracer."

"What's that?"

"A person who tracks down people who don't want to be found. It's not as if she doesn't want to be found. But it's the same kind of situation."

"You look into that. And I'll ask Valor. Hey, Charlie, can you walk over to me?"

Lars led the boy who tested his feet forward, Charlie eagerly trying to get to Mireio's outstretched hands. He wanted her to be his son's mother. Forever. But he had to think of the pack too. And make sure his son got the best guidance through life. This was a tough decision.

And the fact that he even had to consider such a decision? Hell.

Mireio grabbed Charlie and swung him through the air. The boy giggled effusively. He had developed a full-throated belly laugh that always made them both laugh in kind.

"Oh!" She grimaced. "I know why you handed him over to me."

"The one holding him gets to change him," Lars teased. "I am busy reading." He picked up another piece of junk mail and fanned it before his face.

"Fine. But that means I get to feed him his last bottle and tuck him in. So there." She stuck out her tongue at him and wandered into the house.

Lars tossed the mail to the patio floor and sipped his ale. Life had never been better.

Chapter 26

Mireio woke to a strange sound. She couldn't have been sleeping very long after that third orgasm had lulled her into a blissful, sighing slumber. But now she searched the dark room seeking what had sounded like a growl.

Standing near the bed was a shadowed, hulking figure that stomped the floor...with a paw.

"Oh, my goddess."

Lars had shifted to werewolf.

And the baby, likely having been woken by the noise, was crying in his carrier on the floor.

"Lars!"

The werewolf glanced to her and growled. And then he howled a long and rangy sound that Mireio felt sure the whole neighborhood could hear. He stalked toward Charlie, bent to sniff at the infant, then swept a paw through the carrier handle and lifted the infant.

"Oh, no, Lars!" She stumbled off the bed, tangled in the sheets. "You can't. He's not strapped in!"

The werewolf snorted at her and took off down the stairs.

"Oh, shit!" She grabbed her night robe and tugged it on. By the time she graced the top stair she heard the screen patio door open and swing shut. A glance outside saw Mrs. Henderson's lights go on. Charlie wailed.

"Stop!" Mireio cried as she broached the patio and hit the grass at a run.

The werewolf had fled through the pasture that backed onto their neighborhood yards. The corn grew higher than her shoulders, but a werewolf should have no problem navigating it. But a baby, not strapped in…

"Oh, mercy!"

"Mireio!"

"Not now, Mrs. Henderson! He's got the baby!"

"Who? The Sasquatch?"

"No! Uh…" She ran toward the corn. What to say? The last thing Mrs. Henderson needed to know was that Mireio had married a werewolf. Or even a Sasquatch, for that matter. "A stranger! I've got to get the baby."

"I'm calling the police!"

Ah shit, that was not what she needed. Police and a werewolf? That could mean the end of Lars. The end of werewolves. The end of a reality where humans believed werewolves only existed in movies and books. She couldn't let the police see Lars.

But more, she had to get to him before the baby was hurt. She knew Lars would never intentionally harm his son. But how much of his man's mind could control his wolf brain when in werewolf shape?

She followed the path of trampled stalks through the cornfield, tracking the werewolf's grunt up ahead. He was far off, his powerful legs moving him more swiftly than she could run. The long cutting corn leaves slashed across her face and bare legs. She tugged the night-robe over her naked body and tied it as she ran. Should have put on some shoes; the broken cornstalks proved rough to run over.

Charlie's wails spurred her on and his cries grew louder

and closer. She burst out into a clearing where the farmer must turn his tractor, for the cornstalks that lay broken down in an almost perfect circle. The werewolf stood before the baby carrier, which sat on the ground. Not toppled. And now Charlie had strangely settled, his wide eyes taking in the creature who loomed above him.

"I know you couldn't help it," Mireio said as she approached cautiously. She just wanted to get to the baby. Behind her, she heard police sirens in the distance. "You've got to shift back, Lars. Or get the hell out of here. Go!" She clapped her hands toward the werewolf and it cringed from her.

But then it growled and snapped. Actually snapped its teeth at her.

"I'm not afraid of you. I'm your wife, for goddess's sake. Listen to me. If you want to protect yourself and your son, run!"

And of a sudden the werewolf's head jerked to the side and then forward. His shoulder bent painfully backward as his legs bent and he fell to his knees—human-shaped knees. Lars shifted back to his were shape within three seconds. He crouched there on the crushed cornstalks, panting, naked.

Mireio rushed to Charlie and grabbed the carrier. "You have to go, Lars. Mrs. Henderson called the police and I can hear the sirens. Run…somewhere. I'll leave clothes out in the backyard for you. Go! I'll say whoever took the baby got away, but that doesn't guarantee they won't keep looking for the culprit. Please, Lars, go!"

He nodded and scampered off into the cornstalks.

She checked Charlie. He looked fine, though it was dark and there was no moonlight. Lars hadn't shifted because of the full moon. He'd shifted because his body was mutinying and forcing him to surrender to his shift at the most inopportune times.

"Poor man." She glanced down the path he'd taken, thinking he left a lighter trail now that he was no longer in werewolf shape. She hoped it would be an impossible trail to follow.

Wandering back the way she'd come, she met two police officers with guns pulled when she was about twenty feet from her backyard.

"Hands up!" one called.

"It's me," she answered, but she set down the baby carrier and put up her hands. The flashlight beams forced her to squint. "Don't shoot! I've got the baby with me. I'm the stepmother. I woke up and heard someone leaving the house with the baby. I chased after the man and found the baby alone in the middle of the cornfield."

"Keep your hands up, ma'am."

The officers approached her. She'd never been more frightened. Not even a vicious werewolf could make her feel so vulnerable as standing before two men holding guns aimed at her.

"Which way did the intruder go, ma'am?"

She pointed down the path. "That way. But I think he's long gone."

"Let's take a look," one of the officers said to the other.

"You can take the baby inside, ma'am. We'll be back to talk to you after we check this out."

She nodded and picked up the carrier. Mrs. Henderson waited on the porch, wringing her hands. Her hair up in curlers, the elderly woman shrieked when she saw Mireio approach with the baby carrier. And that set Charlie into a new stream of wails.

"Oh, the poor boy," the neighbor said. "The kidnapper got away? Why would someone do that? Was it someone you know? Where is Lars?"

"Lars is…at his cabin tonight. He worked on it all day and stayed over. Just me and Charlie here. And I have no idea why someone would do this. Must have been a burglary. I don't own any valuables, so the intruder must have decided to take the baby instead. I need to go inside and see if I can get Charlie to calm down."

"Do you need me to come in with you, dear?"

"No, Mrs. Henderson. Thank you for calling the police." Not really. But, she had to play nice. "Go back to bed. The baby is safe—that's all that matters."

"All right, but I'll come over in the morning to check on you two. You call your husband and have him come home right now."

"I'll do that. Thanks."

Inside the house Mireio poured herself some water and then picked up Charlie and paced the floor with him. He was wide-awake but no longer crying or frantic. That was a good sign. Could he have known that was his daddy who'd taken him on the crazy run through the cornfield?

"I hope he's okay." She glanced out the back screen door, spying the bobbling orbs from the police officer's lights. With hope, they'd give up the search and mark it off as a failed kidnapping or maybe even drug-induced idiocy. "Please be safe, Lars."

The next morning Mireio awoke to a constant knock at the patio door. She climbed out of bed, checked that Charlie was still sleeping, safe and sound in his baby carrier, then pulled on her robe and wandered down the stairs. She spied the dirt tracked through the kitchen and couldn't recall if the police officers had done that.

Last night two officers had returned from a search of the cornfield and had knocked at the patio door. They'd informed her whoever it had been was nowhere to be found, and then had taken half an hour going through her home and the bedroom. She'd had the forethought to toss Lars's clothes, which he'd pulled off before they'd made love, into the hamper so they wouldn't question where the man of the house was.

And now she followed the dirt tracks down the hallway, even as the knocks sounded gently at the back door—Mrs. Henderson could wait—and into the living room, where she found Lars sleeping on the couch, one arm thrust over his head and hair splayed across his face. His jeans were unzipped and he wore no shoes. He'd found the clothes she'd laid out for him after the policemen had left and must have quietly slipped in sometime during the early-morning hours.

Tiptoeing to the back door, she opened the creaky screen door and stepped out onto the patio so Mrs. Henderson could not come inside.

"Everything is okay," she offered immediately. "I called Lars last night and he came home right away. He's inside sleeping now. And so is Charlie. We're all good."

Mrs. Henderson clutched her arm with a squeezing reassurance. "You know what I was thinking last night as I watched the police search the cornfield?"

"What's that?"

"What if it was the Sasquatch?"

"Oh, Mrs. Henderson, I don't think Sasquatches exist. And if they did, I'm pretty sure they wouldn't have the stealth to sneak into a house and steal a baby. I followed a man through the cornfield. It was probably a burglar who decided to give kidnapping a try. The police said they'd return today when the sun was up to look for evidence."

Of which, she hoped, none would be found. Lars had been naked. He couldn't have left anything behind. Except DNA. No. All they'd find might be a stray wolf hair.

"I brought you some orange cranberry muffins." Mrs. Henderson pointed to the plate she'd set on the patio table. "Are you sure you're okay, Mireio?"

"Positive. Now that my husband is here, we're good."

"You make sure he stays with you tonight. Just in case."

"I will. Thanks for the muffins. Lars will appreciate them."

Her neighbor reluctantly left, waving as she crossed into her yard through the narrow space in the lilacs. Mireio was beginning to wonder if she should plant roses, with thorns, in that space. The woman was a busybody. If she had never called the police everything would be fine.

As it was, she wouldn't stop worrying until the police returned and marked the case off as cold.

She returned to the kitchen and grabbed her phone just as it buzzed with a text. She didn't want it to wake Lars. Eryss texted that she was headed back to town and had left the baby with Dane in California. She wanted to get together to party.

"Will do," Mireio whispered as she texted back.

Then she opened her photograph app to look for a party pic to send, but smiled when the first ones to come up were from the day she and Lars had been kayaking. And the one before that when she'd captured him lying in the tall grasses with the baby snuggled up on his chest. White daisies dotted Lars's beard and he'd beamed as if a ray of sunshine. The man was so happy when he had Charlie in his arms.

Sighing, Mireio tiptoed into the living room, where Lars snored. The poor man. He was degenerating faster. And now, more than ever, she was determined to go ahead with her plan. She had to.

To save her husband's life.

Even though the lasagna didn't have any meat in it, it was hearty and filling. Lars finished his fourth square and eyed the casserole dish. One slice left. His pretty new wife winked at him and nudged the dish toward him.

"Thanks. This stuff is awesome."

"I promise to feed you until you're stuffed every night. That wasn't in the marriage vows, but I will make good on it."

"I know you will. And I promise to help you plant a new lilac shrub where that space is in the hedges."

"Leave it for now. If I end up moving, we'll leave the new owners to figure out Mrs. Henderson. I will really miss that bathroom, though."

"Then I'll make another promise to create a bathroom even more grand than the one you now have. Anything for my wife."

She kissed him, and didn't notice his wince after he'd said that. Would he have the time to do that? Today he felt all achy and his joints were stiff. He felt half in and half out of a shift, actually. Though he wasn't. He was completely in were shape. Yet the shift from last night lingered. Painfully.

By the gods, he'd endangered his son by stealing him away while in werewolf shape. He hated himself for that. Might he have to sleep elsewhere so he wouldn't risk harm to his family? Chain himself up at night? The idea of such a thing sickened him. But even more, if he had harmed Charlie, he would have never forgiven himself.

"Let's go vampire hunting tonight," Mireio said with a hopeful lilt.

He'd been surprised when she'd told him she wanted to perform the immortality spell. But her reason for doing so, because the vampire who killed her mother was the one she'd targeted, was solid. And if his wife wanted revenge? Then he would be the man to stand beside her and support her.

"Sounds like a plan. Do you mind if Sunday babysits?"

"She doesn't threaten me, Lars. In fact, I appreciate all she has done for you and Charlie. She would make a good mother."

"They'll have kids someday."

"I know they will. Sunday will make it happen, one way or another. As for us? I love my little glop of Peanut Butter. Are we going to call him Peanut when we're old and he's grown and married?"

"I certainly hope so." Because that meant Lars would be alive to see such a day.

Chapter 27

It was after midnight and the sky was dark. Clouds blocked the moon. Mireio had brought along all the supplies for invoking the immortality spell. Candles, black salt, lighter, the dragon's exudation, faery dust, a baby's cry and various herbs and crystals. She'd practiced the incantation this afternoon. And had invoked a confidence spell to bolster her efforts tonight.

She was ready to hunt a vampire. And to cast the spell upon herself.

Silently they walked the alleyways they'd followed previously. It felt covert to Mireio, as if they were on a mission and both knew their roles and would only speak if necessary. She wished this night could be as easy as they made it look in the movies.

Lars immediately picked up a scent. Following his silent gesture, she caught up to him.

"You're sure about this?" she asked him.

"The longtooth killed your mother," he said with a strange detachment. "You need this revenge."

"You were reluctant to kill a vampire, no matter what. What's changed your mind?"

"Because I want to remove the threat to you. And if

that means you get the bonus of another century of life, then so be it. Let me give you this, Mireio." He stopped to look at her. "Life."

She swallowed back tears. He wanted to give her something he couldn't grab for himself.

He touched the corner of her eye, releasing a teardrop. "No tears for me. Shed them for your mother. You honor her tonight. Yes?"

She nodded and summoned the bravery she would surely need to make it through the next few hours.

"You ready?" he asked. "It's gone that way. Up on the rooftop."

The vampire saw the two of them approach and stood up from his victim. Closely cropped dark hair shaved with zigzags gave him a ridiculous look. And the gold gauges in his earlobes hung heavily near his jaw. His face was so gaunt Lars at first thought he was starving, but the blood dripping down his chin indicated he'd fed. And well. Lars sensed the human at the vampire's feet still had a pulse and Lars saw his legs twitch. But if he didn't act swiftly, the victim could lose too much blood and die.

"What's this?" The vamp said. He made a show of sniffing the air, then sneering. Gold rings on his fingers clicked as he clasped his hands together. "A wolf? And a pretty little bite?"

At Lars's side Mireio bristled, but he tapped her arm. He wouldn't hold her hand. He didn't want to show the vampire any weakness. Though, he was feeling suddenly dizzy. The world wobbled, and his eyes felt loose in their sockets. Damn it, this disease was challenging him in ways he wished would not show up at the most inopportune moments. But he wouldn't get any better thinking about it.

They had to do this now.

Lars stepped forward and delivered a punch up under the vamp's jaw. His victim was wily, though, and he shook it off, spitting blood to the side. He skipped over the victim's inert body. Lars lunged and slammed him against the wall, fisting him in the kidney once, then again. The bastard didn't deserve to walk this earth. He'd taken a woman's life and had left Mireio alone and haunted.

Gritting his jaws, he narrowed his gaze to see through the dizziness as he delivered another punch that he felt go up under the longtooth's ribs. He would pay for the atrocities he'd served others—

Mireio yelled, "Wait! Don't kill him."

Why was his sweet witch here? She should not be... Oh. Yes.

Lars came down from the sudden murderous rage and glanced to his wife. He'd brought her along with him. For good reason.

The vampire in his grip squirmed and spat blood, which landed on Lars's cheek.

The witch planted her feet squarely and lifted her chin. Thrusting out a hand, she spoke firmly, "Let me have his heart."

Lars nodded. He'd almost forgotten. "Right. Speak the spell, witch." He gripped the vamp by his shirt. "Here is your source."

"Oh, shit! Not this!" The vampire kicked, landing a toe at Lars's thigh, which didn't hurt.

As Mireio began to recite a preliminary spell that she'd explained would put the vampire under a temporary thrall, Lars struggled with the thing as if he were a slimy octopus. The creature was not going down without a fight, that was for sure. And Lars's strength had waned quite a bit over the past weeks. Normally he could have controlled the bastard with ease. But he wasn't seeing clearly right now, and if he wasn't careful, the vampire would slip from his grip...

No, he wouldn't let that happen. He slammed the vamp against the brick wall.

A spark flashed in the vampire's eyes and he suddenly went limp in Lars's grasp.

"It took! We've got only a few minutes," Mireio said. She stepped up and blew green dust into the vampire's face. Then pressed her hand over his mouth and nose, forcing him to inhale. "That'll hit his blood stream and render him incapacitated."

At their feet, the human victim scrambled up and clapped a hand over his neck. "What the hell?"

"Did you work a thrall on him?" Lars shook the vampire. "Tell me!"

"Yes," the vamp muttered drunkenly.

"Go!" Lars yelled at the victim. And when he stood there, stupefied and confused, Lars growled at him, which sent him running.

Enthralled, the human would not remember how he'd gotten the bite on his neck. Nor would he transform to vampire. And with hope, he'd not remember Lars and Mireio either.

Shoving the vampire to the rooftop, Lars stepped over him, straddling his hips with his boots. The dizziness had him wavering over the vampire, but he gripped his shirt tightly to anchor himself. He glanced aside to Mireio, who stood up from setting out candles at four points. Her nervous energy hummed in the air and he wanted to ask her one more time if this was what she really wanted. But there was no going back now. He wanted her to have this revenge. And she would.

"Ready?" he asked.

She nodded. Bending, she sprinkled ashes from a glass vial around her and then placed four black crystals at the compass points between each of the candles. A snap of her fingers ignited the candle wicks. "This is for my mother, Jessica Malory. Thy will be done."

She stood inside a protective circle, but also one that would enhance her magic and make her receptive to the spell. As she began to chant words that Lars suspected were Latin, he bent over the vamp. He knew his role. He tore open the bastard's shirt and tapped his chest right over the heart... This was not going to be pretty. Then he dug in his fingers and pulled up skin, muscles and ribs. The vampire moaned, but not loudly. He was under Mireio's spell and still alive, which was the necessary key to this spell. Gripping the slippery, beating heart, Lars gritted his jaws against the smell and this vile act.

It's not vile. It's punishing a murderer and giving a good woman life.

Life. How crazy was it that he couldn't control his own life, yet could hand over so many more years to someone else?

He gasped, wobbling, but managed to slap a hand to the brick wall nearby to steady himself.

"Lars?"

Mireio's voice startled him out of the swirling dizziness. Shaking his head, he cleared his thoughts. Gripping firmly and tugging, he pulled up the organ from the vampire's chest. Arteries and veins burst and severed. The heart continued to beat as he turned swiftly and thrust it toward his wife.

Mireio took it with both hands and, closing her eyes, pressed it to her mouth.

Lifting his chin and setting back his shoulders, Lars watched. Because he was as much a part of this as she was. Together, this act bonded them in a strange and mysterious way. For life. No matter how long or short that may be for him. She sucked at the blood. And as she did, Lars felt his veins tighten. His muscles cramped.

No, no shifting now. He squeezed his fists tightly, mentally begging for a brief escape from the disease, if only to help his wife.

Beneath him the vampire's body suddenly lurched and then relaxed. Dead. The body began to disintegrate and ashed.

And the heart in Mireio's hands ashed, spilling over her bloody fingers and sifting away on the wind. The candles around her flickered and snuffed out, imbuing the blood-tainted air with sulfur.

"Did it work?" he asked.

"I hope so." She dropped to her knees, bowing her head. And Lars knelt beside her, hugging her against him. She trembled. But he only wanted to hold her and make the world right for her.

"No regrets?"

She shook her head. "I did the right thing."

Once at Lars's place, Mireio jumped out of the truck and ran around the side of the cabin. Lars called after her but she begged him to stay away. She needed time to herself.

What she really needed was to make it to the field of wildflowers so she could... She dropped before the flowers and expelled the contents of her stomach. The horrible act she had committed tonight would not allow her to callously accept the immortality. Had so many witches over the ages done the same without regret? How could they not feel remorse for such a foul act? No matter that the vampire that she'd reduced to ash had been a homicidal madman.

As bees buzzed nearby, hovering over the blood she'd expelled, she spat onto the ground and gasped as tears fell and splatted the backs of her hands. "I'm so sorry," she whispered to anyone who would listen. What had happened to "and ye harm none"? Why was such a spell not considered dark and forbidden? "Oh, goddess. What have I done?"

And then, she shook her head. No. She could not be sorry for taking the life of the vampire who had killed her mother. It was a wish she had held for years. And she felt her mother's soul could feel the revenge and would condone it. Nor could she be sorry for obtaining the one ingredient she needed to give her husband a fighting chance at life.

What was done had been done. She must remain strong.

Standing, she wobbled, then straightened her skirt and stepped away from the spattered wildflowers, which now hummed with hundreds of bees. In the darkness, she wandered around the side of the cabin and into the house. Her shoulder bumped the wall. She redirected but then turned and pressed her forehead to the wall. Lars slipped up behind her and wrapped his hands over her shoulders.

"Don't ask," she said softly.

"I won't. Something happened tonight. Something good and not so good."

"It's a lot to take in."

"You going to be okay, lover?"

"I need to sleep."

"Why don't you let me run you a nice hot tub first? You've some blood on you, sweetie."

"Yes, a bath would be nice." And she needed to brush her teeth. Like fifty times. "Thank you, Lars."

"Sit down." He helped her to sit on the couch. "I'll be back in a few."

He let the screen door bang shut as he raced out and around to the bathroom. Ten minutes later, Mireio was submerged in the hot water, which smelled like Lars's mint shampoo. Very few bubbles, but the man had tried, bless him.

"I'll sit here quietly," he said, settling onto the closed toilet seat.

"No, please. Give me some time alone, will you?"

He nodded, and only when Mireio heard the screen door on the cabin creak once again did she allow herself to cry.

Chapter 28

The next morning Lars drove his family to Mireio's place. She didn't have a change of clothing at the cabin—her shirt had vampire blood on it—and she was kind of cranky, so he decided to do what he could to make her happy. She'd gone upstairs to change an hour ago, so he snuck up to check on her and found her in bed. Sleeping? No, he didn't hear the soft, rhythmic snores. Probably sulking.

After making toast and coffee for breakfast, he took Charlie out to the patio to feed him his bottle. The day was bright and he actually felt pretty good, save for the twitch at the base of his spine. He prayed that did not indicate another unintentional shift. He generally didn't feel it coming on until he was in the midst of it. Which gave him two or three seconds to get away from his son.

Charlie giggled at a passing monarch butterfly that fluttered close to Lars's hair. "Butterfly," he said. "Can you say that?"

Charlie burbled nonsense. And Lars hoped he'd get to hear his son say "Daddy" before life decided to up and leave him.

A rustle in the lilac bushes verified what he'd just

sensed. Mrs. Henderson stepped through the leaves and when she spied him gave a little wave. She carried a plate of some kind of baked good that Lars had no intention of turning down.

"How are the Gunderson boys today?" she asked, handing Lars the plate.

"We're both chipper and eager to chase butterflies."

Charlie grasped out for Mrs. Henderson and she gave Lars a hopeful look. "Can I hold him?"

"Sure." He handed the boy over and the woman seemed to handle him well enough. Charlie was a little chunk and growing heavier by the day, but she propped him at her hip and pulled a face to make the boy laugh.

So Lars peeled back the plastic wrap and dug in to the sliced banana bread.

"It's my grandmother's recipe," she said. "Uses cinnamon and walnuts. You don't have a nut allergy, do you?"

"I don't think so. This is great. I might even save a piece for Mireio to try."

"Where is she today? Inside cooking?"

"No, she's..." He wasn't going to tell the woman his wife was depressed because she'd consumed the blood from a vicious vampire. "Taking it easy today. I'll tell her you stopped by."

"Oh, sure. This tyke is sure an adorable guy. Where's his real mother?"

Lars stopped midbite and swallowed awkwardly. So the woman just came out with the tough questions, eh? She wasn't as unassuming and bat-brained as she made others believe.

"Not in the country," he offered, holding out his hands to take Charlie back. "I should go inside and see if Mireio needs help with the laundry."

"But I thought she was taking it easy?"

Oops. "Thanks, Mrs. Henderson."

She stepped back slowly but didn't make her way toward the hedges. "I could watch the boy while you run in to help your wife."

"No, we're good. Aren't we, Charlie?"

The baby in his arms suddenly tilted back his head and let out a howl that would make any wolf pup sit up and howl back.

"Well." Mrs. Henderson pressed a hand to her chest. "That's unusual."

"Heh. He's making baby noises." But Lars was so excited about the howl, he nearly knocked the table over when he stood. "See you later, Mrs. Henderson!"

He rushed inside the house. Lars held up Charlie and the boy howled again. "That's my boy! Mireio!"

He ran up the stairs. His wife lay in bed, awake, but he suspected she wasn't in any mood to actually rise and face the day.

His excitement could not be contained. "Guess what Charlie did?"

She shrugged and sighed.

"He howled at Mrs. H! Howled! Just like a little wolf. He's werewolf, Mireio. I know he is."

"That's sweet."

"Aw, honey." He sat on the edge of the bed and Charlie reached, trying to grab at her tangled hair. "You feel like lying around today?"

She nodded.

"Can I bring up something to eat? Some tea? Mrs. H brought over banana bread."

"Maybe later."

"Okay. You take all the time you need. I'm going to head to the lumber store today. Need to pick up drill bits. You want me to get you anything when I'm out?"

She shook her head and turned her back to him.

* * *

At the sight of the blinking baby monitor, Lars set his hammer down. He'd considered asking Mireio to watch Charlie today while he worked on finishing the framing, but he hadn't wanted to leave the baby with her since she was still in a funk. She had gotten out of bed this morning and made him breakfast, but she had still been in a robe and her hair had been uncombed when he'd decided to leave around eleven to work on the cabin.

Had the immortality spell not worked? Had something gone wrong?

Or was it as he suspected? She was feeling guilty over taking the vampire's life to prolong her own.

She should not feel that way. A vicious predator had been taken out of circulation. Yet, he couldn't convince himself he'd had such a right to be judge, jury and executioner. That night, in the moment, he had wanted to kill the vampire out of a rage even before Mireio had reminded him she needed to take the heart. They were both responsible for that death.

So why was he here now? He should be standing by his wife, giving her the hugs and compassion she needed. And in turn, he could get the same from her.

Wow. He'd handled this one wrong. But he intended to fix it.

Packing up his tools, he then found Charlie inside in his crib, bubbly and ready for a bottle. Instead of tucking him into the car seat right away, he let the boy roll around on the floor a bit while he reread the will he'd not taken a moment to look at it. Could he do it? Should he do it?

"What do you think, Peanut?"

The boy rolled over and burbled out bubbles, which was his latest trick. He took joy in the sounds the sputtering saliva made, and obviously the drooling mess.

Lars swiped a cloth across Charlie's chin and neck.

He dropped the cloth as the numbness struck him suddenly. His feet and legs began to tingle, as well. The tingling traveled swiftly from his extremities and focused in his spine. So fast! He dropped to his back next to his son and closed his eyes. The numbness was coming on more often and swiftly now, and it seemed to travel toward his center, coalescing at his spine. He had learned that if he lay down and rode it out, it seemed to pass more quickly.

He felt so helpless like this. If a man was going to die, he decided it would be better to be quick. Not debilitating or degenerative. This shit was nuts. He wasn't a weak man. He was a vampire killer, damn it!

Yeah, so maybe he'd had to prove something to himself by killing the vampire. Idiot. And look how the universe rewarded him?

Stretching out an arm, he was able to nudge Charlie onto his back and the infant kicked and squealed, unaware his dad couldn't pick him up if the world were ending.

And with that thought, a tear spilled from Lars's eye.

It had been three days since they'd killed the vampire. And Mireio had, supposedly, gained immortality. Physically, she didn't feel any different. Except tired. But the fact she'd been moping about for days was probably the reason for that. So this morning after Lars had taken off for the cabin with Charlie in tow, she'd gotten up, taken a long bath with Epsom salts and rose quartz crystals, and then wandered out to the garden to pick some lavender. Then she cast a spell to lift her spirits and help her to see the goodness around her.

Sometimes a person could get so mired in one detail that the wide, bright world surrounding them faded into the background. No longer. What had been done was done. She said a blessing to her mother's soul and asked her for a blessing in return. And when the beeswax candle above the stove suddenly flickered to flame, Mireio got her answer.

Her mother approved.

And that was all she needed to lift her head and move forward.

Thinking she might make something sweet for Lars as an apology for her funky mood, she paged through the recipe book she and her grandmother had cobbled together over the years, but nothing leaped out at her.

So when the door opened and Lars and baby entered carrying a little brown bag from Nothing Bundt Cakes, she was thankful the man was on the same page as her.

"You're up," he noted as he situated Charlie in the highchair he'd bought the other day to keep here at the house. He then swung into the kitchen, swept the hair from her cheek and kissed her.

His masculine, fresh-rain-in-the-forest smell drew her to tilt her head for another kiss. And another. And when he landed on her mouth, she turned against him and pulled him down to make it a long and luxurious kiss.

"Wow," he said when he pulled away. "I think you're feeling better."

"Much. Sorry, but I think the enormity of what we did sort of whacked me off balance for a few days."

"I understand that." He took her hands in his. "It affected me too."

"Oh, I know. I've been terrible to ignore you. What can I do for you?"

"What's done is done," he said. "We both need to accept that. And if that's too hard, I picked up something that might help." He grabbed the paper bag and shook it. "Red velvet and chocolate chip."

"Oh, mercy. I'll get the forks!"

Half an hour later, they lay on the couch, naked, with bits of buttercream frosting on Mireio's breast and in the crook of Lars's elbow. Eating cake had started out innocently enough. Until Mireio had dropped some frosting down her shirt, and then… Well.

On the floor, wide-awake in the baby carrier, Charlie gazed at the two of them with a wonder that widened his eyes.

"We'll have to stop having sex in front of the legume," Mireio said.

"Agreed. But we can always eat cake in front of him." They clinked forks together. "Deal."

A shower to remove frosting and cake crumbs was necessary. Afterward, Mireio dried off with the towel and tossed it over Lars's head. He wiggled his butt and then tugged it off and winked at her.

"I hope you don't mind, but I'm going to meet the girls tonight for a gab session."

"Sounds like what you need."

"Why are you so good to me?"

"Because I love you. Because it's easy to want to please you. Because you're the cutest, tiniest witch I know. Because Charlie loves you. Because—"

She pressed her fingers to his lips. "Okay, I get it. You love me. I love you. We're one big happy family. Do you want me to make you something to warm up for supper before I leave?"

"No, I'm good. I can manage a few things by myself. I've survived this long."

"Indeed, you have."

"You could bring home a growler of the oatmeal stout, if you like. I love that stuff."

"That's the only brew I never put a spell on."

He winked at her. "You've already bewitched me. Spells aren't necessary."

"No, I suppose not," she said, but her mind rushed to the plans she had. A spell would be very necessary.

Chapter 29

Eryss had returned from California but had left her six-month-old with Dane. He was flying into Minneapolis in a week. So the party was held in her conservatory. It was two stories high, designed all of glass panes and resembled a Victorian garden house. It had been damaged last year when a fire had started in her kitchen and Dane had broken through the glass to run in and rescue her. But the repairs made it look as if nothing had happened, and the lush plants and real grass carpeting the floor flourished. There were even dragonflies flitting about among the flowers and crystal grids.

Geneva snapped her fingers, invoking her fire magic, which set the candles sitting on the coffee table to flame, yet the flames hung suspended above the wicks. She winked at Mireio. That's how she liked to do it.

Valor's air magic floated those candles above their heads as if in a candelabra. And Eryss's earth magic had sprouted mushrooms about the emerald velvet sofa where they sat. Mireio's water magic spilled a fine mist over the flowers behind them, which released lush, heady scents.

Eryss tilted back the pink and purple drink Valor had mixed for all of them. "Mercy! What is in this stuff?"

Valor winked. "Faery dust. They're called Dust Bombs. I got the recipe from a witch in Paris."

"Seriously?" Mireio dabbed the sparkling surface of her drink with a fingertip. "What do you have to do to get the ingredients? Give your man a squeeze to get it out?" she asked. "Wait. No. I don't think I want to know the answer to that one."

Geneva hooted. "Faeries expel dust when they come. So we all know how she got this stuff!"

Mireio considered her drink for a moment. Kelyn had...? No, better not to think about the collection method. She tilted back another swallow and smiled so widely her cheeks were beginning to hurt. "To faeries!" She lifted her glass, and the other women joined in the toast. "Long may they sparkle!"

"And to wild and wolfy men," Geneva said with a wink. Then she sighed dramatically. She'd broken up with her rustic fellow a few weeks earlier. Truly, his checkbook hadn't had a chance with her expectations.

Valor plopped her head onto Geneva's shoulder. "We need to hook you up, girlfriend."

Eryss, lying on the couch nursing her drink much more slowly than the others said, "Yeah, but none of us knows any millionaires."

"I prefer billionaires," Geneva replied haughtily. Mireio downed the last of her drink. "We need music!"

"I got it!" Eryss snapped her fingers. "Music!"

Panic! At the Disco filled the room with an erratic yet bouncy beat. Geneva bobbed her head and performed a hand jive.

"So Geneva needs a billionaire," Valor said. "And I've got myself a delicious faery man."

"Is it true what they say about faeries and their wings during sex?" Mireio asked.

"Oh, hell yeah. When I touch his wings..." Valor

mocked a shiver and exaggerated it into a lolling collapse back into the couch.

"Tell us about werewolves," Geneva coaxed. "Have you ever fucked your husband in werewolf form?"

"Not yet. But maybe someday. I will never rule it out."

"That sounds creepy." Geneva tilted back the rest of her drink.

"I think it sounds like an adventure." Eryss winked at Mireio.

"You need more faery dust." Geneva stood up to gather more drinks, but she wobbled and landed back on the couch among giggles.

"So tomorrow night, ladies?" Mireio asked. "That'll give us time to sleep off the hangovers we all know we'll have in the morning. I hope you have room on your bed, Eryss, because I'm not going anywhere tonight."

"Last time I remember sharing a bed with you, you kicked me onto the floor in the middle of the night."

"Then lay down some pillows on the floor. Lars loves me for my bed-hoarding proclivities."

"That's a big word for such a very drunk and tiny witch," Geneva said.

And all four of them burst out in laughter.

Lars drove up to the cabin. He'd dropped Charlie off with Sunday, who had asked him again about the will. He'd said he was still thinking it over and she'd frowned. He was beginning to get annoyed that the woman was trying to take away his son. And while he knew Sunday was kind and only had the best intentions, she was making it easier for him to sway toward making sure Mireio got full parental custody of his child.

But first he had to get Charlie's mom to sign the paperwork. Sunday had actually found a friend living near the address listed on the birth certificate, and he'd given

Sunday the email address where they could reach Charlie's mom. She agreed to sign the adoption papers without question and would sign and scan the documents he sent her way, then send them back to him.

A black Firebird and a Prius were parked before the cabin. He wasn't sure who those vehicles belonged to, but he would guess Mireio's witchy friends. Mireio hadn't come home until nine in the morning. She'd texted him last night that she was too drunk to drive. Had they carried the party over here?

Hopping out of the truck and hitching up his jeans, he realized they were looser than usual. He was always rucking them up of late. Was he losing weight? Mireio had been feeding him well, and he always ate like a horse. Was his body somehow protesting? Hell, he didn't want to think about it. So long as he could walk and use his hands and not wince at the ever-present pain that seemed to clench his spine, he would call that a good day.

Wandering up to the front door, he paused when he heard the female laughter around back. Were they out by the hives? Hmm… Better go say hello to the wife and check out what the witches were getting into. Because with a crew of witches gathered together? Something had to be up.

They stood near the entrance to the woods, not far from the hives. Lars wandered over cautiously, not wanting them to see him until he was sure he wasn't sneaking up on anything. Witches were supposed to gather and get skyclad and cast spells. And he did owe the flirty one for seeing him naked. Hmm…

Mireio placed something on the ground. Valor sprinkled sparkly stuff into the air. The one with the dark hair that he remembered seeing that first night he'd met Mireio in the taproom must be Eryss. She was lighting candles.

And the fourth, the witch with the wandering eye for his privates, spun in a circle with a crystal wand held high.

Enchanting the forest creatures this day? Must be some kind of wacky spell. Wonder when they'd all get skyclad? This might require he watch a bit longer.

Leaning against the back wall of the bathroom, Lars crossed his arms and watched, for only a few seconds, before Geneva let out a chirp and clapped her hands, alerting her friends to his presence.

"Lars!" Mireio called, and gestured he approach. But when she looked about to take a step forward, she suddenly paused and stood. She wore a short red dress. Her feet were bare and her hands were bejeweled with crystals and rings. "Come give me a hug!"

He wandered over and nodded to the witches, noting they had set up some kind of ritual. As he got close to Mireio he saw the circle that glinted on the grass—in which his wife stood. He stopped at the outside edge.

"Come here," she encouraged.

A sudden twinge of unease shivered down his spine. He wasn't going to step inside a witchy circle. No way. Not after watching her invoke the immortality spell. He needed a break from witchcraft after witnessing that horror show.

"Come give me a kiss," he tried. If she had no desire to leave the circle, he would grow suspicious pretty darn quick.

"I can't. You have to come to me."

"Why?" He cast his gaze about the circle, meeting each of the other three's gazes for a few seconds. None betrayed their intentions. "What wicked witchery are you ladies cooking up?"

"It's nothing," Mireio said. A flutter of lashes wasn't going to win her any seduction points this time.

Lars noted the three witches who had gathered beside

him gave him sidelong glances. His hackles prickled. And considering how screwed up his instincts and body had been lately, that warned him. Deeply.

"Just a renewal spell," Mireio added. "It's something we do with each of the four seasons. Step inside and you'll feel it, as well."

"I, uh…"

"Don't you want to be renewed?" Eryss asked from beside him. "It won't hurt. Mireio has been in the circle for ten minutes. Look how beautiful she is."

Indeed, his wife had never looked more lovely. Her hair spilled like goddess coils about her face, her cheeks were rosy and her lashes were so thick and tantalizing. The hand she held out to entreat him closer seemed to glow with warmth and positive vibes. A renewal spell?

What could it hurt? It might even settle the ache in his spine. And if he got a few days of relief out of it, as he had with the bathtub spell, then he couldn't argue against it. But why did he suddenly feel like a guinea pig?

"Lover," Mireio cooed. Her voice wrapped about his heart.

Ah hell. He'd do anything for his tiny witch.

Lars stepped over the line and into the circle. And as he did so he felt as if he'd permeated a skein and it wobbled to a bubbly close behind him. The air inside the circle felt electric and cool. The hairs on his arms and chest prickled.

Around him, the witches immediately started jabbering something, speaking in tongues. He saw the candles surrounding the circle all take to flame and they lifted from the ground to float. The crystals on the ground glinted as if they were glowing LEDs. And as he started to back up, Mireio lunged and grabbed his hand, tugging him forward. She pulled him down for a kiss and it was so wanting and deep, he lifted her up until she wrapped her legs about his hips and held her in an intimate connection. He didn't care if they had witnesses. He would kiss his wife and make her know how much he loved her.

And yet...

He didn't feel right. Since stepping inside the circle his muscles had tightened. His fingers began to tingle. And his spine pinched. Would he have another attack in front of so many?

She bracketed his face with her palms. "I love you, Lars. And I'm going to save you now."

"What?" Every hair on his body stood alert. His instincts screamed mutiny.

"I found the spell in the grimoire you tried to hide. Did you think I wouldn't want to sacrifice immortality if I had it?"

Shit. So that's what this was about. "Mireio, you can't. You went through so much to have immortality. What about the revenge you got in your mother's name?"

"The only reason I took that vampire's heart was for you, lover. Only for you. Now. Like it or not, we're doing this."

She wiggled out of his grasp, and in the next instant he felt a burn down his forearm. He was bleeding? She'd cut him. And she proceeded to cut herself with a small blade that glinted with black crystals on the hilt. Then she slapped her arm over his, grasping him at the elbow, and forcing him to do the same to her. The cuts aligned and he felt the electrical energy fuse them together. Bright white light burst out from their clasp. The witches' chants rose in intensity.

Mireio chanted, her eyes closed and her grip tight.

Lars wanted to shake her away. She couldn't do this. She'd only just gotten immortality. He'd killed a vampire for her...

Yet in the next instant his entire body jolted. His free arm swung out, extending with the shock. He gritted his jaws at the intensity of the volatile sensations that skittered over his skin. Was she feeling the same? This was insane. It didn't hurt, but it racked every bone in his body.

Lars fell to his knees. Mireio went with him to maintain the hold on his forearm.

"Listen to the words," she said close to his ear. "Know that my love can heal you. Say goodbye to death. Say it!"

"Goodbye," he managed, feeling his throat close up and wanting it to be real. To not be some silly healing ritual performed in a bathtub. To be something that would really work this time and give him forever with his family. "Goodbye, Death!" he shouted again. "Get the hell out of me!"

"Yes!" Mireio shouted. "We honor the deity Hel, who wishes to take Lars Gunderson's life, but now we request his course be changed and the disease rampaging his body be vanquished. Clear his soul of the darkness. Fill him with light!"

His body hummed with what he could only imagine was light. Vaguely aware that around him flames had ignited the glittering circle and a swirl of wind whipped them around into a wall of gold, Lars spread out his arms. His wife placed her hand over his heart. In that moment he could feel all of her. Her heartbeats. Her joy. Her determination. Her love for him.

Bless her for what she'd done. He prayed that this would work. For he had nothing left to try. And so he exhaled, and let go, surrendering.

And all of a sudden the fiery wall dropped. Tiny spatters of flame scattered across the grass and extinguished with a glint. The three witches, placed at intervals around the circle remained silent, their heads bowed.

Mireio pushed her hands through his hair and kissed his eyelids, then his forehead. "Blessings, husband. The spell is complete."

He opened his eyes to look into pure blue love. Mireio's smile grew slowly. He touched her mouth, then smoothed his finger along her cheek. She felt so soft. So real. So powerful. He still felt the magic vibrating through his system. It was strong. Did her body shudder?

"You two need to stay in the circle awhile, let the magic settle in," Eryss said from outside the circle. "We've done what we came for. We'll leave you two to bind the magic as tightly as you can. Blessed be."

Geneva and Valor both said, "Blessed be."

"Call us later!" Valor called as the threesome made their exit.

"We need to bind the magic now." Mireio stood and pulled off the dress over her head and tossed it outside the circle. "You ready for this?"

Thoroughly taken aback by all that had happened, Lars could but nod and grin. Anything involving his wife's being naked was all right by him.

Slowly she rocked upon her husband's prone body, feeling the glide of him deep inside her being. Becoming a part of her. Owning her. The magic still hummed within him and her. It heightened every sigh, every touch, every slick of skin against skin to an intense sensation. He cupped her breasts as she rode him, and moaned as she used her inner muscles to squeeze him.

They needn't speak. The moon was nearing fullness. Probably tomorrow, Mireio realized. Tonight should be a night Lars had sex until he was sated because his werewolf would want to be set free. But he hadn't had control over his wolf for months. When he'd wanted to shift he could not. And when he least wanted to shift, his body decided otherwise.

But that would all change now. It must. The spell had

been invoked. And they bound it tightly with sex, the join-
ing of their souls and bodies.

Lars slicked his fingers over her clit, drawing up a
moan from deep within her. Her body began to shudder,
matching his tremors. And together the two of them came
in an exquisite blending of magic and wild.

A fierce magic, that.

Later they sat in the center of the circle on the soft
grass that still glinted with the faery dust they'd used in
the spell. Mireio sat on his lap, her head tilted against
his neck. She wanted to set his wild free. To give him
the freedom that his very species demanded for survival.

Had the spell worked? Only time would tell. She didn't
feel any different. As if she'd lost the immortality she'd
only had for a few short days. She didn't miss it. She
hadn't had time to embrace it, so how could she miss it?
She'd never have the opportunity to work the spell again.
It was a once in a hundred years kind of thing. If she lived
naturally for another hundred years, she could attempt
the spell, but it was unlikely that would occur. Another
seventy or so years was enough if she could spend every
day with Lars.

"What are you thinking about?" he asked, softly stroking her thigh.

"How I'm looking forward to spending seventy years
with you. Every day."

"Seventy? Where'd you get that number?"

"I don't know. I'm almost thirty. I figure I'll shoot for
one hundred."

"Sounds like a good goal to have. Do you think the
spell worked?"

"You tell me how you feel."

"Besides the fact that my body was just put through a

wringer and then injected with awesome and now I feel like I'm sparkling like a faery? Who can know?"

"We'll take one day at a time. The moon is watching us."

"I can feel her in my veins. She is calling me to shift."

She gave him an incredulous look.

"I know," he said with the same doubt. "I haven't felt such a calling for a long time. I think I could shift if I wanted to."

"Then do it. Let me meet your werewolf on much better terms than we have the past few times he's come out."

"I don't know. If I can't control the werewolf, he might, you know…"

"Try to have his way with me?"

"Possibly."

"You said that's how we bond."

"But you're not ready for that."

"No, I'm not. But I think you can control that part of you. You would never do anything to harm me."

"Never." He kissed her cheek. "You really want me to try? I could go for a run. It would feel great. I have all this energy coursing through me. I feel like it's ready to burst."

"Then do it." She stood and pulled him up. "We can leave the circle now. Our sex bound the magic. The spell has settled into you. I think shifting might even help it sink in further."

"You don't need to tell me twice. Maybe you should go inside."

"No. I'm staying right here. I want to watch you howl at the moon."

"All right, then." He kissed her, lingered on her soft, swollen mouth that felt as fiery as his heart. "I love you, witch."

"I love you too. Now shift!"

"Here goes. I think I'm going to stay in the circle when I shift. Can I do that?"

"Sure. It still has some minute energies flowing within it." She stepped outside the circle, picking up a red candle and her dress. With a whisper, the candle ignited. Bowing, she touched the flame to the faery dust circle Valor had laid down. It glowed white, a match to the moon. With another whisper, she sent her intentions from her heart about the glow, imbuing it with love, peace and her wish for Lars's healing. "Go for it, lover."

With a growl and a controlled jerking of limbs, Lars shifted from his beautiful, muscled man shape into the befurred and clawed werewolf with a wolf's head and maw that revealed pristine white canines and a soft black leathery nose. His ears were tufted with black fur among the brown, and from his paws sprouted razor sharp ebony claws.

The werewolf turned to her, flared its nostrils and then stepped closer. Mireio held up her palm, and the wolf pressed its paw to it. It was twice as large as her hand and the claws curled over the tops of her fingers, but it was so warm, and the toe pads were as soft as Lars's skin.

"Husband," she said.

The werewolf bowed his head and sniffed at her hair and face. It stood tall, its golden eyes glowing and claws flexing. And then he tilted back his mighty head and howled toward the moon, his chest expanding and back arching.

"Magnificent," she whispered.

And she fell in love with her husband's werewolf that night.

Chapter 30

A week later...

Mireio stood before the beehives after the sun had set. Hundreds of insects buzzed in the air, returning to home base with their pollen loads for the evening. Lars was in the cabin reading to Charlie about how to unclog a drain. She'd suggested he look it up online before going after the kitchen sink that had been causing them issues for days. And her wolfie man was always eager to read and learn.

He'd been exuberant to a fault since the night she and her witch friends had performed the death-dissuading spell. It had worked. It had to have worked. And while she'd suggested Lars go to the doctor to have those tests done all over again, he would have nothing to do with such nonsense. He said he felt great. Leave it at that.

Which, she could do. Mostly. Yet she pined for some sort of reassurance. Some promise that the future she had with her husband would be long and not cut short by a disease that may or may not have been defeated by witchcraft.

"No one ever knows when they'll die," she whispered

to the bees. "I had immortality for a few days. Now it's gone."

And for a good reason. She'd given her husband life. And that was all that mattered. She would never again have a chance to cast the immortality spell. Worth the sacrifice. No question.

"He is such a kind man. I love him beyond words. Take care of him," she said to the bees. "Please. And watch over our whole new family. I promise I will never stop loving him."

The bees continued to buzz, their wings busy and their furry bodies industrious. Mireio said blessings to them and then cast a spell across the meadow, stirring the flowers to tilt up their petals and reach for the setting sun.

Lars gripped the edge of the bed to prevent himself from falling onto the floor and instead rolled to his side, snuggling up close to his wife's warm, naked body. Her hair tickled over his face and he nuzzled into it, seeking the faint cinnamon scent that still lingered on her. She'd made cinnamon rolls last night and put them in the fridge so when he rose in the morning he could pop them in the oven. She intended to get up when the oven timer went off and deliver to him the warm rolls while he worked.

The witch had a curious method to doing things that all seemed to revolve around food and creating delicious memories. He liked that about her. He kissed her head and she moved slightly but still slept. Gliding his hand down her arm, he closed his eyes and drew in the softness of her skin. The warmth that emanated from her. The utter grace and beauty that had agreed to be his wife. Charlie's mother. The witch to his werewolf.

Life was good.

And it was really good lately because he'd not experienced a single symptom nor shifted without volition. The spell had worked. He'd beat the disease.

Maybe.

But he wasn't willing to risk going to a doctor to find out otherwise. Life was to be lived without caution. And he intended to do so.

In fact, he had finally gotten the courage to tell Dean and Sunday that he was changing his will, but only to reflect that Mireio was his wife and, should he die, all his possessions would go to her. And Charlie's mom had signed the papers and emailed them back. Now Mireio was officially Charlie's legal mother. And should Lars ever die, Charlie would remain with her.

All was well with him.

Rising, he pulled on his jeans and a T-shirt, then tiptoed over to the crib. Charlie lay on his back, arms spread and legs splayed wide. He slept like the witch, using up all the mattress. Lars smirked at that. He'd sacrifice all his space for his two favorite people.

He padded over to the fridge, pulled out the cinnamon rolls and removed the beeswax-coated cloth, then he turned on the oven, set the timer and placed them inside. Grabbing his boots by the door, he walked outside and around the back to the framework. The south wall was almost complete. He planned to order windows today and they'd be in by next week.

He walked between the back of the new work and the bathroom. Only about ten feet. He could either craft a narrow hallway that led to the bathroom, expand the expansion even further or move the bathroom up to nestle against the main house. Which would involve a whole lot of plumbing work.

"A hallway to start," he decided. "At least for the winter. Can't have my bride walking out in the dead of winter after she's soaked in her bath."

The Sheetrock needed to be put up today. It was a tedious job, but he had all the right tools, which made it easier. Lars walked over to the stack of Sheetrock. He'd left his tool belt in the bee shed yesterday because, before coming in for the evening, it had started to rain.

Striding over to the shed, he smiled because he realized he had everything he'd ever wanted in life. And more. How had a wolf like him gotten so lucky? And to have dodged death?

Must have been due to the magic that had entered his life. Mireio had called it fierce magic. Indeed, it was.

To his right, the sun flashed on the horizon, pinking the sky and promising a warm August day. Already the bees were headed out on their pollen routes, which would take them across the field of wildflowers, and miles away in some cases, in search of nectar.

He walked past the spot where Mireio had fallen to her knees the night that she'd drunk the vampire's blood. He knew she'd gotten sick and the next morning when he'd come out to toss some dirt over it, he'd seen that it was gone. The bees had landed on the blood-covered flowers and drunk it. Weird. But that was bees for you. He'd once read about bees producing blue honey because they'd gotten into some melted sugar candies tossed into an open factory Dumpster.

And now that he thought of it, he wondered about experimenting with planting some new flowers next summer. Pollinators thrived on a variety of flowers. He'd have to talk with Mireio about it. She knew about things like flowers.

Stopping before the bee shed, he reached to open it, when a sudden twinge in his chest stopped him. He clasped a hand over his heart. Something stabbed at him. And burned. It clenched his spine from neck to hips.

He cried out, but that sound was abruptly cut off as

he blacked out and his body dropped, there on the dew-frosted grass before the hives.

Mireio had listened to Lars carefully place the rolls in the oven and then sneak out. He was so thoughtful trying not to wake her. She loved the big ole wolf. But Charlie had stirred as soon as the screen door had closed. So she dragged herself out of bed, pulled on one of Lars's worn gray T-shirts that fell to her thighs, and picked up the infant.

"You get to taste vanilla frosting this morning, Charlie. What do you think of that? Oh, mercy. The man has a way of leaving the really stinky ones to me. Do you know that?" She kissed the baby's cheeks, and blew each one a raspberry. "Yes, you've got some deadly stuff going on in that diaper. Talk about a witch ward."

She changed Charlie and then checked on the cinnamon rolls. They were done, so she pulled them from the oven and took the frosting she'd made last night out of the fridge. In ten minutes the rolls would be the perfect temperature to frost, then she'd bring them out to Lars.

But she didn't hear any hammering, so she decided to see what he was up to.

"Maybe Daddy is trying to be quiet," she said to Charlie as she skipped down the front steps with the infant propped at her hip. "We'll let him know we're up, then he can go to town with making you a new bedroom. What do you think about that? You're going to have your own room. And I'm going to make sure the other room becomes our bedroom. Lars!"

He wasn't in the framed rooms, so she scanned around the backyard and when she didn't see him, she frowned. "Maybe he went for a run?"

Her vision soared over the meadow, dappled by the rising sunlight and then she spied the opened bee shed. And lying on the ground before it—

Breaths chuffing from her as if she'd been thumped in the chest, Mireio gasped. "Oh, goddess!"

Running toward her husband, who lay on the ground, she called out to him. Charlie bounced at her hip so she clutched him tightly.

Plunging to the ground, she set the baby down as she realized her husband was not moving. He lay there as if he'd decided to take a nap on the summer grass, but...

Panicking, she pressed her fingers to his wrist, seeking a pulse. Mireio moaned. Her throat tightened. And her heartbeats thundered.

"No. Not now. This cannot happen! Lars!" She shook him at the shoulders but he did not rouse.

Why was he on the ground? Had he had a heart attack? He was a young, healthy man. Who'd been on a fast track to death until she and her friends had worked their witchy magic.

Or had they?

"No, the spell had to have worked! Come on! Lars!"

Charlie rolled over and caught his arms on one of Lars's legs. Mireio kept the infant in sight and didn't want to alarm him, but she didn't know what to do. Lars wasn't breathing.

"No, no, no no." Pressing her palms to his chest, she remembered the CPR training she and her friends had taken in case they ever needed it at the brewery. She pumped his chest with both hands. "This can't be happening!"

She had to call for help. Her cell phone was in the cabin. She didn't want to leave Lars.

She bent and pinched his nose. Tilting back his head, she breathed into his mouth. No reaction. She pumped at his chest again. Now she shouted his name and kept repeating "no," aware that Charlie was becoming agitated, but unable to stop her actions. She pumped hard, then breathed into her husband's mouth.

"Please! By the goddess!"

What spell could she work to bring him around? She had none. Had exercised the most powerful spell she could find to give him life... To dissuade death. And it had not worked.

Now Charlie's wails cut the air. Mireio turned to lift the infant. She pressed him against her thundering heartbeats, wishing it were Lars who was reacting, moving, hugging up against her for reassurance. It couldn't end this way.

It couldn't end.

How could it end?

"No!" she shouted and her tears spilled out as she rocked with Charlie before Lars. On her knees, she cried to the rising sun, to the trees and the flowers. And to the bees. "Please, don't take him like this. Not from his family. Not from...me."

A whisk of wind whipped her hair about her face and then the air stilled. Charlie's cries softened, as did Mireio's. She looked about, feeling a weird tingling in the atmosphere. As if magic, but not something she had invoked.

"What's happening? Please don't take him. Please?"

And then she noticed the dark swarm that rose up from the hives. It was thick and wide and buzzed loudly with the flutter of thousands of wings. The susurration of bees moved over their heads and hovered there like a black cloud. Strangely fearful of the swarm, she gripped Charlie closer and shuffled away from Lars's side. Yet, she was also curious. What would cause the bees to act so?

Charlie stopped crying and pointed up at the bees. He babbled something that sounded like "Baa."

"Yes, bees," she said on a tearful sniffle. "What do you think they're doing? Are they flying over your daddy?"

The swarm congregated over Lars's body, lowering as if it was a single entity. Some of them landed on him, crawling over his face and skin. And then Mireio noticed the ones that had landed on him were falling away, dead. Bees didn't just die like that. Not unless they stung someone.

"They're stinging him? No," she pleaded, but it came out as a whisper.

Bees would not sting unless provoked. What were they doing?

A rain of dark droplets began to fall over Lars's body. Mireio thought it could be honey, or perhaps the waxy propolis that the bees exuded after they'd processed the pollen in their bodies. Whatever it was, it was stained red, almost as if it were blood.

Instinctively, she glanced to the place where she'd knelt weeks earlier, sickened after her cruel act, which had served to give her immortality. Or had it? Had she expelled so much vampire blood that she'd never had immortality? And the blood that could have given that to her...

Had the bees taken it up and somehow alchemized it into their honey?

Now watching the bees with awe, she held Charlie as he stood in her arms and pointed at the swarm. The infant was in as much awe as she. If the bees had consumed the vampire's blood, could they possibly have taken on the immortality spell?

Whatever was happening, she had no intention of interfering. Lars had tended those bees with love and care over the years. He had spoken to them, telling him his trials, adventures and about the good times. Surely, he'd confided to them about the bad times. Had he spoken of her to the bees?

Were they now honoring their fallen keeper?

It was a beautiful thing to witness. Lars's body dripped

with the blood-tinged substance. Bees crawled over him, fluttering their wings where he'd been stung. They were forcing it to permeate his skin, making it enter his bloodstream. Amazing.

"Baa?" Charlie looked to Mireio. The boy stretched out an arm and a bee landed on his fingers. The infant giggled as the insect walked along his skin.

She didn't shoo it away. As long as Charlie was curious, she was too.

"Thank you," she felt compelled to say to the insect. "For all the love you have given Lars. You bless us all."

The bee alighted, flew above her head so she could feel the hair move against her forehead a little, then soared back into the swarm. In its wake the swarm lifted and followed their leader back to the hives until finally the sun shone across Lars's body.

Making sure that there were no work tools lying about, Mireio set Charlie down and slowly crawled on her hands and knees toward Lars. Her husband's clothing was soaked from the bees' mysterious honey bath, and while she'd been certain he'd been stung—dozens of dead bees lay around him—she didn't see any swollen stings on his skin.

She dared to touch his cheek, then smoothed her fingers along his beard, thinking this might be the last opportunity she had to touch him so intimately. Her tears dropped onto his chest and she plunged forward to hug him. Drawing in the sweet taint from the sticky substance the bees had left behind, she sniffled and listened as behind her Charlie burbled gaily.

She must remember this moment with joy and give thanks for the short time they had had together, and hope for a future with Lars's son. He'd given her something special. She would honor his wishes and raise his child as her own.

So when the body beneath her suddenly jerked, Mireio let out a chirp and shot upright. "Lars?"

The werewolf groaned and his eyelids fluttered. Bee substance dripped from his lashes as he opened his eyes and looked at her. "Mireio, I love you."

Epilogue

Four months later...

The first storm of the season dropped six inches of snow in the first week of December. The day was bright and the air crisp. Lars clapped his gloved hands together while he waited for Mireio to situate herself on the big red plastic sled with Charlie in her lap. She'd bundled him up in a puffy blue snowsuit that made him look like a ball of dyed wool, but his little eyes gleefully beamed up at Lars.

"You ready, Charlie?" he asked.

"Onward!" Mireio called.

Lars gave a tug and headed down the path that cut through the forest. Snow crystals fell from the tree branches, clattering softly against one another. A red fox darted ahead of them. And life had never been better.

With Mireio's encouragement, he had returned to the doctor for another battery of tests a week after the amazing rescue mission performed by his bees. And...the doctor had been speechless. He'd pronounced him healthy, with no signs of the degenerative failings he'd previously shown. Though he'd warned him that something like this could return, he'd told him to leave and live life.

Which was exactly what Lars intended to do. He'd been given a second chance. He wasn't going to waste a single moment.

The cabin's addition had been completed three weeks earlier, and Charlie's room was currently being furnished. Mireio had talked him into making the other room their bedroom, which he could totally get behind. And with a makeshift hallway connecting the new addition to the bathroom, he had big plans to make Mireio the biggest most awesome bathroom ever come spring. Then they could sell her house in town.

Snowflakes sprayed up in his wake and Charlie giggled. The boy was walking now, with help, and Lars already thought he was growing up too quickly. Good thing he planned to be around for a long time to watch that lightning-fast growth.

The bees had saved him by dripping the vampire blood-infused honey substance over him. He knew that to his very bones. And so did Mireio. Not a day went by that they didn't thank the bees, even as they now hibernated for the winter.

And Mireio. His gorgeous witchy wife with a smile that truly gave him life. There was a reason he'd run through her yard that night so many months ago and had seen her standing there naked. The universe had known they belonged to one another. And now as a threesome, they intended to live, love and hopefully make the family bigger.

Life is filled with challenges, struggles, trials and hardships. We can never know when we will die, only that it will happen someday. Live now. Live for every moment. And bless the bees.

* * * * *

I hope you enjoyed Lars and Mireio's story.
This is a very personal story to me, and I hope
I did it justice with my words.
Most of the paranormal romances I write are set
in my world of Beautiful Creatures.
You do not have to read them in a particular order,
and if you are interested in some of the
characters mentioned in this story you can find their
stories at your favorite online retailer.

Eryss and Dane's story is TAMING THE HUNTER
Valor and Kelyn's story is THE WITCH'S QUEST
Dean and Sunday's story is RACING THE MOON
Raven and Nikolaus's story is KISS ME DEADLY

Get 2 Free Books,
Plus 2 Free Gifts -
just for trying the Reader Service!

STRS17R

Get 2 Free Books,

Get 2 Free Books,
Plus 2 Free Gifts—
just for trying the Reader Service!